After Alyson

"I'm all
hearing aids"
P 84

P 76
Being There

2019

for Lucy,
To enjoy on sunny
days and cloudy ones
too

After Alyson

David M. Sindall

Matador
9 Priory Business Park
Kibworth Beauchamp
Leicestershire LE8 0RX, UK
Tel: (+44) 116 279 2299
Fax: (+44) 116 279 2277
Email: books@troubador.co.uk
Web: www.troubador.co.uk/matador

ISBN 978 1780883 892

British Library Cataloguing in Publication Data.
A catalogue record for this book is available from the British Library.

Typeset by Troubador Publishing Ltd, Leicester, UK

Matador is an imprint of Troubador Publishing Ltd

Printed and bound in the UK by TJ International, Padstow, Cornwall

For the 96 – justice one day.

PREFACE

<u>Shagged</u>

I know one day soon
I will burn all my valentines' cards
in the sun
along with memories of
your perfect smile
kissable mouth
nasty habit and
deeply disturbing body.
You'll catch your flight back
And maybe like you said
I'll toughen up
Learn to be harder
and see that love or a few shags
are different aspects of similar journeys
as cycling must appear to hitch hikers.
They're calling your flight
I'm calling your name
My future ejaculations
May sometimes contain
References to you.

London
2012

CHAPTER 1

I stop the car. I have to. I know in my mind that killing the engine is about parking the past.

The car radio continues to crackle away in the background. I am not actually listening, but football commentary has become the sound track to my life, its rhythms reassuring and comforting. Or maybe I have just become lazy and can't be bothered to find alternatives?

I am sat here gazing out to sea, contemplating the future and the truth is I am very scared – but I don't tell myself the truth. I tell myself that this void of emotion, this empty space in my heart, is excitement for the future. The things we tell ourselves. We tell ourselves we are not fat; that we still have time to fulfil our potential that the perfect relationship is just around the corner. We tell ourselves bollocks.

The light fades from the winter sky and I sense the night taking me in. Birmingham seems so far away. I am calm, I have a huge sense of having left something behind that wasn't good, but wasn't so bad either. So I sit alone on the coast in Devon between the old year and the start of another.

At first glance, so little has changed here. The harbour wall and beach have been frozen like a video still. At the far end of the wall are half a dozen fishing boats – I suspect they are the same boats that were here twenty or thirty years ago on my last visit. Next to the harbour, there is a convenience store that sells groceries and postcards, but it is closed for the winter. I often wonder how such places survive – but this has again endured as a landmark over many years, apparently untouched by the passing of time. Admittedly, a few new houses have been built – modern, box-like homes for retired civil servants. Perhaps the penultimate box they will spend their time in. The only indication of change is the number of satellite dishes that protrude from the side of the houses – even these are fewer in number than in Birmingham. Then again, I suspect this probably reflects the absence of Plymouth Argyle or Torquay United games covered by Sky sports and the like. Or maybe that retired people have less of a need for pornography than the urban population. Who knows?

I grow restless with my meditations. I need to be out beyond the windscreen. I want to smell the sea, feel the wind on my face, to know I really am here.

I open the car door and step outside. I am at once shocked by how cold the wind is. I am sure that my ears will drop off in these conditions. I drag my overcoat off the back seat, thrusting my arms into its sleeves, and pull the collar up high around my neckline. I feel pitifully underdressed, ill prepared for this place. I can sense moderate panic for a moment as thoughts of my stupidity at coming here well up inside me. All too late – now I am here – and there is no place else to go.

I turn my back on the harbour and beach and climb the short hill up into the square. Again, there are only moderate changes. The old bus shelter – where I had my first kiss with a spotty but large breasted 16 year old from Porthcawl (what was her name?) – has been replaced by a modern, clinical glass cylinder. I wonder how easy it is for adolescents to snog in here in the summer, lit as it is by the brightest of lights. The chances of getting a finger onto a girl's nipple have been greatly reduced by the progress of time, and getting your hand in her knickers must now be an impossibility.

The Spar supermarket is also still there – albeit refurbished with a plate-glass front window. Despite the fact that my car is full of most things I need – and tons of things I will never use again – I decide that I should buy some bread and milk for the morning, and thus start to put some money into the local economy for the first time.

As I push the door open, I notice the first real sign of change – and I am slightly shocked. Behind the counter stands a very beautiful Asian girl of 18 or 19. Her eyes, in particular, are fantastic, vistas rather than windows to the soul. I try to hide my shock, but I am convinced – as I am when I silently fart in a lift – that my embarrassment is obvious. You see, I didn't expect this – despite leaving a city where many of my colleagues, friends and neighbours were Asian – my assumption has been that, as it was in the past in Devon, the shop would be run by a middle-aged man, with a receding hairline, brown overalls and hair sprouting from his nostrils. So maybe I should have walked in with a hood over my head, carrying a burning torch and a white cross? Christ I am becoming out of touch!

I wander around the shelves, hoping that I look 'normal' and not like some bigot – but then I calm down. Easy mistake, doesn't make me a member of the EDL does it? Eventually armed with a sliced loaf of white bread and pint of full cream milk, shocked by its fat content and my willingness to overdose on cholesterol, I make my way back to the counter.

The Indian girl smiles at me.

"Hello," she says enthusiastically "down for a new year break?"

I am relieved that she is not surly or suspicious of me. This in itself allows me to feel more relaxed and at ease.

"No, I'm here for a bit longer than that," I say, smiling ironically to myself.

"Oh! Are you the man who has rented Drake House? Mr Garvey?"

I am surprised and a little bit pleased by my local fame or is it notoriety?

"That's right, yes," I respond.

"The new big cheese at County Hall?"

"Hardly," I say "just in charge of bottom wiping and the likes for older people".

She tilts her head to one side, "Can I quote you on that?" She hooks her fingers in the air making quotation marks. "New director of Social Services is only here to wipe bottoms."

"Don't you dare!" I say in mock defence.

"It's OK," she grins back, "I think your secrets safe in Hope Cove."

"Well, given that you know who I am, who are you?"

She smiles – "Just the girl who fills in at the local Spar during the Christmas vacation – but you can call me Alpha."

She stretches out her hand to shake mine.

"Pleased to meet you, Alpha – when do you go back?"

"Oh, another two weeks here and then back up to Bristol."

"Not too far then."

"No – I miss here when I'm away and miss there when I'm here. I suppose Bristol is far enough to stop my mum poking her nose into my affairs and near enough to bring washing home once a fortnight."

I laugh, "Oh well – at least your mum is understanding then."

She rolls her eyes.

"I tend to have to show my mum how to use the washing machine. Like I'm a domestic goddess?" She uses the same contemporary inflection that kids these days do, going up at the end of sentences, too much exposure to Australian soaps is probably the cause.

"I see," I say, smiling. "You know if she's neglecting you I could arrange to have you taken into care?"

She giggles – "No it's alright,Mr Garvey – I'm sure there are more deserving cases than mine."

By now I have paid for my items and she has given me the change.

"Well, if the situation changes – just tell the social worker that you know the boss – OK?"

She smiles and then nods firmly. "OK – I've made a note."

As I walk back down towards the car, I turn and she waves from the window. My first social encounter back in Hope Cove hasn't been all bad.

* * *

It started on a train. I was travelling back from a weekend conference in Newcastle that had not gone particularly well. On the Friday night, I had got sloshed with a bunch of colleagues from across the UK, including Patrice – a lovely raven-haired woman from east Belfast. I was sure I was on for a night of passion with her. It came to my turn to buy the drinks and I left her with the rest of the gang whilst I went to the bar. I came back to find her snogging a guy from Leeds Social Services – Mike Dermott – and thus went any potential bonkfest that weekend. I did, by the way, get my revenge when he applied for a job in Birmingham much later in his career. Despite being the best-qualified candidate, I managed to persuade the interview panel that a far less able visually impaired guy should be appointed in pursuance of our council's equality policies. Affirmative action had never been taken for such negative reasons.

Anyway, I was travelling back to Edgbaston on a train that

gave me a pleasant spring afternoon ride back to the Midlands. I had the *Sunday People & Observer* with me, a table seat to myself and the chance to loll away three or four hours. At York, the train filled a little but there was still plenty of room. So I was somewhat disgruntled when a rucksack, with a bespectacled Aussie girl attached to it, interrupted my intense analysis of the First Division table – I was convinced West Brom could avoid relegation – to ask if I minded if she joined me. I looked up, trying to give her a 'No – fuck off and die look', and grunted.

"Is that a 'yes' grunt or a 'no' grunt?" she asked, grinning to herself.

"Whatever," I said.

"Oh – cool. I'll sit down then."

But she didn't sit down, she played wrestle the rucksack for five minutes – managing to plonk it into the centre of the aisle – and then looked at me helplessly whilst glancing up at the luggage rack. When I didn't respond to her coded calls for help, she took the direct route.

"Can you help me get this up there? Or would you just like to watch me stand here for the rest of the journey?"

Alyson always had a way of making me own her problems. The fact that I missed this the first time was a huge error on my part. I was just too irritated.

Eventually, her inordinately heavy rucksack was comfortably sleeping above our heads. She also had a smaller carrier bag with her and proceeded to unpack its contents. A sandwich, a Kit Kat, a carton of orange juice and a banana. Noticing my glance, she smiled again – her smile was incredibly effective, it's what I now miss most about her – "Can I trade you some Kit Kat in return for the colour supplement from your Sunday paper?"

This seemed a fair trade. I pushed the hostage across the table to her.

She smiled again and said she would share the Kit Kat with me when the coffee trolley came around. It seemed a fair deal.

"You're a man of few words, aren't you?" she said – an observation that was so wide of the mark that it actually forced me to laugh out loud.

"What?! What's the joke?" she asked.

"Never mind," I said, "most people who know me wouldn't have said that – they think I never shut up."

That broke the ice – and we talked. For hours.

She was a trainee physiotherapist from Perth. She had taken a year out of university to come and visit Britain. Her dad was from Merseyside originally and she had spent the past couple of months touring, meeting distant relatives and getting in touch with her roots. She asked all the right questions about me, laughed at my jokes, showed a respectable interest in social work and opened up to me in a very non-stuffy way.

The train was about 10 minutes out of Birmingham when she made a decision that would change both of our futures.

"Birmingham is near Warwick, isn't it?" she said placing her front teeth on her bottom lip in a gently nibbling way.

"Yep," I said "and Stratford-upon-Avon, Ironbridge and the Malvern Hills – to name but a few of its near and illustrious neighbours. Not to mention Spaghetti Junction."

"I've heard of Stratford but not the others. You reckon that there's enough to fill a week then?"

"Well I've lived there most of my life – so it's filled up more than three decades."

"Well I don't have to be anywhere over the next few weeks – maybe I'll get off here."

"Do you know people in Birmingham? I mean, where will you stay?"

"No. The only person I know is you." She lowered her face

but maintained eye contact with me. It was a definite 'go on – invite me' look. She continued, "I mean I'm sure there's a YWCA or something I could go to."

I decided to tease for a moment.

"Yeah there's a really good one near the coach station, apparently."

"Oh" she responded. A flat, emotionally empty 'oh'. The sort of oh that could have wiped the next few years clean if I had left it there.

"Or if you don't mind an antiquated sofa bed and a 10-minute bus ride into the centre you could stay with me?"

"Really? You mean that would be OK?"

"It would be great – I mean I've got work to get to, but I can be around in the evening – show you some good pubs and so on".

She smiled her killer smile again.

"That sounds great – if you don't mind me staying."

"Nope, but I'll have to check with Anita."

She looked flustered again, "Is that your girlfriend?" She was trying to sound cool,but there was a sense of disappointment in her voice.

"No, girlfriend would be inaccurate. I mean,she occasionally sleeps with me. She spends most nights out though. I suspect if she's around tonight she may want to sleep with you."

"Me?! Hey look,I'm not into that sort of thing!"

"What – don't you like cats?" I grinned.

She blushed. "Right! A cat! I, er, really dig cats."

"Well she's never met anyone from Oz, but I'm sure you'll get on with her fine."

We arrived back at the flat 20 minutes later. She planned to stay for a few days. She left 6 months later, when I took her for her flight back to Perth so that she could do her final year. In between, so much did and didn't happen. First night I slept with Anita whilst Alyson slept in the lounge. Second night we went for a curry, had a bit too much to drink, got into a deep embrace, but went to bed alone – Anita choosing an antipodeans' snoring rather than my English variety. It was on the third night – when she cooked me a Thai green curry – that we ended up underneath, on top of and then without the duvet. Too quick? Easy to say that, with the benefit of hindsight.

To begin with, it was just about sex. Here I was with this very enthusiastic and increasingly attractive Australian girl, 8 or 9 years younger than me. When we first met, I was so irritated that I hadn't taken in how fantastic she was. She had dark eyes, straight hair, slightly dimpled cheeks and a wonderfully slim but ample figure. The sex was good too. At what point did it become love-making rather than sex? I have no idea. Maybe after the day we went to see Macbeth at Stratford. She had been with me three months. Al had – as a surprise – bought me tickets for a Saturday matinee. Luckily, the season was over, otherwise I would have been at the Hawthorns – but we wandered along by the river, sat on a bench and watched swans and she began to explain that this was how she had imagined England being. I listened – and I am a very bad listener and didn't stop her. Then after about 20 minutes or so, she stopped. We had been looking into the river but she turned to me and kissed me, a slow, deep, soft kiss.

"Mark," she said, "I, er, think I've got a problem."

'God,' I thought, 'she's pregnant or something,' but did my best to remain upbeat.

"Well a problem shared is a problem halved – tell me all about it."

She glanced away for a minute, looking up the river, in what I hoped wasn't a pregnant pause. Then she turned to me and said, "I think I'm falling in love with you."

I was shocked and moved by this, but not yet convinced I loved her. But when somebody says they love you, it is the easiest thing to convince yourself that you love them, isn't it? And Alyson represented the best I had ever found, so I wasn't going to argue that her love was misplaced -why complicate the uncomplicated?

There were also things that didn't happen. I didn't take her to meet my mates, or drag her along to the sacred temple that is the Hawthorns. Nor did I introduce her to my family, but my sister did have lunch with us one day and said, 'she's hot' in a knowing sort of way. 'You'd be mad to let this one go.'. Hot? Letting go? My sister was echoing some of my own thoughts.

The thing was that nothing really became an issue for us in those early days. I cooked, she cooked. I went to football, she visited a gallery, I got drunk, she got drunk. The equilibrium was perfect and seductive. She even tolerated my dodgy hearing, bad jokes and my habitual inability to remember where I had left keys. So I suppose it was at some point when all the things had gone right and none of the things had gone wrong that we started to realise that we were both in love – for want of a better form of words to legitimise our lust. And at that point, we stopped having sex and started making love. There is no mark in my diary, no one moment that commemorates that change – not even a West Brom victory I can recall that ties the moment to an event (maybe our 3-1 home win over Tranmere at the start of the new season?).

Once I realised I loved her, I indulged in that love. I spent hours at first watching her sleeping. Listening to her breathing and also playing games. She was very tactile, so I would move away at night only to find she would move with me and put her arms around me nestling, her face against my back. And I would buy her things. Meals, flowers, food, pints of beer, Rolf Harris records. My credit card could hardly tolerate the extravagance, but I figured it would recover in the period she was back on the other side of the planet.

It seemed just at the point when we were familiar and comfortable the realities of life hit us. We had both known that she would have to return to Australia. We had sensible conversations about how we would try to keep things moving and yet recognised the challenge of time and distance. Despite this, as the days grew shorter and October came, and her final date of departure -30th drew closer, we both became more distraught. She wanted not to go back, to stay and not to complete her qualifications. I persuaded her that a career in McDonalds would not really satisfy her for long – and that she simply had to become a physio. I don't deny I harboured secret thoughts of her getting a job at the Hawthorns and running on with the sponge bag every time Sean Flynn or someone fell over, but I was also fearful that she would throw her life away and that I couldn't carry that burden of expectation.

When the fateful day came, I drove her to Heathrow, despite the fact that West Brom were at home – this really was true love. I carried her large rucksack to check-in for her and helped her choose a book, some tapes and magazines for her flight. It would be at least 24 hours before I could speak to her again – we'd agreed to call once or twice a week and write letters. Finally, we stood at the gates near passport control, cuddling, comforting and crying, so much so that I am sure West London A-Zs compiled at about that time probably have us referenced as a small lake in the middle of Terminal 3. We pulled apart, and as we did so she pushed something into my pocket.

"Don't look at it until you're in the car, OK?"

I was puzzled, but wiped my eyes, kissed her cheek and watched her go.

Later, after navigating through the throngs of happy people, feeling like death, I reached into my pocket. Inside was an envelope and half a Kit Kat with a note from Alyson.

"Dear Mark, I forgot to share this with you on our train journey from York. I love Kit Kats but love you even more, please eat this and think how great the past 6 months have been and how perfect the rest of our lives will be. All my love and deepest kisses A xxxxxxxxxxx"

* * *

My second social encounter in Hope Cove was less fun. On the phone, Mrs Wilma Mapp had sounded jollier and less of a dour Scot than she seemed face to face.

I sensed and immediate hostility from her was likely to shape all our future relationships.

"You say you work for the county council Mr Garvey?" she enquired.

"Yes, that's right – I start my new job next Monday."

"Oh – I see – and what exactly would that be doing?" Her sentences were precise and slowly delivered.

"Well, I'm the new director of social services"

"Oh. I see." Her response could not have been colder. At the time, I couldn't understand why, but would later find out. "I must say you're rather young to be so senior?"

"Really? Well I suppose so, yes."

She then moved on to explain that she really could get more from renting the property as a holiday let, even in winter, but that I could have the place up until the weekend before Easter at a reduced rate. If I still wanted it after then, I would have to pay the full costs.

"You explained that to me on the phone," I said.

"Yes, well Mr Garvey I just want you to be clear that whilst I am more than happy to have you stay, there is a commercial imperative as well."

"Absolutely," I said, "and hopefully I will find somewhere to rent by Easter."

She showed me around the house, indicating where the central heating controls were, how the immersion heater worked and warning me not to forget to leave the wheelie bin out on Tuesdays. I had visions of public floggings and being forced fed Dundee cake by ginger-bearded Scottish chieftains if I failed to do this, Mrs Mapp looking on with a determined but satisfied look on her face. However she eventually left me and I was alone with Drake House and its wonderful views.

Of course, it was totally impractical of me to rent the place. It would take nearly an hour to get to County Hall from here. It also had five bedrooms, a lounge, a dining room, and a kitchen the size of one of Birmingham's smaller stations. I was reassured by the fact that if I ever got lost in here, the local coast guard would be able to organise a search party to find me, doubtless, huddled in a cupboard under the stairs, surviving on morsels of Kendal mint cake and by drinking my own urine. The impracticality of the place wasn't the point. When I was a kid and used to come here on holiday, Drake House was always my dream home. It stood imposingly on a cliff, an Edwardian edifice that dominated the west end of the cove. What's more, it commanded views across the bay that were breathe taking. So, given half the chance I had to rent it. And despite Mrs Mapp's mean-spirited and money-grabbing attitude, it was easily affordable on my new salary. I had to live here – if only for a short period.

As I unpacked my car, a wind came tearing in off the English Channel below, causing me to wrestle with my shirts preventing, them blowing away to France. 'This,' I thought, 'is truly madness.' I also made a mental note to look up the French for 'excuse me has a size 16 shirt just blown onto the beach near your farm', just in case. But once all my belongings were inside and I had hung up my suits, put some classical music on the radio and got the lighting levels right I knew that the decision was not unhinged. Being here represented a link with the past before failed love and splintered hearts made me into the person I am now. Perhaps Drake House would help me to become the person I was before Alyson? The optimistic kid who would look up at the place from the beach and think 'anything is possible'.

* * *

I am a great uncle. My niece has a little boy who is a delight and insists whenever I see him that I tell him about the 'old days'. I can only assume he means a past where there were only three TV stations, where Sundays meant no shopping and where the height of sophistication and luxury was Leibfraumilch. It certainly was the 'old days' when Alyson first went back to Perth. Now it would be so much easier. We could email each other and speak via Skype. But not then. We would manage a five-minute phone call on Sundays and Wednesdays and in between, we would write each other letters.

She seemed to spend every waking hour writing to me and this put me under pressure to do the same. There came a point when I was convinced that the local postal unions were going to organise strike action simply because a one-bedroom flat in Edgbaston could not generate so much mail from one person without it being a management ploy. Unfortunately, they were wrong.

For the first few weeks, the letters were enough. They kept

coming, and although they didn't contain very much, it was contact. So Al told me about being back at university, stories about the people on her course, things she had forgot to mention to me when she was in England, how her brothers teased her about falling for a guy who could never play cricket or rugby because he was a Pom. All those kind of things. They were well-structured, lovely letters, always ending with her telling me how she missed me, couldn't wait to see me again soon and so on. However, it was becoming clear that the 5-minute phone calls to Perth were not going to be enough, and within 6 weeks, we were speaking to each other for nearly an hour at a time. She'd phone me just before dawn in Perth, I'd phone her just before going to bed at breakfast time on a Thursday on her side of the world. These conversations would cover everything, her mum her dad, her brothers, my family, my friends – she even started looking out for West Brom's results (something that I gained a juvenile, inappropriate pleasure from).

By December, the phone calls were getting longer. Putting the phone down was like holding a loaded gun to your head, knowing that as you did so you faced a kind of death. Gradually, tears and comfort replaced the joy of calls for each other as we were both finding the situation intolerable. My bank account was suffering too as the phone bill went up and I spent money on even more little presents, books and so forth to send to Al. It was the madness that is love. Unfortunately, my bank manager was not so poetic and kept on sending me letters warning me that my account was substantially overdrawn and so on.

A fortnight before Christmas, another letter arrived from Perth. It wasn't from Alyson, but her dad. Before I opened it, I feared the worst. Did he think I was the wrong kind of person for Al? Had something terrible happened? It took me ages to open the letter.

'Dear Mark' it began. 'It is a beautiful summer's day down here in Perth. The sun is high in the sky and everything is perfect. However, we've inherited a little storm cloud that has been sent down our way from England. It used to hang out with us before it went to England and was bright and sunny, at worst fluffy white. Now the only time it resembles the ray of sunshine that it used to be is after your phone calls.

Me and Al's mum have decided that we would like better weather for Christmas. Enclosed is an early Christmas present for Al. We thought of sending her to you, but this way is best as it means she'll finish her training and get qualified. If we sent her to Birmingham for Christmas, we don't think she'd come back.

There are two conditions to this present. Firstly, it is for Al – not for you – so we want you make her as happy as she is after your calls. Secondly, don't tell her. We want to surprise her on Christmas Eve.

Looking forward to meeting you – please call me at my office to confirm you're coming.'

Inside was a return air ticket, Heathrow to Perth.

I was speechless. For a good hour, all I could do was look at the letter and the ticket. My brain couldn't link the kindness of Al's dad with the prospect of seeing her in less than two weeks.

Then the practicality clicked in. How many home games would I miss? And could I actually get the time off work? I phoned my boss at work. The phone call went something like this.

"Nick, Nick it's Mark I need to take time off. At Christmas you see, I mean Al's dad – just fucking unbelievable!"

Nick couldn't make sense of this senseless nonsense.

"Mark – slow down! I don't understand what you're saying."

"No, I know," I said, "I'm sorry, it's just fucking brilliant, I mean so generous and everything."

Eventually, after four or five attempts, I was able to explain that I needed to take 4 weeks off to go to Australia to see Al.

"Can I get back to you later?" Nick finally asked.

"Later?! - Come on Nick, give me a break. I mean if I have to I'll walk out, you can stuff your job if you need to think about this."

"Mark, you're being stupid."

I must've sounded like a thirteen-year-old. "Yeah? In addition, you're being mean – like haven't you ever been in love? You just don't understand how important this is!"

Silence. A long silence. 'Fuck' I was thinking, 'why did I say I was going to resign?'

Eventually Nick spoke.

"OK."

"OK?" I said.

"Go on – go. You're one of my best social workers – it would take three months to replace you. For the sake of a month, it's worth it."

When West Brom score, I cheer with the rest of the crowd, but that winter's morning in Edgbaston I roared so loud that the neighbours must've have thought the whole of the Hawthorns home support had popped around to watch a video of our 1968 cup final win.

"Yes!!!!!! You are the best boss in the world Nick – the best!"

I didn't stop grinning, not for months.

* * *

I now wake naturally in the morning. I never seem to need an alarm clock. This is a new phenomenon for me, until I stopped sleeping with Alyson, I always had to be woken. Now I find that my body kicks me out of bed at about 7am. This is strange, but I guess it is a sign of getting older. First mornings in new homes are strange, but at Hope Cove I woke shortly before 7. It was dark outside. As nobody overlooked Drake House, I had slept with the curtain open. I could see in the half light of the morning that there was rain on the window pane.

My poor hearing means that I don't hear rain falling. Actually, there are quite a lot of things I don't hear. I don't hear birds singing or the wind blowing (unless it's very strong), I get lyrics to songs wrong but convince myself that they're right, I don't hear people talking at neighbouring tables in restaurants (the exception are Americans, who I could hear talking on the next continent, never mind table). Consequently I have tended to rely on non-aural clues. For example, I couldn't hear the boiler downstairs in the kitchen but I could sense it was not cold in the bedroom. Therefore the heating had come on. You get used to living your life in a visual, not a sound-based way and eventually it ceases to be a problem.

So as the light starts to seep through the morning sky, like white wine spilling on to a dark carpet, I pad across the carpeted bedroom floor to watch the day evicting the night that had been there earlier. Down below the cliffs on the beach, Mrs Mapp is walking a dog, a Highland terrier of course. There is a ship out at sea, maybe three or four miles from the shore, and the sky is cloud free.

'So this it' I think, 'this is how the medium term is going to be.' There is the sea, the beach, dog walkers and me. There is the total absence of any contemporary personal history.

I wander down into the kitchen to make myself breakfast. Before I met Al, I wasn't veggie. Now I am. She's gone but the value has stayed, temporarily. I brew coffee and sit at the breakfast bar that looks into town, watching Hope Cove as it wakes up at the fag end of an old year. I can just make out the edge of the caravan park we used to stay at when I was a kid. Are those the fields that I would walk Kips, our mad mongrel through, on summer's mornings? I can remember the excitement of throwing pebbles into the sea for a dog that was convinced it would always find the one I had thrown – not that it ever did. Always the same expression, 'OK – where've you hidden it?' Kips was the first presence in my life that I could truly outsmart. Human 9 years old, canine 3 years old. Human wins. Poor Kips he and I were inseparable and he was the first non-human I ever made a real bond with.

I sniff the satisfying bouquet of the coffee. I drift. As a kid on holiday in Hope Cove, everything was possible. Even if it rained every day here was a good day, promising loads and always delivering pleasures that surprised me. I want to rekindle those possibilities now. I just wonder if I can strip away the layers of grime and dirtiness to leave the scrubbed clean optimism of a kid in short trousers.

* * *

Kay, my sister, dropped me at New Street.
"Don't come back singing 'Waltzing Matilda' and don't come back married, it's too soon – OK?"
I smiled at her.
"Can I come back suntanned?"
"Yes, if you must. Just have a good time and give Al a big hug from me – OK?"
I nodded, grabbed my bag off the back seat and disappeared into the station. I turned and waved at her and she was smiling. She made a sign pointing to her ring finger and nodding 'no!' I shrugged my shoulders and mouthed 'maybe' and Kay slapped her forehead indicating 'What do I have to do with this guy,' but it was all good-natured.

I had no idea what the trip had in store, other than hot weather and a strange kind of Christmas. I was leaving England in freezing weather, surrounded by all the trappings of mid-winter festivities to go to a place further than I had ever been before. Until this journey, the furthest I had ever flown was to Corfu. So this was a whole new ball game.

I had done well to conceal the visit from Alyson. We'd spoken a couple of days earlier. She seemed really down.

"I'm here, it's soon going to be Christmas and there's no you!" she moaned on the phone.

"Well, it's cheaper to phone over Christmas. So maybe I can speak to you on Christmas Eve, Christmas Day and Boxing Day." I was desperately trying to drop a hint just to cheer her up.

"Oh yeah! Christmas Eve!" she said, "Do you know what my dad and I are doing on Christmas eve?"

Had he given the game away I wondered – was this a double bluff?

"No – tell me."

"The neighbours have got their aunt coming over from Greece, so I have to go to the airport with Dad to pick her up. I mean, why can't they pick their own bloody aunt up, we're not some sort of taxi service?!"

"Well you could always hop on a plane to England," I said teasingly.

This upset her even more "Do you not think I want to do that? Every day Mark! Every day I think I just want to get on a plane and see you."

"Sorry," I mumbled, realising I had hit a raw nerve. "Anyway, it's too cold here at the moment. Wouldn't be possible for you to survive in these low temperatures."

"We could stay in bed!" she said, regaining some of her good humour.

"Well, that would be nice."

The conversation ended with me explaining that her Christmas present should arrive by Christmas Eve and that she wasn't to open it until Chistmas Day.

"Is it something nice?"

"You'll love it," I said.

I went over this conversation on the plane. How would she react,knowing that her present wasn't a book on the history of West Brom but me? How would she react to me being involved in a secret with her dad? I also wondered how I would react to her on her own territory. In England, I was in control,but in Oz? It was her place and full of things I didn't know about or didn't know how to do. Like surfing, hot weather, beaches surrounded by sharks, and fit, handsome Aussie guys for competition, not beer-gutted Brummies. It would be a scary few weeks.

By the time I reached Perth, late afternoon on Christmas Eve, I was totally knackered and a bit smelly. Coincidentally, a flight from Athens arrived at the same time. God, Alyson's dad was good. She would be there expecting a little old lady in black to emerge and she would get me. Priceless.

So, picking up my bag off the carousel, I made my way through customs without a hiccup. I'd only seen a photo of Al's dad but knew I'd know him. He was a big guy, broad-shouldered and with a swathe of curly greying hair. Unmistakable. As I emerged through passport control, he saw me and put a finger to his lips, making a hush sign. He pointed across to the bookshop where Al had her back to me, looking at magazines and trying to kill time. As I drew level with Al's dad, he indicated that he would take my bag and gestured so that I could go to the bookshop.

I could hardly control myself but was feeling so happy with the way this was working out. What to do?

I decided that I would speak to her first and slowly walked up behind the magazine rack she was browsing through. I wanted to reach out, to touch her hair, to turn and gently kiss her lips, but I resisted all of this.

She still had her back to me as I drew near, standing the way she always did when she was concentrating on things. A sort of cross-legged stance that was oblivious to how the rest of the world perceived her. "Do they have any Magazines about Christmas in Australia?" I asked.

She put her mouth into gear before her senses had realised it was me.

"I dunno' they'll be,"

And then all hell let loose!

She half turned to face me and at that point exploded.

"MARK!!!!!" The whole shop looked in her direction "Fucking hell, I thought,' that sounds like Mark but it can't be because he's in Birmingham' and it's you! You! You're here!"

She leapt on to me and deftly swung her arms around my neck and her legs around my hip, just kissing me and hugging me.

"You're here! You're here!" She was shouting and just kept kissing me and hugging me and then leaning back to look at me. She way crying, I was crying, she was laughing, I was laughing and the whole shop were smiling at us.

By this point, her dad was stood fairly near to us, laughing.

"This is Mark then is it, Al? Isn't it rude not to introduce us?"

She became flustered, confused. "Yeah, I mean I didn't know he was coming and like we're here at the airport," she was now explaining the scenario to me. "You see were waiting for next doors, Greek aunty and so," she broke off from me and turned to her father. "Dad I didn't know he was going to be here, I mean I just didn't. Is she here yet?"

Alyson's dad smiled broadly.

"Nah, apparently she decided not to come, something about being too worried about the noise coming from you two once she heard Mark was coming."

Al looked incredulous. "You knew?! You knew Mark was coming but didn't tell me?!!"

"Alyson," I said gently, "Your dad paid for the flight over, it was his idea."

"Happy Christmas sweetheart." he said.

This set her off again. She leapt off me and onto her dad. Hugging him, whispering 'thank you' quietly but repeatedly and gripping him tightly in a life-enhancing hug, crying and giggling and smiling all at once. And all around us people were joining in, happy for us even if they weren't really sure why.

All lives should have moments of sheer joy. It might be the celebration of the perfect job, the birth of a child, your first clear round at a gymkhana, or your team winning something brilliant. I have a theory that these moments of joy are frozen on the memory, etched on the happy zone of your mind as a place that you can sometimes return to, forever a place of warmth. In the ten years we spent together, I never saw Alyson happier than that day at Perth Airport. She was ecstatic. Despite the way it all unravelled later, I will never forget the sheer perfection of that moment, on one late warm Christmas Eve afternoon, at an airport on the other side of the world.

* * *

It is New Year's Day. I don't know where the past three days have gone. I know I spent last night in the Ship Inn but left before midnight struck. I was going to go up to Bristol and spend New Year with Giovanni – my longest-standing friend, an actor. However, they have just adopted a five year old deaf kid and I knew that today would've been either a case conference or a need to reassure them that they are indeed 'good parents'. Pity, really. As well as acting, Giovanni is an accomplished musician and had what he described as a 'hot gig, with hot wall to wall tottie,' booked at Ashton Court. Tempting though this was, I wasn't really in the mood. Aside to which, I am nearer to my 50th than my 30th birthday and it just all seems a little unbecoming (who am trying to kid?).

It is now 11.30 and the sun is too bright. I have always been agnostic when it comes to the existence of God. However, it strikes me that if there is one he must have a sense of humour. Thus half the planet is hungover and he makes the weather brighter than it has been since the end of October. Even if the sunshine doesn't induce a migraine, some well-meaning, *Guardian* reading, knit your-own-lentils vegetarian is probably suggesting a brisk walk in the country to the half of the population who can just about resist the desire to chuck up their breakfast from a month ago. The Lord, if he exists, works in wicked rather than mysterious ways and we should always remember this.

I can't remember how much I had to drink last night, but I don't think it was a lot. It was just the mixing of it. I enjoyed a bottle of wine with my dinner. Then I had two or three pints in the Ship, then Jim Pierce, the lopsided headed barman – caused apparently by a drunken accident on his motorbike 20 years ago – insisted on giving me a glass or three of his best malt whisky. Leaving before midnight was a means of preserving my health rather than avoiding the New Year's festivities.

As I was leaving, I ran into Alpha with a mixed group of local kids.

"Hello Mr Garvey!" she said, slightly the worse for drink.

"Hi – how are you?" I cast my eye across the whole group to ensure that there was no way I could be accused of trying to pick up an 19 year old student.

"Here to celebrate the end of that last crap year and the year that Argyle get promotion," belched a horizontally-challenged, acne-infested lad at the front of the group. From the back, a ladette started screaming, "Get me a fuckin' breezer, I want a fuckin' breezer!"

I smiled at Alpha . "Happy New Year anyway," I said, and she smiled and nodded. But the alcohol was clearly having an effect – "Got to dash, we're missing good drinking time!"

So I wandered out on to the harbour side. It was ten to midnight. I wanted to be outside for the close of the year. I reached into my pocket for the box that contained my hearing aids. I have had the same box for years – ever since I was first issued with them as a kid. However, I rarely use my aids socially – largely on the basis that the world is loud enough. Yet on New Year's Eve, I wanted to hear the sea and the foghorns of the ships out in the channel. I wandered along to the wall at the end of the harbour. I felt like I should have a pipe to smoke at moments like this, but instead stood with my hands deep in the pockets of my Barbour jacket, gazing out to sea. I could hear the waves crashing and the wind rustling against the microphones on my hearing aids. I could even make out a car leaving Hope Cove, changing gears as it meandered up the long hill.

I glanced at my watch at a minute before minute. I could tell you that at that point I gazed skywards and, for a moment, as the stars glistened against the last night sky of that year, saw my destiny written in the heavens above. But that didn't happen. Or I could tell you that 30 seconds before midnight the door to the Ship Inn was flung open and there was Alpha stood calling my name.'Mr Garvey, I want a New Years snog!!!,' but again that didn't happen. Or I could tell you that I resisted the temptation to throw myself off the harbour wall into the sea below, realising that leaving Birmingham and coming here was a stupid, stupid mistake. Yet that too would be a lie. In truth, as the church clock chimed midnight, and a few fireworks fizzed pathetically across the sky, all that happened was that a tiny number of ships at sea blew their foghorns, a dog barked somewhere in the distance and I gazed out to sea. Slightly the worse for drink, but entirely happy with my lot.

I turned on my heel and headed back to Drake House, taking my hearing aids off as I did so. The standard lamp I had left on in the hall guided me into the new year. I locked the front door firmly behind me, closing the old year finally shut, then I wandered into the lounge, thought about having a glass of whisky but instead decided sleep would be the wiser option.

Still with my coat on, I climbed the stairs, glancing out of the window at the half landing. I noticed the spotty kid from the pub doing his best to remove the breezer girl's tonsils, but aside to that Hope Cove had not changed between one year and the next.

Now I am contemplating driving to Plymouth as Argyle have a home game this afternoon against Walsall. In the end, though, I know that tomorrow I start my new job, and to be honest pottering, phoning friends and family and enjoying the sheer uncomplicatedness of being here is all I really want to do.

* * *

That Christmas in Australia was magical. I had never been to anywhere remotely warm for Christmas. Well, actually, that's not true. As a kid, we always used to go to my gran's house for Boxing Day lunch and her place was always so hot, with the central heating on full blast, that you lost a stone in weight due

26

to the sauna effect. That aside, I had never spent Christmas in a country where it was, at times, too hot to do anything on Christmas day, and where on New Year's Eve I had to worry about my nose being too red from sunburn rather than it being red raw after the inevitable December cold. Yet with Al and her family,everything was perfect.

Christmas Eve was lost to Al. She sent her family away and dragged me up to her room – which was actually a granny flat at the back of the house, that even had its own entrance. To be honest, I hadn't really slept for over 20 hours and, despite my passion, managed to persuade Al that to make love all night might mean I'd be visited by Leslie Crowther in Perth General Hospital the following morning.

"Who's he?!" she asked, it was then that I realised that our Christmas points of reference were entirely different, and that it was pointless to explain the cultural significance of a man whose main talent as a TV presenter seemed to me to be comforting children in hospital on Christmas Day.

It kept on being like that. Only Al's dad seemed to have any sense of what an English Christmas meant. He'd left Merseyside 30 years earlier, but could still recall seeing Liverpool and Everton play on Boxing Day. Although I couldn't see the scars from the lobotomy, he was an Evertonian and every so often his turn of phrase would belie his scouse origins. Even then, it wasn't always apparent but you got terms like 'sod this!' with the emphasis on the second word, or fairly frequently 'Oh, for God's sake Mo!' to his wife Maureen. Maureen, his better half in at least the good looks stakes, was lovely, a native Australian, who had spent nearly all her life in Perth. In many ways, she was very like Alyson, well, the optimistic half of Alyson anyway. But I guess that there really wasn't much of a family resemblance between either Al or her parents. Added to this was the fact that her two brothers – Simon and Patrick – both looked different to each other as well. So the family appeared to me just like Oz itself – a hotchpotch, a hastily thrown together nation on the arsehole side of the globe. Non of them knew what to make of me with my Brummie accent and ability to mishear the rhythm of their speech. Just before I left, I had finally got to the point where I could contextualise the bits I was missing. At that point, though, I wasn't confident enough to use my hearing aids socially, and – well we just all got by.

Best were the afternoons down at the vast Shell Beach. Me and Al could escape with each other and paddle in the Indian Ocean, making plans and just being together. We would sit, back to back, reading, or occasionally we would swim or just mess around, the heat and the vast blue sky creating a dreamlike sense to our time together. We'd played games too. Odds and evens was our favourite, where we would count the number of waves breaking on the shore in the course of 20 seconds. If there was an odd number, we would stay together for ever, or have 6 children, or become farmers in Scotland. If there was an even number, we would only get half of what we dreamed of. The counting often involved fractions of 19 before we got to 20 seconds. Al stood at the edge of the sea, yelling '19 and a half, 19 and three quarters, wait… wait' -willing the waves to meet the figures to prove or disapprove what we were trying to predict.

In my final week, long after any of it made sense, we were playing a game of odds and evens to see how many dogs and cats we would own. It was irrelevant to anything but we played it with gusto. Al was worked up because she thought the result would upset Anita. I explained that Anita need never know, but it wasn't enough for her and she insisted on playing the game again until the result came out in favour of cats. It took about 20 minutes and I was getting irritated – it really didn't matter, and

Al was placing too much emphasis on a game of chance.

"Come on Al," I said, "we'll come back tomorrow and do this – we've probably mistimed the tides or something."

For no real reason, she started to get upset and ended up crying, big salty tears (I tasted them as I kissed them away) and becoming far too silly for a game.

"You don't understand," she kept on saying quietly, but in a short, breathed, panicked way. "This matters to me."

As she cried, I held her in my arms, confused by the intensity of her feelings over such a daft game.

"Al – we can have as many dogs, cats, horses or gerbils as we want – we can make it work."

She looked up in to my eyes with a pleading I had never seen before,
"Tell me we can," she said softly.

"You know we can," I said, "you're being silly"

She let out a deep sigh. "It's easy for you. You come to the other side of the world, you stand here with a girl who loves you, really, really loves you, and you just don't get it, do you?"

"What? – What don't I get?"

"This love thing," she said, "I love you so much – and I want everything to show that my love isn't misguided, isn't cheapened, isn't seen as temporary unlike the marks made by the waves on the beach. So, you know odds or evens? Life or death? Happiness or heartbreak?"

She looked out to sea for what seemed like ages. There was just the sound of the waves hitting the beach and the heat of a mid-summer's January afternoon, her and me.

I took her hand in mine, turned her to face me, lifted her chin with the tip of the index finger on my right hand.

"I will always love you – odds or evens."

I didn't know then, I had no way of knowing, but this was

the first lie that I ever told her. It wasn't even a real lie, just an attempt to calm her, to reassure her that my love was true, was real. Happiness or heartbreak, dogs or cats, lies or love. They all mean the same things in the end.

* * *

I am sat at my new desk in an office four times the size of one of the meeting rooms in Birmingham. I have just been deposited in here by my boss' PA, having spent a couple of hours going through the plans for my first week or two, in Peter Holland's office. Peter is my new boss and Chief Executive of Devon County Council.

It's my first morning at County Hall. In the first 15 minutes, I was astonished by how different life here is compared to life at Brum. Here there are uniformed catering staff who seem to be retired air hostesses from the 1950s. They are very prim and proper and keep calling me 'Sir'. In fact, everybody has called me 'Sir', and this is a total shock to the system. In Birmingham I was Mark, here I am 'Sir'. In Birmingham if I wanted coffee the most I could expect is that one of my team would make me a quick cup between meetings – but I would always be expected to make them one at some future point. Here my executive assistant – Anna – and my PA Flo – have both already been introduced and both asked, as a first question, how I took my coffee with no hint of irony. Anna was particularly keen to make sure that I got my coffee as frequently as I wanted and seemed slave-like in her willingness to ensure my every comfort was met. I half expected her and Flo to organise a rota for grape peeling, so keen were they to emphasise that they were here to serve me. The only grape I would've had peeled in Birmingham was one that had been grown in a vineyard owned by Mozambique refugees who had established an autonomous, feminist co-operative free from patriarchal value sets – and then I would have had to peel it myself.

Peter Holland had spent the first 10 minutes explaining how delighted he had been that I had accepted the role. He is a friendly affable man, despite his height – he must be 6'4, or something, he doesn't come across as intimidating. He was telling me that at 50 I was the youngest director of social services they had ever had in Devon. In fact, I was the youngest member of the senior management team by about 10 years, it seemed.

"Look Mark," he explained, "this place is like a resting place for the knights of the round table. I need you to help modernise the place and drag it kicking and screaming into the 20th century. The fact that we're now in the 21st century seems to be a shock to most people in County Hall!"

I laughed. "I'm sure it's not that bad," I said. "Anyway, half the appeal of the job is working in a place that's so different to Birmingham."

"Yes," said Peter. It was a long yes and he was silent for a moment. I hate silences like this.

"What?" I asked, a bit too sharply for my own liking.

"Well, you know. Some of the members are a bit concerned that you're going to come in and change everything."

"They think I'll want to make my mark quickly?"

"Things need to change," said Peter sympathetically. "but they're gradualist here not revolutionaries."

"And doubtless I will come across a number of counter revolutionaries and recidivist?" I asked.

Peter chuckled. "Well they're mostly benevolent squires – they just want to make sure that the status quo is maintained. And they're the progressive ones!"

"Well, like I said," I tried to explain, "half the appeal of the place is it's conservatism."

The conversation moved on. Peter took me through what he had planned. Lunch with the senior management team, meeting some key local partnership organisations, lunch with the leader of the council and with the lead opposition members and so on. It was an extremely light programme and seemed to indicate the general pattern and pace of life at County Hall. Everything so very slow, so very genteel.

As our meeting was drawing to a close, Peter moved the discussion to what he described as 'a sensitive matter.'

"Look, he said, "I know about what was being said about you at Birmingham before you left."

I sighed deeply. 'Already?' I thought. 'Have I got to start dealing with this crap now?'

Peter continued. "I've done my own checking and as far as I'm concerned it all seems like total bollocks!"

The word bollocks came out of the blue – almost as if he had decided to drop his trousers and defecate in the corner of his office – and it made me laugh with relief.

"Thank you," I said, smiling.

"You are going to take them to tribunal aren't you?" he asked.

"Well," I began to explain, "these things are complicated and my solicitor is dealing with everything."

Peter nodded, negatively. "Screw them for every penny you can get," he said, "You'll have no trouble like that here."

I could feel the relief dissipating inside me. I laughed.

"Thanks," I said, "that's a great comfort."

My reflections on the meeting were interrupted by Anna knocking on my office door – which I had left ajar.

"Hello Mr Garvey," she said from the other side, "can I come in?" Yet another amazing change. I sometimes felt in Birmingham that if had've dug a trench three foot deep, put searchlights, barbed wire and landmines along a 30-metre radius and had guards trained to shoot to kill, colleagues would have still pushed open my closed office door without thinking twice. Closed doors were seen as a symbol of secrecy and coercion. It was only by virtue of the fact that I had to hold confidential meetings that the right to an office space had been acceded. Anna? Knocking? This was weird.

She stuck her head around the door and smiled.

"Of course," I said.

"What do you want to do about lunch?" she asked. I thought I could detect a slight nervousness in her voice.

"Well," I said, "I was rather hoping that you and Flo would keep me company and show me were the canteen is."

Anna's eyes widened.

"Canteen?!" she said. "There's a senior manager's dining room where you can book a table or there's the staff refectory."

"Which is best?" I asked.

"Best?" She seemed puzzled by the question, "Well Mr Frampton, who was here before you, always used the dining room."

"Right, right," I said "Well, that settles it – me, you and Flo are going to the refectory."

She smiled a happy, bright smile that seemed to indicate she was pleased.

"Ooh," she giggled "that'll be fun. Just give Flo a call when you're ready and we'll go down together."

She left closing the door behind her. The quiet revolution was about to begin.

* * *

The holiday ended. We agreed we were still in love. She would come to England in the summer. We would live together in Edgbaston. Anita would have to get used to Al being back, Al would have to get used to missing her parents, rain and not being able to walk on glorious beaches, although I suggested a trip to Weston-super-Mare as soon as it could be arranged, even though it would never compensate.

That was it. My fate was sealed. She was happy, I was happy. The future was there for the breaking and break it we would.

CHAPTER 2

I'm lying in the bath in Drake House's cavernous bathroom. The water is hot, probably a bit too hot. I always seem to draw baths to the wrong temperature – much too hot or much too cold. I wonder if there is an internet website to give me details on the best formula.

Outside, the rain is lashing against the bathroom window and the wind is howling. It is not yet dark. Classic FM, its cultural appeal on a par to believing that if you drink Chardonnay you're a sophisticate, is playing in the background. Again, I'd left the dial on the radio down a little too low, so I'm only getting the louder bits. This is easy on the pieces I know – they played the first movement from 'Rhapsody in Blue' which was a doddle, but they've also played a couple of songs by Mozart and, well, I was lost. Anyway, when did Amadeus last have a top ten hit?

I have been contemplating the idiosyncrasies of Devon's plumbing. Above me, in the corner of the bathroom is a spaghetti-like maze of pipes that all seem different in age. One, with a strange Perspex ending, strikes me as particularly odd. Almost out of place amongst the older more antiquated ends. Probably a recent addition and, knowing Wilma Mapp's preference for economy over quality, it will represent the cheapest repair possible. I have always hated stereotypes, but Mrs Mapp fits that which represents mean, dour, middle-aged Scot to a tee.

I am looking forward to eating dinner early and popping across to the Ship for a few pints and to watch Man Utd v

Liverpool on Sky. I am also looking forward to eating the freshly baked bread that is coming to the end of its baking cycle down in the kitchen. I didn't think much of the home bread-making kit that my nephew bought me for Christmas when I first opened it. Now I can't stop using it and hardly ever have to buy a loaf.

I am really pleased about how well things are going. The first six weeks in the new job have been great. Yes the place is antiquated, yes the conservatism of most of the staff is a wonder to behold, but I have a sense of making headway. With Anna and Flo working alongside me, anything is possible. The chief is being supportive in a very subtle way. Even the members are starting to see that some of the things I'm doing make sense and aren't just gestures. So now I have a regular open table session in the County Hall canteen on Tuesdays where anyone in my directorate can join me and talk over ideas. The first couple of times, I got the usual spoilers – people arguing about unpaid expenses cheques or being forced to move desks, etc. Over time, though, these have given way to people who want to make more constructive suggestions and who are really keen to improve what we do. Everytime we do it, Flo and Anna are there, Anna providing the context which I don't have so that when somebody complains of a decision taken three years ago she can explain the background or the reason. Flo on the other hand is super efficient at making things happen after the meetings, visits to district offices and the like.

Building on the success of this, we're now planning to do the same at day centres and care homes. The idea is that we simply listen and explore and where we can problem solve. So there's a buzz about my office that is great and people have commented. One of my colleagues – David Sparrow, Director of Library Services – keeps stopping me on the corridor and asking if we can help him do similar stuff, and how he hasn't seen Anna or Flo being so positive in years. So the signs are that success isn't too far away.

Socially, though, things could be better. To be honest, I am really missing the physical things that come from being in a relationship. After recent events I've promised myself I would rule out anything with people I directly work with. In my current role I have to be more careful. I've promised myself I will be but, well, promises are made to be broken. Shagging people at work is a last resort. There must be a way to meet people. But how on earth do you meet people here? The only 'action' I have seen is geriatric, old ladies walking older dogs! Maybe I should buy a dog? Maybe I should buy an old lady?

All these musings are interrupted by a hammering noise coming from downstairs. It took me a while to realise but it sounded like somebody was trying to get in.

I hop out of the bath, pad across the bathroom floor, pulled my dressing gown around me and descend the steps to the hall. Silhouetted against the frosted glass front door is the unmistakable shape of Wilma Mapp.

"Hang on," I yell – making sure that my dressing gown is tied and that there is no danger of a one – eyed snake making a dash for freedom.

I edge open the door, feeling the cold of the February evening air against the v in the middle of my exposed chest.

"Och, I've been hammering away on this door for ages, Mr Garvey," says Mrs Mapp, bad temperedly.

"Sorry" – I say – "I was upstairs in the bath". 'Cheeky cow', I think, 'I would have left you there for a while longer if I'd have known it was you.'

Before I can invite her in, she is pushing her way through into the hallway. This is quite something.

"You'd like to come in, would you?" I say as she brushes past me.

"I can't stand out there, I'm soaked as it is!" she says.

37

There is no point, I just have to get this over and done with.

"OK" I say "so what is so urgent? Has war been declared? Is the house burning down?"

She changes her tone. "No, no Mr Garvey" she says with a forced laugh "it's just that next week is half-term week."

"And you decided to come around and tell me? I must say Mrs Mapp it's an excellent service but working at County Hall as I do, I already knew."

"Well," she says, "you see the thing is that I have had a couple phone from London, they've a wee bonny son, and they usually come down here for half-term week."

I am non-plussed.

"To stay at Drake House," she says by way of explanation. As if this obvious ploy would immediately result in me bounding back up the stairs to pack my bags and be outside in three minutes flat.

"Yes?" I ask, knowing full well what was coming next.

"Well, I was just wondering if you're going to be here next week."

"Yes. I am."

"Oh – oh well I see. You're not going away."

"I'm at work Mrs Mapp."

"I know, but the thing is that they're willing to pay double what you're paying to have the house for the week. It's a very attractive proposition to me."

"Mrs Mapp," I say, beginning to lose my patience "We have an agreement. I am renting Drake House from you until Easter weekend. I am at work next week. There is nothing to discuss."

"Oh!" she says. "I really think you're being unfair now. I let you have this place when I didn't need to but now all I'm asking is that you just let me have it back for one week. Is that really such a big thing to ask?" She is looking at me, trying her best to appear sincere, but coming across as the money – grabbing, mean spirited lump of haggis that she is.

In the past, when I was younger, I would probably have given in to this sort of nonsense, but not now.

"I am wet, I have dinner to cook and there is nothing else to say about this," I say. "I will vacate Drake House on the Sunday before Easter and not a day sooner. Good Evening Mrs Mapp."

She starts again. "I really think you're being"

I interrupt her.

"There is the door, Mrs Mapp. Use it. Go!"

"Really!" she exclaims and turns on her heel, walks out of the front door and slams it behind her. The old Victorian weather barometer on the wall shakes with the force. But she is gone.

I wonder if I have made my first enemy in Hope Cove? All the indicators suggest I have.

I take a deep breath. There is still the rest of the evening ahead and I don't want that nasty Scottish apparition to spoil it for me. Life will have to go on.

* * *

It was strange, being back in England, having spent Christmas and New Year down under. At times, I wondered if the whole thing hadn't just been a deep sleep containing a long and beautiful dream. But there were the realities of my visit to deal with. The fading suntan, the holiday snaps, the sun-kissed memories and the long and tired aching for Al that was now worse, not better.

Everybody at work was really great. Nick knew that my first few days home would be hell on earth, so he organised a light workload for me. There were messages from my clients, saying they had missed me and that they were glad I was back. At that time, I was working on mental health support, so lots of the people I had left were more than happy to have me back. This gave me a sense of purpose by day, but by night I drifted.

I'd spend hours at home just listening to music, mostly melancholic Leonard Cohen tracks which ensured that any mice at the flat in Edgbaston simply left on the grounds of manic depression. If I wasn't playing Uncle Len's dirges, I was writing even longer letters to Al. They were nowhere near as well-structured or as passionate as hers were to me. Each time I tried to emote, it would seem stilted or clumsy. So I'd leave my expressions of love to our telephone conversations. Still long, still made at the wrong time of the day for the sides of the planet we were on, but still a lifeline.

February was hell. The Baggies kept on losing and I had stopped going to every other home game so that I could pay my phone bills. At times, I felt more down than the people I was supposed to be helping. It would be 6 months before Al would be here, and we were only 10 weeks away from the anniversary of our first meeting. I knew that without her that would be torture.

One day I was at my desk at work, thinking about how shite my situation was, rather than celebrating my good fortune for having a woman in my life that loved me and having had a free holiday to Australia. My phone ringing interrupted this downward spiral of self-pity.

"Hello," said a voice I thought I recognised, "is that Mark Garvey?"

By the time she had said Garvey – with an over lengthened 'a' – I knew who it was.

"Patrice? Is that you?"

"Oh hi, yeah, yeah. How are you? I hear you've shacked up with an Aussie."

'God,' I thought, 'how the hell does she know about Al?' So

I spent 10 minutes explaining the situation and she seemed interested and enthusiastic for me.

"What about you?" I asked, "Last time I saw you, I was thinking there's the new Mrs Dermott."

She laughed. "No way!" she said, "I mean he's very nice, but he's not really my type – a bit too much of a social worker."

"But Patrice – we are social workers!"

The conversation bubbled along and I admit that I was enjoying having somebody to flirt with and pleased that the Dermott prick was not really a fixture.

"Anyway," she eventually asked, "are you coming over for the conference?"

My mind went blank. Conference? What conference?

"It's just that I was thinking we could do a paper together on the differences of dealing with minorities in Northern Ireland and in Birmingham? What do you reckon?" She pronounced Birmingham as three words Bir-ming-ham the way people do from the six counties making it sound like a little-known, exotic, Thai island.

It seemed like a good idea. Maybe it would get me focussed on the thing that paid for the phone calls to Oz, the occasional Interflora flowers and food for my belly, namely my job. I promised to get back to Patrice by the end of the week. I needed to clear the trip with Nick, but knew that it wouldn't be too much of a problem. If I was presenting a paper, the conference organisers would pay for my flight. Brum would just have to pay my subsistence which, given the conference was only for three days, would need to cover the price of about 30 gallons of Guinness.

I'll say this now, but I was really naïve. At no point did I think that Patrice might have any ulterior motive, although if I had've given the matter much thought, it would have been obvious that I wouldn't have been at the top of most people's list. The fact was that my love for Al really blinded me to the possibility of anything other than a professional-ish relationship with Patrice. Unfortunately, because love is blind, I should've consulted a guide dog before I so enthusiastically accepted her invitation in principle.

* * *

I am looking at the TV screen in the corner of the Ship. It has been a dull, dull game with every pass and kick exaggerated by the TV commentators to convince the viewer at home that they have been watching a classic. What nonsense.

Worse still, Jim has spent the whole evening talking to me. This conversation has been strange. He is fascinated by my stay at Drake House, keeps on telling me it is too big. Nobody, it seems, is keen for me to be there. Then he was waffling on about this coming Saturday night being Valentine's Day and how it's normally 'cracking' on Valentine's Day.

"You'd be mad to miss it Mark, a handsome bloke like you."

I could happily force my pint glass sideways into his mouth. Does he really think I'm going to be interested in the local spotty 17 and 18 year olds standing around making eyes at one another? I smile weakly at him.

"Oh I'm not sure; I might be back at the Hawthorns on Saturday."

This sends Jim off romanticising about the days when Bryan Robson played for West Brom and generally getting 95% of his facts wrong. Still, it is a relief to steer him away from any interest in my nonexistent love life. Whilst he is wittering on, I try to work out when was the last time I had a night of non-Baggies passion, and but realise that it is at least 6 months ago, if not longer. There are mornings when I begin to worry that the only use I will have for my willy is for bodily rather than pleasurable will be functions. Neither me or it are happy about this state of affairs, but we both recognise, like Palestinians caught in the tension between terrorist and the Israeli army, that we have to get on with our lives and hope that the future becomes a better place.

I'm about to go when the door is pushed open and in walks Alpha. I haven't seen her for weeks, assuming she was back at Bristol.

"Hello," she says to me and the turns to Jim, "you're not torturing Mr Garvey are you Jim, you'll know you'll have the international court of human rights on your back if you bore one more person rigid ever again. I can get an injunction, you know?"

I laugh a little bit too much for my own comfort at Alpha's comment to Jim. She turns to me

"Can I get you another drink?" she smiles, enjoying my laughter at her comment.

"Here, let me" I offer, and before I know it she has pulled up a chair and is chatting away to me.

She is home for a reading week – that coincidentally coincides with half term and means that she doesn't have to be up in Bristol.

"Are you coming in here on Saturday?" she asks

"Oh, not you as well!" I protest and explain the Jim situation.

She smiles but then looks serious again. "No," she says "you've got to come in because I'm bringing my mum in here on Saturday and I have told her all about you. In fact, she's surprised you haven't been to see her."

"See her?" I ask. "Why would I need to see her?"

"Well," says Alpha thoughtfully "I suppose not everybody would register with their GP if they were here on a temporary basis, but it's always a wise move."

Alpha begins to explain that her mum is the local doctor, a fact I have missed from the local gossip, and that she covers the Cove and the surrounding area.

"So what does your dad do?" I ask.

She looks annoyed.

"What do you call a man with a nose like a penis?" she asks.

"Sorry?" I say, not sure what she is on about.

"Fuck nose!" she says, "same can be applied to my dad. I haven't seen him for about four years, not since he went back to Portugal."

She explains that ~~her dad~~ left her mum several years ago ~~and that~~ she never sees her dad, who was also a doctor ~~but was~~ who Portuguese, not Indian. "I know my mum will have nothing to do with him now, thinks he's a right tosser, yeah?"

It seems that Alpha's mum, who I later discover is called Kalpna, also has little time for her dad, so the two of them have become mutually supporting.

"You know," she says, "its not easy for her ~~sometimes~~ down here, we know we're ~~always~~ outsiders, and unlike the other outsiders, we have to deal with a stupid undercurrent of racism. At least up at Bristol people call me 'Paki' to my face, here they want to but are just too scared to do it."

I'm not sure if this is the drink speaking now. Alpha has gulped down her pint of lager far too quickly and looks like she's keen for another. On the other hand, it could be bitter experience rather than the drink speaking.

"You know if we ran the local supermarket or Indian restaurant it wouldn't be too bad, but we're seen as uppity because my Mum is a GP and I want to be a barrister. You really have to know your place in Hope Cove."

I blush inwardly, recalling my assumptions on the first day – which must be detected outwardly because Alpha apologises.

"I'm sorry," she says "but you being new means that I can have a rant. It's really ~~nowhere near~~ not as bad as I'm making out. At least ~~here~~ I haven't got the pressures of other Asian families

44

calling me a slag for drinking in pubs or for going out with local guys, and nobody is trying to arrange for me to marry an anethesist from Southall."

Before I can respond, Jim rings the bell for last orders. I see this as a good enough reason for making my way back up to Drake and leaving Alpha to her musings.

"I have to go" I say apologetically, "committee meeting tomorrow."

"Oh, OK," she responds flatly. "Just make sure you're here Saturday." I nod but I'm not sure if I will be here. "And wear something nice, a collar, but not a formal shirt – my Mum doesn't go for that, OK?"

By now I'm at the door. I'm still not sure if I'll come in on Saturday but.

"OK, see you on Valentine's night," I say. With that, I am out into the wind and the rain. For the wind blows and the rain falls and life continues around it.

* * *

"You didn't call! Why didn't you call? I mean I was worried, I thought something might have happened to you." She was in a real state.

When I walked back into the flat, the answerphone was blinking at me accusingly. 'Come on' it was yelling, 'get out of this one huh?' There were half a dozen messages from Al. Each more insistent until the last one, which went something like

'Look, it's 3 am. here; I don't know when you're back, but call me as soon as you get home. If you ever get home.' It was flat, defeat, showing in her voice. And now it was 2pm on a Sunday afternoon and I had woken Al's dad, who in turn had woken Al, and I was now officially a prat on the other side of the world for waking a house in Perth in the middle of the night.

"I'm sorry," I began to explain, "the hotel phone rate was mega expensive" – which was true – "and all the sessions ran on and on" – which was not really true at all.

"I went to the airport, you know? To meet a flight from Dublin, to see if I'd missed any news about a bomb or a shooting or something. They just laughed at me!"

I sighed. "Al, I'm really sorry for putting you through that – but look, I'm OK, and nothing happened to me. I've still got all my limbs; everything is working as it was before I left."

'Was it?' I thought, 'was everything working?' My guilt pushed me into ending the phone conversation quickly.

"Look, go back to sleep." I said, "I'll call you in about 5 hours – we can have a long talk then. OK?"

She seemed a bit more reassured by this. "OK," she said, "OK – I'm just really pleased that you're OK. Sorry if I've been silly Mark. I was just worried."

"It's sweet that you were worried," I said, immediately regretting how patronising that sounded. Then it came.

"I love you, you know," she said.

"I know," I said and there was a nanosecond of silence, dead air filled with hesitation because I would normally go straight into telling her that I loved her too. She sensed the delay.

"Look, you still love me don't you?"

"Al! You're tired, come on. Of course I love you – more than ever." This was also true.

"Right." she said, "Well," with a deep sigh, "I'll go back to bed and dream of something other than identifying your body under a sheet in a morgue in Belfast."

'Stop this,' I thought but realised that all Al was doing was putting her real concern into a melodramatic costume.

"Sweet dreams – dream that I'm next to you with my arms

46

wrapped around your waist, breathing in the scent of your hair, kissing the nape of your neck."

"Stop it!" she said, "you'll make me horny and then I won't be able to sleep." I laughed.

"OK sweetheart, I'll talk to you later. Night, night."

"Night," she said, "I'll dream of you."

I put the phone down. I was full of self-loathing and bile and the crazy thing was that nothing had really happened. It just depends on how we interpret the word 'really', I suppose.

The conference had gone well but from the moment I arrived, Patrice had been after me. First, it was just stuff about how we were going to organise the session and that led to her suggesting I join her and some colleagues who were also staying at the conference centre for dinner. I knew, don't ask me how, that she was after more than a chat but I thought 'OK, at least the colleagues will stop her misbehaving.' _Belfast?_

We were in Newcastle and the fact that we were in a seaside resort added to the sense of this being more like a holiday than work. And on holiday you can have holiday romances and they mean nothing, so what is there to worry about? After dinner, we wandered into a local pub and she sat very close to me. I could feel her thigh pressed against mine as we sat crammed in a group in the corner. Slowly, without realising, we were just talking to each other, not joining in the group conversation. But nothing was 'really' happening, I mean we were just flirting, and I mentioned Al so often that Patrice must've got the message that there was nothing doing.

Eventually we all left, walking out into what was – for late March – a surprisingly warm spring night. As we were walking down the street, at the back of the group, she linked her arm through mine. Although I wasn't comfortable with this it was nothing 'really'. _but_

47

And by the time we got back to the reception and the others had gone into the bar, I'd already decided that I was going to bed and that I was going to call Al. Her disappointment was obvious, but I really wasn't that bothered.

"You're going to dream about *her*," she said. And it was the emphasis on 'her' that made me realise the situation was straying into dangerous territory. What did I expect in Northern Ireland? Didn't us Brits come here for the danger and the excitement?

I tried to make a joke "Go on," I said "there are loads of blokes in there, you don't need to tie yourself to a lovesick looser like me for the weekend." But it didn't work.

"Well don't I get a goodnight kiss?" she asked.

'What's the harm in that.' I thought. Certainly qualifies as 'nothing really' happening. So I went to give her a peck on the cheek but she deftly manoeuvred herself so that the peck on the cheek somehow became a kiss on the lips. Being Patrice, her tongue was not going to keep still, so it decided it would get to know mine and before I knew it there was a deep French kiss taking place. I pulled back.

"Stop it," I said, still trying to make a joke, "you'll unleash a battalion of vengeful kangaroos onto yourself."

She just put a finger to her cheek, innocently. "Oh that would be terrible" she said mockingly.

I left her in the reception and made my way back to my room. It was nothing. Really.

The following evening, when she wouldn't leave me alone and was really pleased about how our particular session had gone, nothing 'really' happened. She monopolised me at the disco, pushing in between me and any other male or female colleagues who tried to chat to me. She was being bloody stupid, really. But discos work to a formula that inevitably means they always end with 'The Woman in Red' or some other sentimental

Lady

48

nonsense. And whilst I had managed to lose Patrice for a little while, she grabbed me just as they put 10cc's 'I'm not in love' on (us social workers – we may talk like revolutionaries but it's all talk – check out the music at our discos).

So there we were on the dancefloor, me feeling trapped, her rubbing her crotch deep into mine. Of course, it wasn't long before something was stirring causing her to get more excited as she sensed my erection growing. This led to her deciding that the tongue of doom would like to explore my tonsils again and although I restricted her to one deep probe, she was off. By this point I was also a bit drunk and a lot turned on.

We ended up back in her room and things then got a bit out of hand. I don't know why I was there (ask my prick), but there I was. No sooner had the door shut than she was tugging at my shirt. She lifted it and was licking my nipples. It took all my will power to stop her but I managed to do so.

"Come on Patrice," I said, "I don't do one night stands."

She continued to busy herself with trying to get my fly undone.

"Who said anything about one night?" she said, giggling, "I was planning on more than that."

This was stupid. I pulled away from her.

"Look," I said, "stop it now!"

"Don't you fancy me?" she asked. She turned her back to me and hoisted up her skirt, revealing a naked bottom – what the fuck had happened to her knickers?

"Don't you think I've got a lovely bum? All men love my bum, you know." She was wiggling it at me, leaning with her elbows resting on the bed.

She was right, it was a grade 'A', class1 bum, but that really wasn't the point. It wasn't Al's bum.

I took my chance. Her back was turned. This was a no win

situation but I knew that it was now or never.

"Well, let me be the first who has resisted it." I said, and quickly picking up my jacket that had fallen on the floor, turned and made my way out through the door and back to my room.

As I hurried down the corridor, I felt both noble and cheated. Surely one quick shag wouldn't have mattered? But I loved Al, and knew that it would. Yet there was this throbbing erection that was demanding action plus and a throbbing conscience that was telling it to 'get fucked' – just what it wanted in fact.

My sleep that night was light and fitful. I woke really early, with a slight hangover and an urge to get back to the airport and get back to Anita and Birmingham. I called down to reception. I asked them to get me a taxi to Belfast City centre immediately and left before even the kitchen staff had arrived to start breakfast. My flight from City Airport wasn't for ages; I had loads of time to kill. So I can now say, without doubt or qualification, that Belfast is the worst city in the world to spend for a Sunday morning in with a hangover. But I can also say that nothing happened 'really.' Except that a spell had been broken.

* * *

Along with postmen, who I assume hate the bloody thing, I can't stand Valentine's Day. I think it dates back to my first Valentine's Day rejection when I sent a girl at school a bunch of red roses, only to be laughed at by her. Romance? Nah, just an excuse to market schmaltz to the masses whilst, for the other 364 days of the year, with the exceptions of birthdays and Christmas, we behave like arses.

I have the same trepidations about Valentine's Day in Hope Cove and tonight I have made a bit of a mistake. I mean, I didn't really want to go to the Ship and I was trying to relax myself before I made the short walk down across the quay and inside. I decided to have a simple meal – a light salad of Puy lentils and goats cheese. But I opened a nice bottle of Barolo and before I knew it one glass became three and three soon became the bottle. Now I'm slightly sloshed and I've got to go down to the pub and meet Alpha's mum. I'm sure she'll think her daughter has introduced her to some dog breath-like alcoholic. Why did I have to drink so much? My forehead feels like it is cotton wool, too soft in the middle, and my eyes can't focus on anything very much. I wish I'd have had something more that a tarty bloody salad too – what was that about? I'm not some sort of male model. I toy with the idea of putting some chips into the microwave but dismiss this. I'll probably end up microwaving my head in error.

And what did Alpha say about what not to wear? Did she want formality or informality? Oh fuck the formality, I wear a suit every bloody day for work and look like a bag of shit tied up in the middle. Why should I wear something smart for tonight? I stumble up to the bedroom pull out a pair of black corduroys from the wardrobe and a black Moss Bros angora v-neck. Too black? Ah, the jacket will sort that out- nice denim jacket, the Hugo Boss one. Cost me a fortune in Selfridges before I left Birmingham, but I think it makes me look a bit rugged. I catch myself in the mirror and worry that it makes me look a lot like Bruce Springsteen, some old fart who hasn't outgrown boring people about driving fast cars and girls called Candy. I mean, Candy for fuck's sake – who ever met a Candy, particularly in Hope Cove? Flossy maybe, Candy Floss even, but not Candy.

I'm in the kitchen now and I drink two pints of water to try and dilute the effects of the red wine. This just fills my bladder, but I can't work out if it was full anyway and end up sitting down on the loo rather than standing for a pee cos I'm worried about slopping wee down my trouser leg. God this is so pathetic, what am I doing?

Eventually I'm meandering down the road towards The Ship. I'm worried I'll meet somebody and they'll ask me where I'm going and 'Ship' will come out as 'Shit.' I'm trying not to think this is such a waste of bloody time but even I'm not convinced.

I push the door of The Ship open and I'm struck by how busy it is. Jim waves to me as I enter the lounge and points to the corner where Alpha is sat. Is she alone? Where's her mum? Then I notice a really attractive Asian woman who looks like…well a goddess, I think, like Anna Ford but more exotic and younger with big brown eyes and great, fantastic dark hair is waving at me. She makes the sign of a pint at me. 'For fuck's sake woman' I think 'a whole bloody pint?' but I nod and mouth 'bitter' to her, hoping that she doesn't think I'm saying please in German. This is all too much.

Now Alpha is waving at me and smiling. She gesticulates for me to come and join her.

"Hello," she says as I finally reach the table. Luckily it is so busy that nobody can tell that I am unsteady on my feet. As I get towards Alpha, she is giggling and mouths 'fly.' My hand instinctively reaches to my zip and I do my trousers up quickly. As I'm sitting down she says, "nice boxers Mark," and I think 'this is no time to be saucy or foxy.'

Then her mum comes back and joins us and I am immediately struck by her voice. It is so clear, so English, and so bloody beautiful. I must look like some little puppy; I'm sure I am going to start humping her leg, such is my sense of desire for her. But I just sit there, feeling the wine leave my body, only to be replaced by the bitter that does a good job of clogging my brain with yet more fuzzy alcohol. 'Say very little,' a voice inside my head tells me.

And then Alpha's mum, whose name I now remember is Kalpna, is talking to me about my bloody hearing and how well I seem to be following the conversation. I do my best not to get uppity – 'fucking doctors' I think, 'we're not here for a public case conference.' And I want to make this point to her, but I don't, because I know if I do I'll come across as an arsehole. She's only being nice and Alpha looks really pleased that I'm listening to her and she's talking to me.

"So what do you think of Devon County Council?" she asks and I'm off like a racehorse, talking too quickly, throwing too many words into sentences, trying too hard to impress, and I feel like I've developed verbal incontinence. I want Alpha to interrupt with a change of subject, but she is just smiling and listening. In the end, the three pints (two water, 1 bitter) start hammering on my bladder. 'Let us out before we blow this baby,' a voice is yelling from within my boxer shorts. So I make my excuses and go to the loo and stand there with my knob out, pissing into the urinal for what seems like a lifetime. 'For fuck's sake,' I'm thinking. 'Get a grip man!'

I can't remember much after this. Alpha went off and talked to some kids her own age and her mum just chatted, but I am buggered if I know about what. She could have been telling me I was the ugliest man in the world for all I knew. It wasn't that I couldn't hear her, I was just concentrating on not being pissed. I was trying really hard not to be leery and at the same time getting intoxicated with this beautiful woman sat next to me. Her clothes, her voices, her perfume and her general presence all had the sober part of my brain thinking, 'Wow! Bin-fucking-go!'

I decided at some point to quit whilst I was ahead. I think I could've only have been there for just over an hour and a quarter but I knew that I was already pushing my luck. Any second now I would forget I was not watching some wonderful porno movie and start masturbating in the middle of the pub. So I quit whilst my hands were still away from my groin and made my excuses.

Now I'm lying here on my bed. The Brucey jacket is crumpled on the sofa in the lounge, I'm looking up at the ceiling which is spinning and I can't get Kalpna's face out of my head, or her voice.

I drift asleep, aware that I haven't brushed my teeth, aware that I haven't done half the things I normally do and wondering why my head hurts so much. But I'm grinning, I can feel this big cheesy grin spread across my face and I know that I must look stupid and pissed and whatever. It's the happiest and silliest I've been in ages. It's the happiest and silliest I've been since, I lie there thinking, and then realise. It's the happiest and silliest I've been since Al left.

* * *

I remember my first brand new car. It was a little red Fiat Punto. Not particularly flash, but I loved it. It did everything I wanted and more and, from time to time, I would get the occasional smile from people as I drove around in it, singing along to cassettes or maybe listening to football commentary. I adored it, kept it sparkling clean inside and out and was always careful where I parked it. Always under a lamppost, always somewhere bright. Anyway, one day I was coming home from work and wanted to pick up a few bits and pieces from the supermarket. So I parked it in a tight space in Sainsbury's car park.

When I got back to the car, weighed down by a couple of bags of shopping, I noticed that somebody had put a dent in it and scratched the paint just above the wheel arch. I was furious that somebody could be so cruel to do this to my little car. The car was repaired, but I would always look at the wheel arch where the scratch and dent had been, convinced that the rest of the world could tell that the car had been marked.

After Patrice, I think I felt the same way about Al. The incident in Newcastle had been the same as the first scratch on a new car. It was the same car, I was the same driver. I even continued to lavish the same amount of time and attention on it. Just every now and again, I'd forget to put an old can of diet coke in the bin, or notice that I hadn't thrown away an old crisp packet that had somehow drifted under the passenger seat. With Al, there were no discarded sweet wrappings or anything, just a sense that I had made us vulnerable and I was convinced that she and everybody else could see this, so I tried all the harder to show that everything was more than hunky dory.

What I really wanted was to have a conversation with Al about what had happened and to explain that I had walked away, that I found the whole thing terribly embarrassing and was really annoyed with bloody Patrice Hardy (particularly as she had subsequent been leaving messages for me at the office for me to call her – but I'd probably leave that bit out of the conversation). That Al was the only woman I wanted, that nobody could be better than she could and that nothing really had happened. And why didn't I have that conversation? Because I was scared that to have it would raise the risk of Al never speaking to me again.

In the screenplay that is written in the hearts and mind of the protagonist, in the gender war males are sex-obsessed demons and women are angels who only get their wings broken by bastard men. My experience of this is a bit different. Certainly, in Patrice's world, she was more devil than cherub, and whilst I wasn't searching for beatification, I certainly didn't feel that I had been ignoble. Yet that fear thing, fear of the consequences of telling Al the truth, had me by the short and curlies.

So instead of addressing the truth, I tried to be even more

loving and passionate in my letters. I sent flowers, chocolates, Kylie Minogue scrapbooks and increased the quota of phone calls from twice to three times a week. Anything to cover up the scratch on us from Northern Ireland. I also spent lavishly on planning our journey back to Britain and insisted that, rather than wait for her result, she came here in late July, I would come out to Perth to meet her, rather than meet her in Kuala Lumpur as planned. That way we would have more time together and still get the benefit of the few weeks of what we laughingly called an English summer. But no matter how much I practised polished prose, or cleansed myself from what had happened, there was always a crisp packet lurking in the back of my mind, the crumbs of a silly night of indiscretion spilling out to spoil the glow of our nice, clean, loving relationship. As with the Punto, I knew exactly where the dent was. I also kept on seeing Patrice's perfect bottom and, despite myself, knew that I would see it again, in all its glory, at some point in the future. And the worst thing about it was knowing that I was like every other man, pretending to be above it but infatuated by her bloody bum.

* * *

"She really likes you, you know."

I can't believe this – how the hell does Anna know about Kalpna and how does she know that she 'really likes me.'?

Anna was sat next to me grinning, she could see I wanted to know how she knew.

"Come on," I say, "have you been hiring private detectives?"

We were in my car, I was driving, and she was doing her best to cause an accident.

"No, no nothing like that. People just have a habit of telling me things – I mean, I don't ask them to, they just sort of tell me. I must have a trustworthy face I suppose." Which is true, because Anna does have a trustworthy face. She would have made an ideal police officer except that nobody trusts the police anymore, so her face would've been wasted in the Devon & Cornwall Constabulary.

"Jim," she eventually says.

"Jim, at the Ship??" I ask, incredulous that there is a link between Anna and the lopsided-headed, humorously challenged, barman.

"He watches Argyle with my husband, has a seat near him in the stand, anyway, he reckons that on Valentine's night" Anna interrupts herself, "I mean that's a long way to describe one evening."

I'm irritated.

"On Valentine's night?" I repeat, wanting her to finish the sentence.

"Oh yes" Anna continues, "well after you left, she was crestfallen for a bit. Then Alpha cheered her up and by the end of the evening Jim heard her saying how much she liked you. That's all."

Anna's expression was amazingly earnest, there was nothing malicious or gossipy about it.

"I mean," she continued, "me and Flo thought it would be good. You know, her being a Doctor and everything."

I let out a sigh, a deep exasperated sigh.

"So," I asked, "have you done a paper for the Social Services Committee approval? I mean, obviously, if you and Flo approve the whole council will back the plan unanimously."

"Mark!! Look, there's no need to be like that – we were just talking between ourselves and we thought it would be good. For you. If you want our advice, that is."

"Well you've given it now so I'll just have to think about it."

I dropped Anna at the corner of her road in Honiton. She was looking a bit worried as she got out of the car, which was another vocational skill that she seemed to have had no real opportunity to apply – her worried look was, well, worrying.

"Will Liam drop you in the morning?" I asked.

Then she started giggling.

"Mark, you always do this! Liam is two and is my son! Dom is my husband. If Liam was going to drop me, we'd have to set off now. Even then I don't know if we'd both fit into his Postman Pat peddle car."

The humour broke my annoyance. I laughed.

"OK, OK – well, whichever one of the men in your life it is that brings you – I'll see you tomorrow." With that I left her on the corner and drove off.

I have driven about half a mile when my phone vibrates in my pocket. There is a text message, but oddly, when I open it, there is no number.

'She is evil – beware!' it reads. I have to concentrate on not crashing the car again! I glance around me as if there will be some electronic fingerprints around the car will leading me to the sender of the message. What on earth is this about? Who is the 'she'? Anna? Kalpna? Surely not, I wouldn't put either of these people down as being evil. I am convinced it is either a wind up or a strange mistake, a faulty text message going to the wrong person.

Once I am on the A303 heading back towards Exeter, I glance at the message again.

"She is evil. Beware!" There is no time date stamp, nothing. This is totally weird.

I notice that the petrol warning light has flashed into life on the dashboard. I make a detour to a Tesco near to County Hall and stand with the petrol nozzle in one hand filling the tank. 'I must replace this bloody Car,' I think as it swallows as much petrol as it can. Just as I am finished, I notice somebody waving to me from across the forecourt.

58

It takes me a second to register it, but I realise it is Kalpna. She has just come from the pay kiosk and instead of returning to her car, she wanders across to me.

"Hello Mark," she smiles "How are you?"

I'm pleased to see her, I wonder if it shows.

"Oh, maintaining body and soul," I say by way of introduction, "what about you?"

She sighs. "Well to be honest," she says in that gorgeous, erection-inducing voice "I am really frustrated."

'Join the bloody club,' I think, but instead raise my eyebrows.

"Oh? Why, what's the problem?"

"I've just spent an hour in there, shopping for the weekend, only to have just got a phone call to say that the person -" then she corrects herself, quickly, "people who were meant to be coming for dinner tomorrow night aren't coming. Sod's bloody law, isn't it!?"

Sometimes in life you get one shot at open goals. You either blaze them over the bar and are laughed at by the crowd and admonished by the commentators or you bang the ball into the back of the net in a moment of inspiration. Its either Rooney the hero or Wayne the donkey. I decided to lunge at the ball.

"Well you could always cook for me," I say.

Is the ball going to bang into the net or is it going to balloon way up over the petrol station forecourt out of the ground, only for the other customers to start a chant of 'would you like to know how wide' to add to my humiliation?

Kalpna smiles.

"You're a fast one," she says but doesn't seem offended by the idea, just amused. "OK – a deal – you can bring some wine, but yes, I'd like that."

In my head, the crowd are going wild. I am punching the air and being surrounded by players on the pitch and the big screens

59

around the stadium are showing an instant replay. How did the boy do it, where did he find that from?

"Would 8 o'clock tomorrow be OK?" she says.

"Great," I say "Looks like I won't have to brave Tesco's myself now."

She smiles and walks back to her car. I'm still celebrating the goal when she stops.

Oh fuck! Did the linesman have his flag up? Me and the other players are glancing left and right,what could be possibly be wrong with that? Perfectly good, opportunistic strike. The crowd fall silent, my teammates look worried.

She walks back across "Mark – do you actually know where I live?"

This is a really good question, because I don't.

She reaches into her handbag and scribbles down her address "It's Hampton View, number 8."

I laugh, "Ok – I'll find you – otherwise I would've spent the evening knocking on every door in Hope Cove."

She smiles, wanders back to her car, which I now see is a sporty soft-top affair, waves again and the drives off.

Back of the net! The celebrations continue. I run off to the end of the ground, occupied by the visiting supporters – who just happen to be all the women who have ever turned me down for a date – and I put my index finger to my lip whilst using the other hand to cup my ear so that I can hear their silence. Ha! Ha-fucking ha! Then I'm racing back towards the 'home' end where friends, family, my favourite long forgotten school teachers, waiters in restaurants who I've generously tipped in the past, helpful estate agents, considerate motorists, Alexi Sayle, Eric Morecambe – they're all stood, ecstatic for me in my moment of genius, my moment of triumph. Yes! Yes! Come on!!!! Are you watching, Wayne Rooney!??

But then I'm not in a football stadium. I'm stood on a petrol station forecourt. Grinning, again, after Kalpna.

* * *

In July, by the time we stepped off the plane in Kuala Lumpur, I had no doubts about Al & I having a future together. My credit card paid for a flight out to Perth and the stopover on the way back. I did wonder why I had to behave like a gaoler collecting a prisoner, but dismissed this. I enjoyed her company – that was all there was to it, wasn't it?

The last few days of Al's time in Perth had been filled with relatives coming around. She seemed to have thousands, and I couldn't remember half the names, other than if I said Bill or Mary I tended to have a 50% chance of getting the name right. They all wanted to see her and to meet me, the Pommie person who was taking her away. She seemed genuinely sad to be leaving Perth but also excited about coming to England.

On the day before we were due to leave, her dad suggested we go for a drink. It wasn't in reality a suggestion, more like an order. So we found ourselves at a beachside bar, sipping Fosters and at first talking about pleasantries. How, for instance, he missed Liverpool. But he only had to see a news programme about the decline of the docks, the way the city had become, to realise that he had made the right decision to come here. Then he switched the conversations.

"Yeah," he said, "I've always been good at decisions. What about you Mark?"

It struck me as a strange question and one that I really had no easy way of answering.

"I think I'm good at decisions. Yeah, my judgement's pretty sound."

"You see," he said quietly, "I'm worried that you and Al could be making mistakes. I mean, I know Al. She's lovely, but she can be as difficult as hell too, a real handful if she decides she wants to be one."

"I think I've picked that up. But, you know, I love her."

"Well that'll help, but she could try the patience of a saint, not to mention a few devils."

"It's part of the attraction," I said. I didn't mention the great sex or the fact that I just wanted to spend as much time as I could with her.

"Look" he said, now being more direct, "if it goes wrong, I won't think any the worse of you. You're a decent bloke Mark and as long as you do your best with her that's all I can ask."

I felt myself becoming emotional. Mates had called me a decent bloke before, but never a mate's dad, well not a girlfriend's dad anyway. I was also getting upset at the prospect of it going wrong.

"It won't go wrong. I promise."

"Mark, mate, that's not entirely within your gift, OK? I know you'll do your best, but there are two of you in this. it's not all down to you."

'OK,' I thought, message understood.

We sat silently for a moment both, staring into the middle distance. I took what he was saying at face value – just a man-to-man chat about how impossible his daughter could be. Nothing more, nothing less.

Eventually, out of boredom of the silence, I suppose, I wanted to move us on.

"Another beer?" I asked.

"Well," he said, "it's a beautiful day, I've got stacks of work to be doing back at the office, but bugger it, another beer would be smashing."

I left him nursing the remnants of his glass and set off to the bar to buy us both another drink. The rest of the afternoon passed with him and I talking about football, about Birmingham – a city he claimed never to have had a good time in, which I found unbelievable – and him relating stories to me about Al as a kid. All very civilised, all very pleasant. Yet in reality, his comments about devils and saints unsettled me.

Checking into The Colonial hotel in Kuala Lumpur, most of this sense of unease had disappeared. It felt a bit like catarrh left over from a cold – you thought it had gone, but you were sometimes aware that it stopped you doing things quite as quickly. So we were in the bar in the Colonial, splendid place that made me feel like somebody out of a Graham Green novel, and we had splashed out on cocktails. I'd splashed out on a Singapore Sling for Al, I can't actually remember what I was drinking. I noticed anyway that her eye was roving around the bar, almost like she was looking for somebody else. It wasn't something overt but more covert, like she was weighing up the scene for something. I noticed too that she seemed more than friendly with the local Malaysian barman.

"Your wife is very beautiful," he said to me.

"Ah, she's not my wife," I began to explain when Al interrupted,

"Nah, I'm just his floozy," she said.

The barman looked a bit shocked – I could sense that he thought it might well be possible that Al wasn't lying.

"Will you stop it?" I said over-protesting so that the barman could see I was joking. "This is what happens," I said, "when you go for something other than a mail order bride."

The barman smiled, understanding now that this was that famous, ironic English humour.

"Oh, mail order brides are from Thailand – not Malaysia," he said, smiling.

Yet later as we wandered through the night market in China town, crammed with fake watches and pirated DVDs, Al and I had our first serious row.

Al had been uncharacteristically quiet to the point of being cold for about 40 minutes or so. I could feel the storm clouds gathering.

"Come on Al," I asked eventually, "what's up?"

"I don't like being called a mail-order bride," she said. "It cheapens me."

I was astonished.

"So what about suggesting you were a floozy? Doesn't that kind of devalue your currency?!"

"Yeah but – ah look, it doesn't matter, you know I'm just tired from the flight."

"No, no this matters," I said. "Look, the barman was really confused and I sensed his embarrassment. I was simply trying to put him at his ease. Anyway, I don't like you pretending we're anything other than lovers."

"Lovers?" she said "Isn't that a strange term? It suggests impermanence and like we're just passing through. I mean you're more than my lover."

"OK, OK." I was getting irritated, "How would you like me to describe you as? My girlfriend? Bit possessive if you ask me. My partner? Makes us sound like a pair of accountants, or how about her indoors? Again, too parochial for my liking but, you know, you're the boss."

"Well how about just saying 'this is Al,' let them work it out."

We continued in this vain for some time. It was a game of verbal tennis where we seemed to be more content with smashing the volley than the affects this game was having on each other.

By the time we'd eaten, I'd grown fed up with the row. I wanted to turn the clock back to the scene before we were sat in the bar a few hours earlier. Yet no matter what I tried, Al seemed happy to pursue the argument until she was vindicated.

The evening wore on, we continued to argue as we wandered through the streets back to the Colonial, ignoring the charms (actually lack of if the truth be told) of KL and instead just continuing to wind each other up. Later in bed, I tried to make amends. I held Al in my arms but she pushed me away. I tried again, but again she moved my arms off her.

"Look," she eventually said, "I'm too hot and too tired – OK?" and then she turned her back to me.

It was the first time we had slept together and never made love. I lay there awake staring at the ceiling and the ineffective fan that was whirring away above me. This stank. Here we were at the start of our whole future together and we were fighting. What happened to the girl on Shell Beach?

I got up and I went to the bathroom for want of anywhere else to go. I sat on the loo, looking at the patterns the white tiles didn't make on the floor. Eventually I grew bored, finished my toilet business and made my way back to bed.

Al seemed deep asleep, which irritated me even more. She could just ignore this and go off to dreamland? I contemplated going to the bathroom again and bringing myself off, but to be honest I just felt totally depressed. What on earth was I doing here? How stupid could I be to think that me and this strange, ultra pretty, Australian kid had a future together?

As I churned all these negative thoughts around in my head, Al moved from off her side and rolled across the bed towards me.

"I'm sorry," she said, but she said it below the threshold of my hearing.

"Sorry?" I said, which she took to be me asking for an affirmation that what she was saying was sorry.

"Yeah," she said.

I then had to explain that I didn't hear the first thing she said,which made her physically tense for a moment. Then she sighed deeply and turned on the lamp at the side of the bed. She was naked under the thin sheet and I found myself getting excited, stiffening as I saw the contours of her perfect breasts moving against the harshness of the white sheets. She placed herself so that her elbows were resting on my chest and then gently pressed the end of my nose like it was an on-off button. She was speaking a bit more clearly now but had a lovely gentle sexy, sleepyness to her.

"I said I'm sorry. I'm tired, it's been a long day. I'm sad about leaving Perth and I was a bitch earlier on. It's me not you," she raised an eyebrow "OK?"

"OK," I said. I think I must've looked a bit down because she smiled and said "I love you the most when you're looking like this."

"Like what?" I said.

"Ah, you have this little boy lost look, like somebody took all the toy soldiers, all the cricket bats and all the footballs home so you can't play."

I laughed gently,

"Well my favourite toy wouldn't come out of the box," I said, trying harder to look sad, deliberately playing with the edge of the sheet in order to add to the impersonation of the little boy lost.

She paused. "I want to make love in the morning – not now – I'm too hot and too tired. OK?"

I sighed "Promise?" I said.

"Promise" she smiled.

"OK then," She kissed me, not passionately but sweetly on my mouth, rolled back to her side of the bed, turned off the light and we both drifted off to sleep.

With Al, she could be a devil and a saint in the space of a few hours. She wobbled between the two. I didn't dislike her devilment, I just missed her saintly side when it wasn't there. Yet loving her was loving her as the whole person, not just the loving, gorgeous, caring angel but as the fire-breathing, halitosis-ridden dragon that she could also be. When I was a kid, I was told that dragons came from the West, from Wales. Now I know they come from western Australia too.

* * *

I'm sat in Kalpna's dining room. It is plain white with a beautiful bay-fronted window, dressed in cream muslin curtains, draped rather than hung to dress the window.

Number 8 is the last in a row of Victorian villas, all four storeys high. There is no road outside, instead, a path runs along the front of the house and means that you feel like you won everything you can see. The view is phenomenal. We can only be 100 foot above Hope Cove, but it looks picture perfect from here. The main road winds down into the town square, where the Spar supermarket and the bus stop are easily visible, then it drops away again down to the harbour. I can see The Ship quite clearly and Drake House, sat on a hill above the quay.

The table is littered with the remnants of our meal. Kalpna seems to have culinary skills that match her looks, and although I didn't know, she is also veggie. I spent the whole day worrying about this, so when she said I was unbelievably relieved. Earlier in the evening when she told me, matter of factly, that she was veggie and hoped I wasn't a meat and two veg man. I think the look on my face must have given the game away.

"If I'd have served meat, would you have eaten it?" she asks, looking attentively at me.

"Well," I begin to explain, "there is a Buddhist view that you should eat whatever is placed in front of you and not to do so is disrespectful. But no, I wouldn't have eaten it."

I wonder if this is the right answer, but also wonder why I'm so bothered about giving the right answer.

"Good," she says, "I like people who hold to their principles."

For a moment, I am irritated. Why can't I ever meet unprincipled women? Why do I always have to fall for the bloody stroppy ones with opinions and ideas? I sometimes wonder about relationships with traditional women – Tories perhaps – who have failed to open hostilities in the gender wars. I'd even settle for a Switzerland type, who hasn't joined the battle. Perhaps men who only drive Ferraris feel much the same way about Morris Minors? Who knows?

So the food, all Italian dishes, all perfect, has gone down like manna from heaven. We've also, over the course of two or three hours, consumed a couple of bottles of Barolo. So we are both on the 'hic' side of mellow.

My musing is interrupted by Kalpna's footsteps coming down the hall. She is looking stunning in a little black number, her hair clipped back, her skin perfect, all so understated, given her obvious sensuality.

"Shall we have our cheese and coffee through in the lounge?" she suggests. This sounds like a good idea and I nod my approval.

Kalpna has disappeared to finish making coffee, so I decide I'll go down into the kitchen to see if I can help.

The hall walls have black and white photos of Alpha at different stages of her childhood. One of her in a paddling pool naked, she must have been about 2 I guess, and then a quite breathtaking one of her and Kalpna in the bath together. In both they're naked. I have to quickly glance away, feeling voyeuristic

68

at having seen Kalpna's naked body. I feel like I've seen the pudding before I've even looked at the starters. As I get to the kitchen doorway, Kalpna turns from a vast Aga and sees me.

"Oh no! Out! Out – go on!"

She is shooing me away as if I am a stray cat that has come in from the garden.

"I just wondered if there was anything I could do to help?" I say in defence.

"Yep. Be patient. Coffee won't be long."

"I'm not very good at being patient," I offer.

"Well go and practice. Practice makes perfect, you know."

'I like this. This feels good,' I think.

"OK, I'll go back and study the view and the rogues gallery on the walls."

I want her to know. I want her to know I've seen her naked photos. I wanted to see her reaction.

"Oh, those," she says "Yes, you can tease Alpha that you've seen her bum. She'll be mortified." She's smiling. "Now leave me to it, OK?"

So I wander back along the hallway to the dining room and wait, taking in a few more photos as I do so. These are all of Kalpna and Alpha together,or of Alpha on her own. They are innocent photos of a little girl playing on a beach, of a six year old on a pony and her mum on a horse (this looks like it was taken abroad), of a 10 year old girl at a birthday party with a big cake that says 'Happy 10th Birthday Alpha' and lots of very well-behaved looking kids smiling to the camera with Kalpna in the middle of the scene holding a knife and smiling at the camera. I wonder what happens in the scenes that follow, the slicing of the cake? The unwrapping of presents? The inevitable fight between badly behaved little boys?

Before I can answer my own questions, Kalpna calls again.

"Do you want to come across into the lounge now?" cafetière

I wander in to the Hallway and she is stood with a cafeteria of coffee and a round marble cheeseboard that seems to have a ton of all sorts of cheeses on it.

She kicks the stripped pine doors, that have a distressed look to them, and I follow her into a room that is the mirror image in shape to the dining room, but which has a totally different feel.

The windows have wooden shutters across them and the walls are a dark burgundy colour. There is a real fire with a modern wood burner and the far wall is dominated by a huge oil painting that depicts Kalpna with her back to you sat naked with a towel around her midrift. It has the feel of a Degas, but again exudes an undercurrent of suggestive eroticism.

"What a fantastic painting," I say, "I love the size of it."

Kalpna smiles. "Daniel, my ex-husband, did it – I like it because it captures a time in the past when he and I were happy."

"So it is you?" I ask, knowing the answer.

"Yes," she says gently, "a version of me that was then."

By now, the cheeseboard and coffee have been placed on a big round oriental looking, low table. I decide I want to move the conversation away from her nakedness, and what could become a discussion about failed love – never a good thing. So instead we chat more about Hope Cove, life in Devon and joys and disappointments of the place. the

"Do you think you'll stay here?" she asks.

I smile. I wish I could tell her the truth and tell her that I could stay in this room, right here, right now, until the moment I die, such is the sense of calm and space that has been created. Instead, I give a factual answer.

"Well, I'm not sure. It's totally impractical living here from a work perspective. Takes me longer to get to work now then when I lived in Birmingham and I've got to be out of Drake by Easter so…Well, we'll see."

"Oh," she says "I really hope you decide to stay."

Something about the way she says this implies more than a discussion about estate agency.

We are not sat close – in fact, we are sat in two armchairs opposite each other near the window. This adds to my sense of longing and brings an additional charge of repressed lust to the way things are going.

And then there comes a point where I know that we've exhausted the possibilities of the evening. A time when less will indeed be more.

"Look," I say, "this has been great. I have really, really enjoyed being here. The cooking, the food, our conversation. I'll have to hire in a catering company, or brush up on my beans on toast, but I'll return the compliment before I move out of Drake House. OK?"

It's credit to her ice-cool stylishness that she doesn't come out with a 'Oh going so soon' or 'Stay for another coffee,' but instead merely responds with;

"Yes. I'd like that," she smiles "And the beans on toast might make a pleasant change."

We wander into the hall. She ~~goes and~~ collects my coat from a hat stand in the hallway.

We are stood on the doorstep by now. I turn to her, she smiles and then I think 'bollocks – if this fails it *will* be beans on toast' and then kiss her, on the mouth.

She accepts this and returns the kiss. And then she smiles.

"So," she says, still very cool, "there is some passion in there after all?"

"Some?" I laugh. "Let's leave that for another time, shall we?"

She nods. I wander down the path to where it meets the

road. I turn to look and she is still stood in the doorway and waves. I return the wave, mouth 'thank you' and then turn towards Drake. As I do so, I noticed I am being watched. Stood in the shadows, with her less than savoury-looking terrier, is Wilma Mapp. She has a look of horror on her face- perhaps she isn't keen on inter-racial relationships?

"Evening, Mrs Mapp!" I say.

She ignores me, turns and walks off in the opposite directions, doubtless marshalling her resources for the battles that lie ahead.

* * *

It is strange how a familiar place begins to change and everything in it. Before Alyson came back from Australia, my flat in Edgbaston was as familiar to me as my belly button, possibly more so, as I rarely paid much attention to my navel, whereas I would spend hours in the living room at the flat, or lazing in the bath, listening to football commentary or just generally letting the time wash over me. Anita and I were perfectly happy doing our own thing, although I never did quite master her ability to perch on a window ledge for hours on end, preening the top of my head.

Alyson's arrival changed this. For instance, Anita and I had to get used to a new concept that neither she nor I had ever had any need for. Houseplants. It seems strange now, but I had actually managed to survive for over 30 years without knowing the difference between a spider plant and an umbrella plant or without the chore of having to water them. Within 6 weeks, though, the flat had taken on a greener look. Anita didn't seem to mind, particularly as the large Swiss cheese plant that arrived one weekend gave her a nice new place to crap in wet weather. I admit to being a bit jealous of Anita. I gained no such advantage. Nor did we ever seem to yield a crop of umbrellas or Swiss cheeses. However there was a marked increase in the numbers of spiders around the place, as I seemed to spend a good deal of my evening removing them from baths and other places where they liked to chill. Until this point, I had never realised that spiders were so loud, they seemed to scream, and I often confused this with Al, but what was there to scream at?

After KL, I also had my worries that the bright, warm sunny Al that I had first met was being replaced by the storm cloud version her Dad had referred to back in Oz. In reality, the current weather system that was present in Edgbaston was prone to hazy sunshine at times and the occasional squally shower, but as time went on she gradually became the person she was before she went to Australia. I put the spat in Malaysia down to a short, brief monsoon.

As August became September, and Al's birthday approached, I was at a loss as to what to get her. One Friday lunchtime, I was sat talking to colleagues at work and one had mentioned that they had just got back from Hydra, 60 miles south of Athens and unspoilt. It sounded perfect; no traffic, the remnants of an artistic community and good food. A call to my travel agents, who by now were getting used to me sticking hotel rooms in Malaysia and flights back and forth to Perth on my increasingly over-burdened Access card, suggested that we could both go for a mere snip of £200 each. I knew it was mad, but also wanted to give Al a birthday surprise.

Another thing I loved about Al was that she was never a 'girly'. I would buy her things and would never get a 'No you shouldn't have' – a very English response, anyway – but instead I would get a 'That's really cool' or 'yeah, fab!" to most positive things. So despite the fact that we had no money, and she was only doing locum work, we ended up on the morning of her birthday at Pireaus, taking a Flying Dolphin through the waves to Hydra. Al just seemed to love it; the fact she was in a new country, the fact that Greece was still relatively unspoilt, the donkeys in the harbour instead of cars to carry our bags to the hotel, with shuttered rooms that had no air conditioning. The whole thing just melted her, turned her into a puppy in the sunshine where she was coy, playful and occasionally sexily naughty. In fact, frequently sexually naughty. Actually, continuously, to the point of not leaving me a-bloody-lone naughty. I didn't complain.

We had had three or four days and in the middle day of the holiday we were sat on a harbour wall above the town. It was dusk and the daylight was fading whilst the villas on the hillside around town began to slowly light up. There was a customs house on the end of the harbour wall which was occupied by two rotund Greek customs officers. They appeared to be in disagreement over something. One would pop out, look towards town, turn, shaking his head and go back in. The other would then come out, repeat the same movements and then also go back. Each time, it seemed, that as one went back in another house would light up.

I explained to Al that they were not customs officers, but people I had hired to turn the day to night. They just weren't very good at it. We sat chuckling together as, unbeknown to them, they continued to act out a fantasy of lighting the town just for us. It was a warm night, it was a perfect night, in a perfect place. Romantic, artistic. Leonard Cohen had lived on Hydra for many years with his muse Marianne. It must have been the combination of the warmth, the constant sex, and the laughter at the efforts of the lighting customs officers -the whole perfection of the scene that led to the next moment.

I was sat with my back against the harbour wall and she was sat between my legs, her back against my chest. I could smell her hair and kiss her head and I just loved having her in my arms like this.

"Al," I said.

"Yeah," she said, giggling.

I didn't want her to giggle.

"Al, I've got something important to ask you."

"Important? What could be important here?" her tone was still jovial.

"Well, there's a question I need to ask you."

"Oh, like 'do I think they'll be a bar here that will have the West Brom game on tonight?'"

"No," I said, "More important than that."

She leaned her head back and looked toward my face, but for a moment her head was upside down.

"You mean there is something more important than the Baggies? Hey I gotta hear this!"

"OK," I said "Will you marry me?"

"Will I what?!"

"Will you marry me?"

For a moment, nothing mattered: I wanted her answer, but she gave me the answer I didn't want.

She was quiet for a moment and then she moved from between my legs, swung her body so that her feet dangled over the harbour wall and leaned towards me. She kissed me deeply on the mouth.

"Yes," she said "I would love to marry you!"

And the night was warm, and the air was still, and she gave me the answer I really didn't want. Fuck!

* * *

Sunday morning. I am in the bath at Drake House. I am enacting one of my favourite, favourite fantasies. I hold the loofah in my right hand.

"So," I say to myself, in a tone that is learnt from too much exposure to this kind of thing. "Mark Garvey – give the listeners at home your thoughts on last night's game."

"Well," I say in response to the journalist's probing question, "it was a tough game, you know, I mean it's been a while and I really wasn't sure how well I'd do."

"But you're happy with the result, happy with the way you performed?"

"Well you know Brian," they are always called Brian, "since my move from Birmingham, I haven't really been playing, so I saw last night's game as a warm up. Hampton View is always a tough place to go and not many people can come away with a result."

"Yes Mark, but not quite the convincing victory you had in mind."

"I'd disagree with that actually Brian. I mean we've got the second leg down at Drake and I always do better on home soil, so as to speak. I mean the Kalpna girl never made it easy for me, you know Brian, she really is world class, but I think I did enough to suggest that the second leg will be worth playing."

"So you don't see this match as being dead yet then?"

"No, don't be daft Brian. Everything to play for. Fat lady's not even gargled her mouth out yet."

"Any particular high points for you from last night?"

"Well obviously towards the end there were a few nice touches, felt I was back to my best form. Unlucky not to come away with a full result really but, as I say, I'm saving myself for when we get her back here. I've given her plenty to think about."

"And any last word for your fans?"

"No, just hope they're as happy as I am with the way things are going here in Devon."

He switches off his microphone. We exchange a few pleasantries, he walks off to the radio car to file his report. Tonight it will be broadcast on the sports desk that is the TV station that transmits from my head.

Everything to play for. Everything is going well.

* * *

Athens airport. Al is on the phone. She's been really wanting to make the call and mouths to me 'it's my mum'. She breaks her news about my proposal and starts to makes those girl noises that only girls and their mums seem able to replicate together. Halfway across the planet I imagine her mum smiling, being animated, happy. I can see that despite my private discomfort she is enjoying telling her mum the news. Happy at the way things are panning out.

Then she changes tone and mouths 'Dad'.

"Yeah, OK," she says "you can have a word with him." She seems silent. I sense that something is wrong.

She passes the receiver to me.

"Hi!" I say, trying to be as light and OK as possible. "How are you?" then he is off.

"To be honest Marky lad I am not that chuffed." For some reason he sounds very Scouse. "You know, when I was younger a lad used to have to ask a girl's father before he asked her to marry him and I think, well words fail me really."

I am really stunned, what the hell is this all about?

"And another thing," he continues, "I think you've been really rude actually. I mean I bloody paid for your flight over to Perth and the least I would've expected is a phone call from you!"

I try to explain "it was a," but he interrupts me.

"Oh I know what you're gonna say," he says, "a spur of the moment thing and all that but, well,"

He goes silent for a moment. I turn around and Al is actually laughing – why is she laughing? Then it clicks, but not before he says:

"Hey Mark, you're going to make a brilliant son-in-law. You are so easy Mark Garvey, you are so bloody easy!"

He is laughing now.

"Do you seriously think I'm that pompous? Do you?! You daft bugger you!"

Bastard! Bastard! I think, you were offering me a way out there, but -

"I'm delighted for you both, excellent bloody news, I'll even forgive you for supporting West Brom!"

Al is giggling in the background – she bloody knew that this had been a set-up, a private joke between her and her dad.

I felt like a man on a desert island who for a moment has seen the ship that will take him back to his old life – in my case, of being single, of being free to make my own choices – sail on by in the ocean beyond. Ever since I have never seen Scousers as funny. They're cruel, not funny. And Al's dad stole my freedom for the sake of a cheap joke on the back of a cheap proposal of marriage from me to his daughter. So, when I think about it, maybe at that moment in time I deserved everything I got.

CHAPTER 3 & p. 187

I am awake but my head is hurting. My mouth is really dry too
and other parts of me hurt like they haven't done for a while. I
have a sense that the room is spinning and I know that opening
my eyes is going to be bloody painful. I drank two pints of
water before I finally got into bed last night but that hasn't
seemed to work. *worked.*

I pluck up the courage to open my left eye and in so doing hit
the pain barrier. I feel like a marathon runner when they hit that
point in the race where the only thing they know they can do is
carry on. Pain, like shame, must be conquered. My one functioning
eye takes in a glass of wine on the bedside table next to me, my
trousers crumpled on the floor and general chaos around me.

It had started so well. I had managed to put together a
reasonably competent meal. It was only really minestrone soup,
some pasta and a few side dishes but even I thought everything
tasted about how it should. I returned the compliment of a
cheeseboard for afters and had bought some good coffee beans
to grind later.

When Kalpna arrived, she was very complimentary about
Drake House, even though she had been in here several times
before. She kissed me lightly on the cheek as she came into the
kitchen. I noticed her perfume again, subtle but musky – I still
didn't know the brand. And she looked as gorgeous as ever.
Trousers, a light diaphanous black top with a plunging v shaped
front, finished off with a pair of what Giovanni would have
called 'fuck me from behind' shoes. Wicked beyond words.

"Ooh," she said, "I admire your bravery – I threw you out of my kitchen."

I laughed, "Well to be honest, there's very little to see and I haven't got all my cookbooks so it's not a very adventurous meal." The second point was a barefaced lie. All the cookbooks I had ever owned where with me. There were no cookbooks in Drake House. It seemed like a convincing lie, though, because she didn't probe about whether I thought Delia Smith was better than Nigella Lawson, so I think I got away with it. All my recipes had come from Kay who had coached me over the phone on how to prepare everything.

Kalpna made the right noises, complimenting on the smells and so forth, and even admiring the freshly cooked ciabatta that had come out of the breadmaker.

Over the minestrone, we chatted about nothing much in particular, and I sensed that things were going to go well because there was no tension. None whatsoever.

I cleared away the soup bowls from the starter and set about getting the main course ready. I left Kalpna in the dining room admiring the sea view. We had already polished off a bottle and a half of wine I think, so it wasn't as if we weren't merryish. Anyway, I found her standing in the window nursing a wine glass, held against her chin.

I thought 'that looks like a woman who wants to be kissed'. The sensible thing to do would've been to wait and just acknowledge that I had a gorgeous woman in my lounge who might, if I didn't totally blow it, give me the chance to be more intimate later. I am not sensible.

I wandered over to the window, placed my hand on her shoulder and she turned towards me. I kissed her on the mouth, it was not just a 'hello' kiss, more of a 'those shoes are going to be useful tonight' kiss. Stupid! Stupid! Stupid!

She went berserk.

Within seconds, she was tugging at my clothes, pulling me down on to the floor. Somehow or other I found myself with her lying astride me looking down at me, ripping my shirt buttons off and just raining kisses down on to my chest. Then in a flash she had taken off her top and her bra exposing – well they were the most gorgeous breasts I had seen, the perfection of which were almost clinical. I can't remember what I was doing at the time, I think I was just too overcome with the pleasure that hit me in the way that pleasure hits you when you ride a rollercoaster or similar.

I could smell her hair, her perfume, but I could also smell dinner burning in the kitchen.

"Hang on! Hang on or we'll be joined by the bloody fire brigade."

I rushed to the kitchen and turned everything off, only to be met by Kalpna stood in the hallway. My trousers were the first to fall, hit by a shrapnel of passion fired at me from Kalpna's markswoman-like hands. And it just continued and continued and all I went over to her for was a kiss.

My head is still aching. I roll from my side to my back and look at the ceiling. I reach across to Kalpna and touch her outer thigh, she sighs and hums contentedly.

"Tea?" I ask.

"Hmm," she says, "that would be lovely. It is so long since a man made me tea in the morning."

I nervously get out of bed. What is happening here? What the hell is going on? I fight my way through the lust-strewn passion field that is the hallway. There are condoms, like some form of latex house parasite, all along the route between the kitchen and the bedroom. Scattered along the way are abandoned items of clothing, like tanks left by a retreating army. The mess in the kitchen is unbelievable. I rub my bottom as I pass the kitchen table and the sensation reminds me that we, at some point, had sex in here. Something about the edge of the kitchen table pressing into my buttocks jolts the memory.

I watch the kettle boil and the water turn to steam. Everything this morning is in slow motion. I have a beautiful woman dozing in my bed upstairs, I have had a night of passion unlike any before. I have a sense that life, in a strange way, has just got more complicated that it need ever be again.

ever need

* * *

I had never had a fiancée before. It was strange. I couldn't get used to using the term. I wondered if people with artificial limbs had the same problem with the word 'prosthesis'. It seemed to me that having a fiancée and having a false leg were pretty much the same thing. An appendage that had been grafted onto you rather than something that was actually yours.

On the other hand, Al seemed more than happy with her new status. She stayed excited, in every sense of the word, long after we returned from Hydra. We set no date for a wedding but still got sackfuls of congratulations cards from Australia, from aunts and uncles demanding to meet 'the lucky fella' and asking us what we wanted. So we also got pressies too, some of which were nice, some of which were dutiful but all of which ended up being put in nooks and crannies around the flat.

At work, everybody was happy for me in a PC sort of way. I got cards from some of my clients and my team (both of them) also bought me a present – a book by Germaine Greer on men in relationships. Good-hearted stuff, but typical of where I was at.

In the interim, Al found herself a permanent job and started to develop a social life. She was working up in a hospital in Sutton Coldfield. This created its own tensions as it meant we took it in turns to use the car or use public transport. So that gave us a bone of discontent, as it meant I could complain to myself on the bus on the way to work about the harshness of life. I always seemed to have to use public transport on days when the rain would fall, whereas Al always seemed to get to use the train on days when the sun shone. Or on the days she didn't have the car, she would always end up going out with friends after work and expect me to pick her up in a slightly, actually very, tipsy state. These were minor tensions at the time, but started to hint at a pattern of things to come and started to get to me subtly, slowly, stalking me emotionally.

Then, how I still don't know, I got another promotion to lead a bigger team that was more policy based than field based. So this created a disparity in income that again created a tension. I found that the pattern of me paying for meals out, tickets for the cinema and so on, that had been established when Al was a backpacker, continued even when she was earning. At the time, I didn't really resent this, but it became a running sore, a pimple that I would occasionally scratch in private but keep hidden from Al.

Just before Halloween, don't ask me how I know it was Halloween but it was, I got a call from Mike Dermott.

"Hello Marky," he said in a singsong voice that made me cringe. Nobody calls me Marky, with the exception of Al's dad.

"Mr Dermot," I responded, "How's life in the county of sheep-shagging?"

"Ooh," he replied, "you are so non-PC. Anyway, we're in Leeds, the sheep shaggers are all in Bradford and Calderdale."

"Funny, that's not what a colleague in Wakefield reckoned." And on it went. We were being jovial but I wondered why he had called. Eventually, having insulted most of West Yorkshire, he got to the point.

"I don't know how to put this," he said, adopting a sincere, caring, social worker tone that grated even more, "but there is a sensitive thing I need to discuss with you."

"I'm all hearing aids," I responded. "Fire away."

"Well, it's about Patrice really."

The moment he said her name, I got a flash back to her perfect bum, her skirt hitched high and her elbows leaning on the bed. I adjusted my seat just in case any of this was showing in the office.

"Oh yes," I said "what about Patrice?" I thought, 'what gives you the right to raise points about her with me?'

"Well," he said and then sighed. There was a long silence.

"Yes, go on Mike."

"Well she keeps on calling me about how she has really, I mean really, got the hots for you."

I thought 'oh just fuck off will you,' but decided to let him continue.

"Mike, if I had a penny for every woman who had the hots for me at work I'd owe people 50p. You know, I mean it's flattering and everything but I've just got engaged, very happy with it too and I'm afraid it's unrequited lust on her part."

"Oh," he said, "she knows about the engagement. I think all she wants is closure. Just a chance to do that face to face."

No. No. I knew that this would not be the case. She wanted me. Not closure.

"Well, it's impossible. No way. I'm here. She's in Belfast. End of story."

"Yes, but she wants to come to Birmingham to meet you".

Bloody hell! Oh for goodness' sake, somebody stop this.

"Well she'll just have to want," I said, trying to be as cold as I could.

"Look Marky, you know give her a break. She really wants to do this."

"No" I said firmly. And put the phone down.

The last 'no' must have been quite loud because in the open plan office around me a few people looked up. Gemma, a social worker who had a desk near me, spoke up. "Well Mark, who *doesn't* need to go on assertiveness training then?" A few people giggled. I just mouthed 'piss off' to the delightful but nosey sod.

Yet there was that bottom, haunting the remnants of my conversation with Mike. Not much else could be said, but events had been set in motion and there was little I could do to resist them. Not with that arse.

* * *

I like Bristol, always have done. I like Browns too. Something about it that exudes an air of easy living. I have just finished lunch with Giovanni. It's a Saturday and I have come up for the weekend but in an old-laddish couple of hours we have got together alone to discuss life, the universe and everything.

It is good to be with him. We always seem to spend most of our time together doing my favourite things which include talking about music, reminiscing about life in our band as teenagers, talking about women, generally just drinking and laughing. If only he liked football, the guy would be perfect.

We are discussing life in Hope Cove, which is a precursor to discussing my sex life. I have hinted, and with Giovanni my hints are about as subtle as an elephant farting in a boiler suit, that something is happening. He has this ability to get me to tell him things I don't tell other people. He was the first to know that Al and I were serious, for example, and he was the first to know that we were breaking up. Even in the interlude between Al finally going and me moving to Devon, he became priest-like in hearing my confessions of immorality and seemed quite interested in the revolving door that led to my bedroom. So each conquest or failure was discussed ad infinitum.

"So is it someone at the new place your working at?" Geo asked, getting bored with the wait after so many bloody hints.

"Nope," I responded. "You know me, I'm trying to stop bonking colleagues, at least for the moment."

"OK," he was into guessing mode now and we had time to kill, "Is it someone from the past, like Patrice the Scottish girl."

I sighed "Oh for goodness' sake matey, she was from Northern Ireland. And no it is not Patrice, it's somebody new."

"New?" said Geo. "Go on."

"Well look," I said, "We've only really slept together once and, you know -"

Geo knew that all I really had to do was sleep with somebody once and I fell in love with them. Was I flattered that somebody dared to venture into my bed with me? Did I just have an open heart? In reality, this wasn't true any more. Before leaving Birmingham, I slept with too many women, none of whom I fell in love with (well OK, one, but that was infatuation) so I knew that I wasn't as vulnerable to my heart ruling my head as I had been in the past.

"OK," Geo continued, "She's new and you haven't met her through work. She's not the Asian girl in the shop you mentioned, is she?"

That was below the belt "Come on matey, you know my views on sleeping with women that young, it's just too perverted. What was it the Leonard Cohen said 'there's nothing worse than seeing an older man come on to a younger woman.' Or something like that anyway."

"So???"

"So it's her mum!"

"Ah-ha!" Geo responded. "You've always had a hankering for Indian women anyway."

This was also true and showed that Geo in his priest-like role kept fairly accurate mental notes of my tastes and preferences. He could for example always give you a list of actresses that I would or wouldn't sleep with. The list included people like Nicole Kidman, the young Juliana Moore and Kate Winslett. The 'wouldn't' list always amused me as really I think if push came to shove, and she asked, I probably would sleep with the younger Meryl Streep or Cate Blanchett. They just must've mislaid my phone number.

"So what does she look like, and more importantly what's her name and what does she do? What division is she in?" Geo probed.

This last comment went back to a stupid game we used to play whereby we would rate females as being Premier League, Championship, and so on, going all the way down to Sunday League park football. There were also variations so we knew that some women thought they were Premier League when in fact they wouldn't even make the bench in the Second Division. I also rated myself on this scale, too, which meant that I saw myself in the same category as West Brom – Championship, with occasional seasons in the Premiership.

"She's like Al," I said "Definitely Champions League."

"Hmm," said Geo "I thought you said Al was only First Division in the end?"

"Well, yeah I did. But in her prime she was Premier League. She would've won the odd cup too, but," I was getting bored with the analogy, it didn't feel right talking about Al as if she were still to be rated.

"And what name does this new woman have?"

"Kalpna – she's a doctor"

Geo imitated a sort of Frankie Howard voice, "Ooh I say, missus – make sure her hands are warm, ooh, yes."

"Stop it," I said laughing. "You're cheapening something that could be," my toned softened at this point, "special."

Geo teased me. "Mr Garvey! Well you can't keep a good plonker down, that's what I always say. You impress me. Been there less than three months and already you've started with a local doctor. For that reason alone I'll buy lunch."

'Oh here we go,' I thought. We never ever seemed able to do this bit graciously. No matter who paid the other made a fuss so this time I thought 'bollocks – let him do it.'

"OK – thanks," I said.

Geo was taken aback for a moment and gave me a suspicious look. "Hang on, there's a catch? Go on, what's the catch?!"

"No, no. If you want to buy me lunch that's great. I'll buy you, Jane and Matty lunch when you come down."

"OK," he said, still suspicious, "she's not put you on anything, this doctor, has she?"

I laughed

"No," I said, "but I could always arrange for her to spike your food with something horrible!"

He knew I was joking. Now, though, I had crossed the Rubicon, moved over a threshold. I had told Giovanni about Kalpna. This was now in the open. So Jane, his wife, and Matty would know her name, I'd even have to come up with a sign for Matty so that he didn't have to fingerspell it every time. A little part of me was slightly unsure; had I told too much too soon? Was I tempting fate? These musings were interrupted by Geo's mobile phone.

"Shit!" he said "No darling, we'll be there ASAP."

He turned to me, "You are a bad influence, Mark Garvey – come on, we've got to go and pick Jane and Matty up – you've made me late."

We left in a hurry. I was relieved and Geo was decent enough not to push me any harder on details about Kalpna. Perhaps he shared my anxiety; perhaps I had said too much too soon. He knew me too well. I was always telling him about beautifully-wrapped Christmas presents that turned out to be empty boxes.

* * *

She was tense and I really didn't know what to do.

"You're sure?" I asked, more in hope than in any sense of her having got it wrong.

"Yes. Yes Mark, I'm absolutely bloody sure." she was starting to cry.

I went over to her on the sofa to comfort her. I put my arm around her. It was just so bloody typical. Life could never be sunshine and smiles, it always had to be drizzle and thunderstorms.

"What am I going to do? I'm not even qualified yet! I mean, this is so bloody-" she let out a deep sigh, her shoulders were heaving; she was more upset than I had ever seen her.

"It's a 'we' thing sweetheart, not an 'I' thing."

"Oh fuck off!" she said. "That's fucking easy for you to say – you haven't got to either carry the thing for another 8 months or go through the termination." She got up and stormed out of the room, slamming the door behind her. Anita, perched high on a shelf above the TV, leapt into the air, nearly dying of the shock. I just didn't know what to do.

After about 5 minutes, I went through into the bedroom where Al was lying on her back staring at the ceiling. I stood in the doorway, looking in.

"Can I come in?" I asked.

She nodded agreement, silently.

"Al, I'll go along with whatever you want to do. We'll find a way to get through this. I'm sorry if I occupied your space by saying it was an 'us' thing. I just don't want you to feel on your own. That's all."

She held her arms outstretched in front of her, I climbed on to the bed and just held her while she cried. She sobbed. Huge tears. Her body just shook, and with her tears I started crying too. This was a horrible situation.

We lay on the bed together for hours. Mid afternoon became late afternoon, and then passed to early evening. We were silent, distressed, wanting nothing but the comfort of each other, the occasional holding of hands or sometimes I would kiss away her tears as it was all I could think to do. Eventually Al spoke.

"Mark, I can't keep it. It's just not right. Not at the moment. I don't want to marry you with a bulge under my wedding dress. You know, all my family, they'd only think we were getting married because of this." She pointed to her stomach.

"Al, don't think about what people will think, what about what you want?"

"I want to have fun. I don't want to be a mum, not yet. We've got so much to do and I want to do that. I think it will be 3 or 4 years before I'm ready to be a mum".

"Well," I said "if that's what you want."

She started panicking again. "The thing is, that if I have a termination, if I get rid of it, what if I never get pregnant again? What if I get punished and can never have kids in the future?" She started crying again. The illogicality of it all was just too much. For the first time since we met, I felt a tenderness towards her that was protective, that wanted just to shut the world out and let her do what she wanted. The emotional equivalent of running away to the circus together.

The next few days were awful. We were both all over the place, but very tender with each other. We seemed to spend hours sat in silence on the sofa, Anita looking on, trying to make sense of these humans. 'One minute they smile all the time, the next they cry – they're weird'. The nine lives of a cat must've seemed so much simpler.

Eventually, after a visit to the doctors, it was agreed. Al wanted a termination. Even the word avoided the reality. Abortion. No matter how you dress it up, you know that you're taking a life away and you know, one way or another, that you've swooped down to the depths of morality. Yet there is no other choice.

The day came when I had to drive Al to the clinic. We tried to stay light and sort of made out that she was going to the dentist, but we knew. I kissed her on her cheek as she got out of the car and watched her walk through the door into the clinic. She looked like a kid, not someone old enough to have a baby. Thoughts raced through my head. 'Nobody is ever old enough to have a child, I don't care what people ever say. It's too much responsibility, too much of a bind. We fuck up our own lives, how can we be expected to sort out new ones that are supposed to model themselves on us? Madness.' So I made that promise to myself, sat in a little Fiat Punto, that I would never be a parent.

The days and weeks that followed were surreal. Al came home, had a few days off work and then we carried on as normal. There was only one thing missing and it was the one thing that had drawn me to her initially. But I could understand it. I mean, no inquest had been held, but it was obvious that as well as being repulsed from the termination Al was also scared. We had taken precautions, using condoms all the time. But now was off the agenda. Every effort, every potential moment of passion ended in the same situation. We'd get to the point of penetration and Al would clam.

91

"No, I can't," she'd say and I'd be understanding but still frustrated. So we could do lots of things but we couldn't have penetrative sex. We'd kiss in places where we had never kissed before, we'd do strangely erotic things in strangely erotic places, but we didn't actually do the business – she wouldn't have me inside her. And even when she made me come, she would move away from me as if my sperm was radioactive waste, the touch or taste of which would kill. All that sperm, all that life, going to waste on my thighs, into paper handkerchiefs.

Then a final twist. To cheer Al up, I decided to take her to the Lake District for the weekend. And although it was surreal, and I spent a fortune at a veggie country house hotel, it seemed to work. We walked and talked and she loved the scenery and the feshness. We finally got back to Birmingham late on Sunday evening. We were laughing and chatting as we came in through the flat door. There in front of us was a note that had been pushed under the door. It was from Pete, our neighbour.

"Dear Mark and Al, please, please come downstairs when you get back."

Something about the tone wasn't right. Pete was normally a light bloke who would leave a message on the answerphone before a note, he wasn't the note-writing sort, he never even sent Christmas cards.

Al had already wandered through into the kitchen to put the kettle on. She called through:

"Hey, looks like Anita is dieting – she's not touched her food!"

Then I knew.

We went downstairs. Pete was fantastic, he knew how much Anita had meant to me, and he was also meant to have been feeding her. She had been found dead, in a gutter, just round the corner from the flat. He handed me an old box, a supermarket cardboard box that had previously been used for dog food. Inside was Anita. There was blood stained into her tabby coat and her midriff was twisted. She looked like she was asleep. But she was dead.

Then, more than over the termination, more than any of the missing I had felt for Al, I cried, really, really cried. All I could do was shudder as I realised that there was no Anita. No one to listen to the football commentary with on the radio, nobody to share my bad jokes with, who didn't grimace when I told them, and nobody who simply listened when I talked without judging. Just a void, a horrible empty void between me, and the world now and the world that had been.

* * *

I have a confession. Life scares me. It's the speed of it.

I'm sat here now and I've just got back from viewing about half a dozen properties. Nothing wrong with that, except that Kalpna and Alpha are in the kitchen discussing the relative merits and demerits of the ones I've viewed. I can hear them talking but can't really hear what they're saying.

It's only three weeks since Kalpna and I have slept together and we're starting to feel like Terry and June. I'm not really sure if I want this but I'm going with the flow.

How life happens. There I was, happily sexually frustrated, now I have a sex life. There I was, happily making my own mistakes, now I have an angel watching over me, helping to guide me to the best decisions.

Alpha appears in the doorway to the lounge. "Mark, didn't you like the last one best? I thought it was lovely." She is carrying a tray with biscuits and a pot of Darjeeling tea. Her mum appears behind her, carrying cups and a jug of milk. I catch her eye and she raises an eyebrow and smiles. She's enjoying the precociousness of her precocious daughter.

"I think they were all interesting," I said "But they're only to rent. Not to buy."

[handwritten margin note: say]

Alpha looks frustrated at this. "Yeah, but I mean you want to be happy, don't you? Anyway, I don't know why you can't just move in here."

This brings Kalpna and I up sharply. Kalpna speaks.

"Alpha I think you're making too many assumptions, don't you?"

Alpha looks embarrassed. "I'm sorry," she offers. "If you were students you'd be living together. Loads of people move in together at Bristol, only takes days there.."

"Maybe I should move to Bristol," I say to Alpha smiling. but this causes Kalpna to give me a strange look, a look that say 'Hoi – don't bloody encourage her," except I have never heard Alpha swear in this sort of setting – only in the bedroom.

[handwritten margin note: Kalpna]

I start to feel uncomfortable, like I have let my defences down far too quickly. Kalpna is beautiful, there's no doubt about that, but this is claustrophobic. I'm getting caught up in a grown up-world when I just want time to be a child for a while. I want to make my own decisions, not share them with others, or to seek approval for what I'm doing.

I go quiet. Alpha hasn't noticed and is still continuing a running commentary on what, I don't know, but Kalpna has. She is stood behind her and mouths 'Are you OK?' but I just turn away, look out at the view down into Hope Cove for the moment. By doing this, I feel like I am committing an act of betrayal. So I immediately look back and whilst Alpha is wittering away her Mum mouths 'Come on – she means well'. I nod.

[handwritten margin note: she's]
[handwritten margin note: Alpha]

I want an excuse to leave and just in the nick of time my

94

mobile vibrates and shows that I have a new text message. I hit the button and it opens.

'I've tried to warn you. You have to stop.'

It's identical to the last one – no identification signs on it, no time or number showing.

"Look," I say, hiding behind the excuse of the text message. "I have to pop down to Drake, something has cropped up. Work."

"Do you want me to run you down there?" Kalpna asks, who has been doing all the driving, on account that she knows the area better than I do, which has only added to my sense of my life being hijacked.

"No, you're OK." I explain. "I'll take my car. It might take me an hour or so to sort this so I'll call you later, is that OK?"

"OK," she says nodding. She comes across and kisses me on the cheek and I don't know if I imagine it but I get the impression she is trying to look at the mobile to see who the message is from. I stuff it into my jacket pocket quickly.

A moment later I am out walking down the path back at the front of Hampton View. I know that tonight I need time to myself because if I don't get it I'll kick back too hard. I decide there and then to unplug the phone, leave myself alone. Decisions on where I live can wait until I know that they will be mine.

* * *

We were reaching the first unravelling. Al was depressed, a form of post-natal depression that is apparently quite common after abortions and I was depressed because, well it seemed the easiest thing to be. Neither of us was were obviously down to the outside world, we just knew that we weren't right. Al's passion was just not in the neighbourhood; every time I called, it seemed to be out. Equally, on the few occasions that she tried to find me in, it just wasn't the right time.

Fortunately for me, things were going well at work. I felt a bit like Chancy Gardener in 'Being There.' I wasn't doing anything particularly brilliant but I found myself gradually being given more trust and responsibility. Then I managed to get a secondment as Executive Assistant to our Director, Geoff Times. It was only a 6-month thing, but it exposed me to stuff that had previously not been on my radar screen. And Geoff liked me, which was reassuring. The secondment also brought me into contact with councillors more, so I found that my status in the department was going up. Little things, like I'd be walking out of City Hall with colleagues from my old team and the Chair would approach me with a 'Mark, can you just let me have the latest District Auditors report on...' Well, it made people think 'God – he's on first name terms with the Gods.' I found myself having to be around at meetings in the evenings or getting involved in consultation things that ate into my free time.

Al initially liked that fact that I was earning more money and that I seemed happier with my lot. Yet she started to feel a bit neglected too. The sort of conversations we would have over a cup of tea in the morning went like this:

"Hey, why don't we go for a curry tonight?" Al would say brightly.

I'd try to respond positively but it never came out that way.

"Well I've got a meeting tonight, so if you don't mind eating later?"

"Later? OK. How late is later?" You could sense the tension and you knew that there would be no curry.

So the more this went on, the more I found myself going for a drink with Geoff and councillors and not rushing to get back home. And often when I did get back home, Al wouldn't be there, because she'd decide to go and see a film, or meet up with people from work or she'd go to bed early.

I think we both still loved each other. We were just changing. Actually, that's not fair on Al. I was changing and in the process I was becoming self-absorbed with work.

About midway through this, we had a horrible Saturday night where we both got smashed, something else we seemed to do more of than when we first met, and ended up trying to have sex. At some point, Al just seemed to die on me and lay there whilst I thrusted away, but it was like making love to a corpse. Neither of us came. Instead midway through, I stopped. Then, unexpectedly, she started to cry and went on and on about how it wasn't her fault.

"I know you're not happy are you? Nobody can be happy with a zombie cunt like mine." The word 'cunt' just hit me like somebody throwing a cricket ball in my face.

"I could go back to Perth if you want me to, I could leave you to find a normal woman. Somebody who fucked properly." And then, in this drunken and horrible state she just cried and cried and cried.

I was telling her that I loved her, I was trying to explain that she was still the only woman I wanted and she just got angry.

"You say that now, but for how long?! How long will you put up with this, huh?! When are you going to have some fucking self-regard? When are you going to have some self-respect?" She started pointing down to her pussy "This doesn't work! – Get it? It doesn't work!!"

More tears, more histrionics. A horrible night.

"We'll work it through," I kept on saying. "We'll work it through."

And I'm sure we would have done, but for the fact that on Monday morning, exhausted by the fighting, I decided to let

Geoff's secretary put a call through to me. A call from Patrice.

* * *

I've been wandering the streets for hours, trying to work things out. About once an hour, Kalpna has called or texted me. Unusually, I have ignored these calls, either turning my phone to voicemail or ignoring the text messages totally.

I don't want to see her tonight and I can't explain why. I'm enjoying being on my own and keep asking myself why I've chosen to get involved with her anyway. I wander through the streets that are wet after an early spring shower. Hope Cove in the darkness has a different quality to Hope Cove by day. It's quiet at night, particularly in the main High Street. I stand by the memorial clock tower, a strangely shaped wrought iron affair erected to commemorate one of Queen Victoria's jubilees. Its dullness has been broken by a coat of blue paint, a light blue that used to be used for municipal transport, buses and the like. What strikes me is that for 11.30 at night, on a Thursday, there are so few people around. Then again, I'm up in the centre of town, away from the harbour. I pass The Kingfisher, a pub I never use despite its aesthetic appeal. I realise that most of my time in Hope Cove has been spent around the harbour, away from the heart of things, and it strikes me that I have been making some strange choices.

It starts to rain again. I am feeling like the loneliest man in the world as my phone starts to vibrate. I can feel it in my pocket and I've grown bored of not answering. It can only be one person. I pull it from my pocket, its face illuminated showing Kalpna's name.

"Hi," I say, without any sense of emotion.

"Mark. You're OK, aren't you?" Her voice is calming, tranquil, and almost hypnotic.

I am OK. "Of course," I say, ignoring the sense of claustrophobia that I'm feeling, "How are you?"

"Wanting," she says, using one word to convey so much.

"Oh?" I ask, "what are you wanting?"

She goes silent for a moment, then speaks:

"I want you. I want you here next to me in bed. I want to feel you inside me. I want to feel you coming. I want you with me, Mark."

Her tone isn't pleading but cool. She's collected, in control and I'm struck by how 'wanting' is such an underused word.

"Hmm," I say, "that wanting sounds enticing."

"So come and explore it," she says, "come and taste me, on your mouth, on your tongue, come and smell me, come and have me."

I know I'm not in the mood, I know that I want to go back to Drake House, where I could indulge myself in music or just have having a deep bath. Yet there will be other nights for that sort of thing.

I pause and I'm interrupted by Kalpna.

"You still there?"

"Yep, I'm still here," I say. Her calmness is infectious because — I find myself being calm too.

"Come to me. Please."

I think 'hang up. You don't have to do this' and I know that going back to Drake House is the best decision I can make.

"Give me 5 minutes." Before I have even put the phone back in my pocket I have changed course, set sail for Hampton View. I smell the sea in the air, taste the salt. Yet I know that if I wanted to spend the rest of the night tasting salt I could go home and sprinkle as much as I like on to a table top and stick my tongue straight into the middle of the white heap of nothingness. Salt isn't as satisfying as the muskiness of vanilla, or the taste of

Kalpna's nipples, or the scent of dark, lustful sex in the delights of her dark lustful crevices.

My pace quickens. The speed of life still scares me but this life of lust anaesthetises my fear.

* * *

It's strange what we notice and don't notice. When eras end we get no warning. The world isn't crafted in the neatness of events like 9-11; that was a one off and atypical. Instead things crumble without you even noticing them. Like when a great defender suddenly loses the ability to time the tackles as well as they used to. At first you put it down to the fact that they're carrying an injury, then you notice that they keep picking up bookings or conceding free kicks where in the past they would never have done so. And before you know it you're with the rest of the morons around you, baying for their substitution, suggesting that they spend time in the reserves, ignoring the fact that everything changes and that you in your arrogance have lost the ability to see your own imperfections. You like to think that you're above hunting with the pack, above the consciousness of the mob. So you lie to yourself and pretend that the mob is being led by you, and then it's easy to ignore the hurt you inflict or the misplaced self-belief you follow. All that matters is being seen to be right, even if you know that you're wrong.

Al and I played out our first disintegration fixtures in Edgbaston. Edgbaston had its range of pubs and hostelries, some of which were very dull, some of which were a bit livelier. One, The Lost Weekend, seemed particularly popular with straight and gay people. I've never understood why particular pubs develop in this way. I mean OK, there are places in Soho or on Canal Street in Manchester, but these are well-established gay communities. As far as I was aware, at the time anyway, Edgbaston was hardly known as a bastion of sexual tolerance, so it always struck me as odd that the Weekend had this sort of mix.

It was a great pub – the sort of pub where you could happily spend two hours with a pint and not be bothered by the bar staff, so I guess its relaxed atmosphere was probably its appeal. Al loved to hang out in there on a Sunday afternoon. So at first I just thought it was the relaxed atmosphere that made her chatty with the sisters. Al was chatty at the best of times anyway, except when she was on her own with me, when she could've won gold medal in the 10,000 metres being miserable event. Yet the sisters always seemed keen to chat with her, and the keenness was more than a way of passing the time. She always seemed to attract gay women and didn't do that much to repel them.

It ate at me. She seemed to enjoy the flirting. Was it my imagination, or was she followed into the loo a couple of times? Or was I just trying to find a reason to justify my own actions?

I was feeling guilty about Patrice. The phone call had been so easy -too easy- and I wasn't comfortable with how I was slipping into the role of love rat.

"Hi. I thought I'd never speak to you again," she said. Her tone was soft but her Belfast accent made everything sound as gentle as sandpaper being stroked against a nipple.

"Well – we just couldn't go on avoiding each other, could we?"

She was silent for a moment. "Look, I really want to come and see you. You know, I know it's silly, and I'm really sorry about what happened in Newcastle, but I just want to chat really."

'Yes,' I thought, 'and Gerry Adams would much rather be a painter and decorator than a mouthpiece for Sinn Fein?'

"OK" I responded, no longer regretting the decision, just keen to get the fixture off the books, "when do you want to meet."

"Well look," she said, brightening, I could feel her enthusiasm down the phone line, "I have got to go on a training course in Bristol, so maybe we could meet after I've done that. I mean, Bristol's not far from Birmingham is it?"

So for a while we got lost in the practicalities of dates and what have you.

"Look," she said "I'll book myself in to a wee hotel. We can meet for a drink and talk things through."

I had no problem with this. It had now been 12 weeks since anything sexual had happened with Al. As far as I was concerned, if she'd had said, 'we can meet for a quick fuck', I would've gone along with it. I hated the clinical aspect of it all but she'd satisfy a need.

I was thinking about this as Al came back from the loo at the Lost Weekend. So what if she snogged the odd dyke in the loo? Compared to what was going on for me, this was nothing. Absolutely nothing.

She sat down on the sofa next to me. She seemed brighter.

"Hey, why don't we order some food?" she asked, smiling at me.

"OK." I thought that there was a glimpse of the old me and her, through the crack in the curtain of resentment that seemed to have been hung between us. I wanted to touch her and to kiss her and to take her home and to make love to her gently, slowly.

Instead we ordered two veggie lasagnes and sat like brother and sister, to go home to sleep like brother and sister and not to explore the possibility of any incest in the future. I was prepared to wait, anyway. Until after Patrice and after the flavour of the sauce from my feeding had become a distant memory. So what if I conceded a free kick here, picked up a booking there? I was leading this not responding to the baying of the crowd and their warped logic.

* * *

Then the bollocks. It has been a less than easy meeting.

"Let's go over this again. If you take them to tribunal, there's a huge risk you'll get less than this," said Pat Quinn, my scary but very effective solicitor. "If I were you Mark, I would take what they're offering."

This wasn't what I wanted to hear. I wanted to set the record straight because I knew I was dealing with lies. The worst sort of lies – lies that actually questioned my integrity. I fingered the edge of my glasses, something I always do when I'm unsure about things. Pat looked at me, trying to work out what was going on behind my frames.

"Look," she said, "if it's any consolation I totally believe you – everybody I have spoken to says these allegations are stupid and you and I know that they are only allegations. There's no evidence, Mark."

I sighed. Hindsight is great. With hindsight, I would never have gone to a Diwali party with a group of colleagues. I would never have agreed to going to the pub with them afterwards or to having sat next to an over-sexed, straight out of university basic social worker called Uma. And I wouldn't now have been dealing with an allegation that I sexually assaulted her, I mean I didn't even talk to her for that long. And I knew it was revenge. Social work at the best of times attracts a type of woman that is, at best sceptical about men, at worst who hates us. I mean, sometimes I share their hatred too. We can be the most obnoxious species around, male humans. But we're not all the same; we're different. We don't automatically see women as only sex objects. But they

103

knew about Al and I having split up and the knives were out. Time to add the scalp of an Assistant Director to their display that documented the success of their own Stalinism. The

Pat looked across again.

"Well Mark, it's your call."

'If only it were,' I thought, 'it would be great if all this could be put to the scrutiny of a sports phone in programme with the presenter arguing the toss with viewers at home.

'Next we've got Keith in Stoke-on-Trent. Keith, you want to talk about the Mark Garvey affair?'

Keith, an inarticulate Port Vale fan, would be heard down the phone line – half-pissed because these things always go out after pub closing time.

'I think it's diabolical,' he starts to rant, 'Mark Garvey just isn't the sort of guy to do this kind of thing. You know I've never been a fan but he's decent. Anyone knows that."

'No smoke without fire though Keith, and he is meant to like Asian women.'

'Oh, I like Swedish women but it doesn't make me a Viking rapist does it, eh?" he responds quickly.

I drop this line of thinking; I have to concentrate on what Pat is saying.

"Look, I can buy us 48 hours or so for you to decide. But you have to decide."

"OK," I say, "I'm moving house tomorrow anyway so can we leave it until Monday morning?"

"I'll do my best," she says.

I so much want to nail the bastards for this, to hit them where it hurts, because allegations like this destroy people. I saw it happen in the past and I am not going to let them destroy me. But I pay Pat an awful lot of money to tell me the things I don't want to hear. I get up to leave.

"There's one other thing," I say.

She brushes her blonde hair back off her face. She's not unattractive, but a bit too mumsy for me.

"Go on," she says, glancing at her watch making sure I know that the clock is still running; her time for me is professional, not personal.

I explain about the frequent strange text messages. I just want to share the information with someone.

"Sorry," she says, "sounds like a criminal matter. I'll have a word with a colleague about it if you want," which means 'pay me more and I will do it.' "I suspect they'll advise you to either go to the police or change your mobile phone. Not much we can do about that one. There's a limit to the powers of solicitors even," she says this with a big smile. I know she doesn't believe it. Everybody in the legal profession believes they're omnipotent. It's why so many of them go on to be politicians and end up bombing innocent countries and betraying principles whilst still managing to grin their inane smiles with the forcefulness of a child wronged.

"OK," I say as I rise to leave. I glance at my watch too – playing the same game of keeping time.

"I'll call you – let you know what I want to do next."

I make my way outside. I look at the trees with their spring apple blossom, I catch the sight of a guy walking down the road with his guide dog, a mum and toddler chatting to each other about nothing in particular, a shop keeper exchanging a joke with a traffic warden. I am annoyed that they are so, so what? Oblivious? Detached? Then I realise that bollocks only matter to the people who are having theirs cut off. The rest of the world carries on, oblivious that they could be the next to go under the knife. I realise that by and large this indifference makes the world a better, not worse, place.In the end we all have to get happy – everything else is just self-indulgence.

* * *

The Hagley Road is despicable. I hate it. It grinds on for miles out of Birmingham after Five Ways, taking the motorists who use it back to their suburban lives with a warning. 'Look,' it says to them, 'your lives may be empty but think about the poor bastards who end up staying in these hotels." The comfort of a semi-detached house, with a semi-detached marriage and a semi-detached love, must be infinitely better than having to spend time in a hotel on this rain-washed strip. Staying in a hotel on the Hagley Road is the nearest that mortals can come to purgatory.

Patrice didn't know Birmingham, so she booked herself into the Oak Lodge on Hagley Road. It was a Friday and I lied to Al that I had a conference to go to.

"On a Friday?!" she asked, which was a good question.

So I lied and said it was a residential thing for day centre staff that I was opening because Geoff was indisposed.

"You mean he's going away for the weekend?" she said. If the lie hadn't been a lie, I would have risen to defend Geoff's honour but instead I ignored her comment.

"Anyway," I continued, "I've got to stay for a buffet dinner and then I'll be back about 9.30. We can go to a late movie if you like."

Al looked distinctly unimpressed.

"Nah," she said, "I'll hang out with Joy from work, catch you when I get home."

I have to say that Joy was not my favourite person. I mean, she was nice enough and could be fun to be around when the mood took her, it's just that the mood never took her very often. Worse still, she had introduced Al to the music of Cheryl Crow, an unforgivable crime in my eyes. She always seemed to bring out the excess in Al, too. Still, if she was with Joy, there was less chance of a confrontation whatever time I eventually chose to turn up. Her and Al would spend the night drinking, talking about Joy's life as a physio and probably allowing her to complain about the absence of romance in her life. A common complaint, usually accompanied by confessions of deepest love for me and Al after a bottle or three of wine too many.

So on a Friday afternoon, about two weeks before Easter, a not very good Friday I suppose, I found myself in the lobby of the Oak Lodge. It was dingy and smelt of stale cigarettes with an undertone of antiseptic. The owner, obviously used to such situations, made no fuss when I asked him to call Patrice's room.

"She says you can go up," he said. with a half smile that conveyed he knew all he needed to know.

The rooms were much more pleasant than the lobby area. Although the décor wasn't really that important to me, not much was that important to me.

I found Patrice's room. She opened the door. We chatted for five minutes or so, she ordered some wine – a cheap bottle of some Italian white that was neither sweet nor dry, or chilled come to that. Then we fucked. No poetry, no lyricism. It was sex and that's all it was.

Before I left, we agreed we'd meet again but made no firm dates.

I arrived home. It was late evening. 'Friends' had just reached the commercial break and there was a note from Al on the kitchen work surface.

'Out with Joy. Be back late, gone clubbing. Sort yourself out. Al x.'

No poetry there either. Just the harsh realities of life after straying into the gutter on the Hagley Road.

She is on the phone arguing.

"Mr Garvey, the place was really a terrible mess."

This is nonsense. I left Drake House spotless and I know it.

"How do you define mess?" I asked, "Everywhere had been vacuumed and dusted before I left. So I fail to see how you could deduct £200 from my deposit."

"Look Mr Garvey, this is pointless. You have a cheque from me for the balance of your deposit; I suggest you pay it into your account and we'll say no more about your goings on."

"My goings on? I think that needs explanation, Mrs Mapp."

"You know very well what I'm referring to. But I never pass judgement on other people's morality."

This was rich. It was like the Pope suggesting that he really wasn't that interested in hearing confessions.

"Mrs Mapp, you steal £200 off me and then have the audacity to comment on my morality. I find the poverty of intellect on display at your end of the phone line breathtaking."

She snaps back, "Look, don't you try being clever with me. It cuts no ice, do you understand sonny?" There is more a hint of Glasgow than Edinburgh to her once refined accent. She has moved from Morningside to Paisley in the space of 30 seconds, and she's still heading west of Queen Street station.

"Enough," I say firmly. "I'll put this in the hands of my solicitors Mrs Mapp," and slam the phone down. It echoes around my office and Anna, who must have been passing, sticks her head around the door with her concerned look well to the fore.

"Are you alright?" she asks.

I am but I'm still angry at the interfering old haggis. I nod.

"Who was that on the phone, a member?" Anna asks.

"No, no – just Wilma Mapp my landlady".

"Ooh, you need to watch her," says Anna, "she's evil!"

I blink. Did I just hear that correctly?

"Sorry, Anna, what did you say?"

"Wilma Mapp, she's as evil as they come that one."

The text messages flash into my head. The words are almost identical.

"Is it you?!" I ask.

"Me what?!" says Anna, shocked at the ferocity of my enquiry.

"Text messages. I've been getting anonymous text messages that say things like 'beware she is evil.'

Anna is wide-eyed "I don't even have a mobile phone!" she says – "and besides Mark, I'd tell you."

She's right. The most gorgeous thing about Anna is that there is no hidden agenda. WYSWYG. That's Anna.

"Sorry, sorry," I say. "I don't think you're sending me stupid text messages. Look, forget this conversation, OK?"

She nods "I'll make you some tea. You'll feel better after a brew." And she is gone.

'Why is so much getting on top of me?' I think. But I don't really need to answer this question because I know.

First there's my new accommodation. It's not Drake House. OK it's good, it's got everything I want, has fantastic sea views, but it's not Drake. Stockwell Cottage is away from the harbour, a good 10-minute walk from The Ship. I've got it for the next 6 months, but it's not what I want. I compromised. Worse still, Giovanni phoned me the other week to say him and Jane have managed to book Drake House for the May Day week. That feels like he's managed to bed one of my previous girlfriends – not that he would ever do a thing like that. Not that any of my previous girlfriends wouldn't go to bed with him.

Then there's Kalpna. I mean I really, really like Kalpna. I lust after her continuously, but I don't think it's love. It's great sex but not love. In fact, our sex games are becoming a bit- well I'm not sure what the word is, but 'strange' is the only one I can think of. At first I didn't mind her occasionally biting me, or even pulling at my nipples, but now she's really getting much more aggressive and domineering. It's a strange kind of dominance. More of a maternal sort of thing. Take last night – last night she wanted me to wear some rubber pants in bed. Rubber pants? OK, so it was an interesting idea, and yes I did put them on but, well I'm really not too sure if this is all healthy. It's dirty though, and sometimes it's nice to be dirty.

The bollocks trundles on. I finally persuaded Pat to push for more than the £30K they were offering and to put in the relevant documentation for employment tribunal. She wasn't happy, but I think of what they have accused me of and I think £30K is like being pissed on (something that Kalpna has yet to do!). I know, though, that all I'm doing is pushing up my legal fees, eating into the money I will finally have and just being stupid. Point is, I know this. I know this and I'm still pushing in the wrong direction.

Anna returns.

"Tea," she says. She smiles as she puts the cup down on to my desk.

"And I thought you'd like some of these too." She offers me a packet of custard creams.

I smile. Custard Creams. Tea. Is this the route of all happiness? I wonder at her ability to distil the simplest acts into something that is more important, something that has a deeper meaning. Dominic and Liam probably don't even know how lucky they are. But then who does? Do I? Or do I just sit here complaining that the glass is always half empty and cracked at best?

I pull a custard cream from out of the pack, dipping its corner into my tea. And through one small gesture, I discover that life can be simple again and fun if we just enjoy the moment.

* * *

After the Hagley Road incident, things went quiet on the Patrice front. She phoned me a couple of times at work and we chatted about nothing in particular, but there that was friendship rather than affection. I think we both felt that the urgency, well her urgency, actually, had gone for the moment. Given that I had nowhere else left to go with her, it was simply a case of now being able to relax into the friendship. In effect she had become a fuck-buddy. The first one I ever had.

Meanwhile, Al also became a bit less grumpy, a bit more OK. She was still hanging out too much with Joy and drinking lots but she was moving back to being a bit happier. Oddly we didn't talk at all about weddings or how we were going to progress the engagement. It was almost as if the termination had forced her into a vow of silence.

The other thing that sort of helped was that my secondment also came to an end. In June I returned back to my post as team leader, leaving the glamour and glitz of being an executive assistant behind me. I also lost a hundred quid off my salary so I needed to tighten my belt a little. On the plus side, I managed to have had more evenings free, which meant Al and I could start to do more together. It was little things really, like going to the cinema, cooking for each other and just having time to sit down and chill out with each other. I think we had become strangers over a short period.

But it wasn't a bad summer, all things being considered. Al was affectionate without being sexual and I was more than happy with her company. I didn't even feel guilty about Patrice. It was just something that happened really. A shag is a shag is a shag. Nothing more to say about it. Yes, I knew what I had done was wrong, but under the circumstances? It was just a shag. I still loved Al, still desperately wanted her, could still only see myself spending the rest of my life with her – even if I didn't really want to marry her. So the episode with Patrice was like feeling guilty about getting a carpet wet when you use a fire extinguisher. It was something that really had to be done and in so doing I could convince myself that far from drifting into the gutter I had taken steps to save the most important relationship in my life.

And yet, sometimes I would wake in the night next to Al. I would pull her near to me and I would be filled with this horrible sense of guilt. All I could do at these times was to hold her, as gently as I could. Occasionally she would pull away from me, at other times she would role to face me and kiss me, kiss me passionately, raising my hopes. Then she seemed to remember it was me and, like a singer who suddenly realise they don't know the song after all, she would stop before we got to the chorus. Yet I know that I lived for those halted moments of passion because they could take me back to a place where things where still OK.

It was a good summer. We even managed to get to see England play Australia in a test match at Edgbaston. Al loved it, teased me over every ball, every wicket, every moment. And I'd tease her too and it was for moments like these that I had asked her to marry me. She could always be fun and the great thing was, neither of us was trying. On the way home after the test match she broached the subject that hadn't been discussed.

"Mark, I'm sorry you know."

I misinterpreted this as more teasing.

"Nah, we're just crap at cricket – well, compared to Australia."

She punched me playfully on the arm.

"No," she said softly. We'd been walking back through the streets away from the cricket ground and she pulled me to one side.

"About the....." and glanced around surreptitiously. In my usual sensitive way, I missed the point.

"What? About the what?"

She paused. Then, and I'll never understand why, she smiled her gorgeous smile.

"Sex," she said.

I was silent for a moment. I was moved as well. I never expected an apology, but it was good to at least break the ice on the conversation that could never be spoken.

"Oh, that." I said "Well, look,.....Al, I'm sure all this is only temporary."

We stood there for a moment in silence. The odd car passed us and we just looked into each other's eyes. All I could do was put my arms around her and hug her, gently.

She started to cry.

"I promise you," more tears, blubs and sobs. She tried again. "I promise you it will be alright. I just need some time. Just need a bit of space to sort it out." Yet more tears, I stroked her hair, held her tighter in my arms. I didn't want this. Not her self-torture, not her anguish in the face of my own unfeeling acts of betrayal. My response was also so false, about as genuine as the breezy 'have a nice day' offered by the pimpled, surly teenagers from Solihull who serve in McDonalds. Lacking in truth, like a synthetic apple pie lacks flavour.

"Shsssh," I said "It's OK, it's OK."

And then her voice was firmer.

"No Mark, it's not OK. It's crap for you. It's crap for me too because I really want you, I just can't have you, you know?"

"It's OK."

Then she was quieter again. "It's not OK. I know that you love me. I know that you'll be patient. Just wait a while longer. Please, Mark."

I nodded. 'Yes of course I will wait,' I thought. Yet I knew that I hadn't waited, that I couldn't even be honest with her about that. So what did I do? How did I get myself off the hook? Three simple words.

"I love you."

I wished then – I wish now – that I had never ever gone to Hagley Road. Hagley Road stole any truth from my life.

* * *

I am sat with Peter Holland on Friday evening in his office. We have taken to sharing a bottle of wine together at the end of the week. Convivial, civilized, not really like work, but we are in work mode. In the beginning, these Friday afternoon sessions started with tea. One afternoon I arrived and Peter had been into his favourite wine merchant's in Exeter. So when it came to a drink, he pulled open a rather nice French red which was allowed to breathe whilst we had a cup of tea and then we drank a couple of glasses each. Now we always seemed to end up taking our time, not getting inebriated but knowing that to have more would more than dull our senses.

Peter has been teasing me for the past few minutes about my car. It's a raw nerve for me, but I guess he's entitled to his opinions.

"It's virtually vintage," he says "I grimace every time I pull in next to it!"

"Oh Peter! Come on, just because I don't want a penis extension car like yours."

He laughs. "Your not the first one to suggest that. But I assure you the Z4 is a simple pleasure, my treat for having to put up with you lot. Anyway, if it was a penis extension it would have to be a bloody juggernaut!"

I'm not sure what he means by this, but the glance down towards his fly suggests that he is suggesting something very male and sad about the size of his appendage.

I move the conversation back to cars.

"I'll change it once I've finished my probationary period."

"Oh!" says Peter. "You're that confident we'll let you finish it!"

"Well – if I decide to finish it."

This pulls Peter up sharply, he seems to have missed the point that it is a joke.

He goes quiet for a moment.

"Come on Mark – you know you'll sail through it. We'd be really up shit creek now if you left."

I explain that I was only joking but I'm also pleased that he's been good enough to give me an encouraging sign.

"Come on Peter," I end up saying, "do you seriously think I would leave with the possibility of Argyle playing West Brom next season? That's got to be worth staying for."

His phone rings. His wife.

"No my love, leaving any minute, just got that idiot Garvey here having our end of week debrief." He pauses whilst he listens to the conversation. "I know, I told him. But he still insists on driving that heap of rust." He turns to me, "My wife is just saying your car is a disgrace to the County Council." He laughs to the phone. "No darling, I know you didn't say that, and yes I'm sure Mark knows that you wouldn't. I'm just winding him up; God knows something has got to happen to move him on."

He smiles. It's spring. My boss is happy, I am OK. I might even consider changing my car. The world is set for better times.

* * *

Sometimes I think about all the little mistakes I made with Al. Not the big ones, the little ones. These include not telling her I loved her often enough; losing my temper in traffic jams and cursing other drivers; always passing the phone to her when her mum called and so giving the impression I didn't want to talk; leaving the loo seat up too often; brushing my teeth whilst running water into the basin – apparently disrespectful to people in the developing world; reading the paper in the loo; leaving wet towels on the bed; laughing at my own jokes; not laughing enough at her jokes; not keeping my New Year's resolutions – particularly not learning Italian when I said I would; never taking her to see Paris; eating Bombay mix which would inevitably make me fart for days; buying own brand-label teas rather than the Tetley's she preferred; never spending enough time or effort buying her birthday presents; deliberately washing up badly so that she would do it; ditto the washing – never properly hanging it up to dry so that she would do it; ditto her clitoris – sometimes failing to make an effort to properly find it so that she would do it and, along the way, give me another cheap kick.

So when I think about it, fucking Patrice was probably only another nail in a well-holed coffin.

nailed ')

* * *

I have been toying with this for ages. And now here I am, moments away from signing a piece of paper, just about to make a huge commitment. What is it with me and commitments that when I

116

get near to making one I either duck the issue or freeze out?

Doing business down here is different to ~~in Birmingham~~. When I bought the Volvo, I walked in, chatted, haggled over the price and that was that. Here, buying a car is more like buying a carpet in the Grand Bizaar. Tea is served, options are discussed and only after the car salesman has told you his life story are you able to even think about test-driving the damn thing.

Now, ~~though,~~ the car salesman, an exiled Mancunian who it turns out is younger than me, is waiting with me to make a decision.

"It's a lovely motor isn't it Mr Garvey?"

Fuck, I hate being called Mr Garvey in these situations. It reminds me too much of servile waiters in Indian restaurants. And it also always forces me to use their surnames.

"You're right Mr Davis, it is lovely," I say.

"Not bad at the price either, is it?" Davis continues. He allows me to contemplate the silver chrome, the soft-top roof. "Not many Directors of Social Services will have had one of these in Devon, eh? Not too bad for 16K either."

This to me seems a ludicrous price to pay for a car. The Volvo was only 7K and I've blown a hole in my budget.

I try a final haggle.

"There's something about spending this much on a car, the psychology of it. You couldn't drop it to 15.5 could you?"

Davis' tone changes.

"Do you think I've got time to waste, Mr Garvey? I know you think that we're in a sleepy backwater here but I've had people phone from as far off as London for this one. I've been keeping them away, thinking you were taking it. I've only to get back on phone and they'll all be back you know."

Fuck! Fuck! 'And fuck off with the whining Mancunian accent!' I'm thinking. 'I want this car!'

Davis's tone changes yet again.

the

"Look Mr Garvey, I'll tell you what. How about if we split the difference and make it 15,750. ~~I don't know why but I suppose~~ I've sold a few this month. I won't tell the missus cos she'd beat me black and blue if she knew but, well, that's the best I can do."

Somehow or other I am not shocked by this idea. Ryan Davis seems a slight man whose wife could, I imagine, knock him down with a single flick, never mind blow. How come car salesmen know how to do this to me? Is it part of my inability to say 'no'? I can imagine Alpha coming back from university and wanting to drive it. Most sane people would tell her to clear off; me, I'd say yes and regret it. Alpha knows this too. Waiters know I'll tip, taxi drivers know I'll round the fare up and yet nobody treats me any better. It's not even ~~moralistic~~. Nope, it's just weak, sheer unadulterated weakness. *a moral issue,*

~~But~~ I'm thinking of Peter Holland's face when I pull in next to him at County Hall, thinking about driving up the M5 and parking it at the Hawthorns, spring evenings driving across Dartmoor, picnics with Kalpna, maybe even passion in the grounds of Castle Drogo, the car smelling of sex as we make our way home. I'm thinking of the renewed respect I'll get, Jim's reaction if I pull up at the car park in the Ship. I imagine now I will be able to stay at the sort of hotels where somebody parks the car for you and not worry about the guy's reaction when he takes the keys. Maybe he'll slip the car in next to a visiting footballer's or a successful barrister? All this from simply changing my car!?

A nod. Two smiles. Then handshakes and an agreement to go in and complete the paper work. Now I'm the owner of a Z4.

* * *

It was towards the end of the summer. Nothing for weeks; just silence. Then a phone call.

"I want to meet up again." she said. "I've really got the need to see you."

I knew what this wanting to see me was about and it wasn't anything other than a shorthand for needing to have her lust fulfilled.

"Well it's difficult, I'm still with Al, you know."

And things were better. We hadn't exactly started making love again, but there was passion back in our lives. It just didn't cover penetrative sex.

"Well, you see, I've got an idea. The thing is that your team – West Brom?"

"Yes," I said, a long yes.

"Well they play away at Crewe on 16th August. So you could pretend you were going to the game and meet up with me."

'God,' I thought 'she's even working on alibis for me now.'

"That's an interesting idea, Patrice." I was trying to sound dispassionate but already the possibilities were appealing.

"I can book a hotel, and I can get cheap flights across to Manchester. It'd be easy, don't you think?"

I wondered how far the planning had got. I thought any moment now she'd have told me she had already bought tickets for the game.

"Let me think about it – I'll call you in a couple of days."

It was still pre-season. Al knew that I was planning on buying my first season ticket at the Hawthorns, and I was pretty sure that she wouldn't be interested in going to Crewe.

That weekend I broached the subject with her.

"You know Keith who I work with?" I asked her.

"Keith – have you mentioned him?"

"He's a Baggies supporter in HR. Sad really, he's got a really bad stutter so conversations take hours."

"Oh, Football!" She looked at me like I was talking about

119

toilet habits, pulling a face as if I had gone into too much detail about my last bowel movement. ✗ ("oh! football.")

"Well I feel sorry for him. I mean he likes me because we talk about matches together."

"So?"

"Well he's asked me if I want to go to the away game at Crewe. Would you mind?"

"Where's Crewe? Isn't it just a railway station?"

A forced laugh on my part.

"No, it's only about two hours away by car."

"I'm not coming with you! OK? Don't drag me to some dreary place where there's only a buffet and trainspotters!"

'Yes!' I thought. Perfect, she thought I wanted her to come. So we chatted and she said that the same date was the weekend of Joy's birthday and she was planning on doing girlie shopping with her.

"Oh – like I don't matter?" I responded, pushing home my advantage.

"Oh come on! You'd much rather go to football. Anyway, Joy's invited us round for dinner with some other friends so, you know, you can join us in the evening."

This was getting better.

"Oh god! Dinner? At Joy's?"

"Ah, come on. She really likes you."

I was silent. Played with my food for a minute. This would be worth having a sulk for in normal circumstances, but now the effect would be even better.

"Please?" Al asked gently. "Come on, come to Joy's. You can make your way to her place after the game and meet me there."

And yes, I felt guilty. Yes, I felt like a lump of shit. But I felt like a clever lump of shit who was going to Crewe for an afternoon of passion ~~and who, because~~ he was a decent guy, was ~~even going to have~~ an evening of being a nice guy ~~after by going~~ to a person's birthday party who I didn't care to like. Devilment and beatification in the space of one conversation.

I'm not proud of what I did. But Patrice made all the arrangements. I was just going to be a spectator in my own life for a few hours. A foolish, idiotic, nasty, spectator playing at playing away. Back of the net!

* * *

They say love hurts. I'm not sure it should hurt this much, and I'm not convinced that she loves me.

I am working late. My mobile is switched off. This is a high risk as a member might have an urgent ward matter, but it is also my insurance. I can also screen calls on my desk as it shows the number of who's calling. She's tried me here four times in the past hour. I daren't turn my mobile on, I know there will be too many messages, and my text in-box will be full. She also sent a cryptic e-mail with a read receipt. So she knows I've read it. ~~It said;~~

'Mark, you never mentioned you were working late, not like you to slip up is it? Come around after work – we need to talk.'

I don't want to talk. ~~I know what she means.~~ She wants to punish me. I don't want that. I just want things to be OK.

Sometimes (now) I find that my hands have started shaking for no reason. I'm like Tom Hanks in 'Saving Private Ryan.' This is sexual guerrilla warfare, it's more like a terrorist war than an open war. There are moments of real tenderness when she holds me in her arms, touches me so gently, kisses me so delicately. But then she gets a radio message from the command post deep in her psyche and everything changes. Things crash

121

into me, I am slapped or a bulldog clip appears from under the bed and is applied to the skin of my erect penis. 'And this is love?' I ask, not daring to even answer my own truth.

Tonight I need a break from all this. I need an evening in Geneva, protection from the UN forces who will guard my testicles and chest and maintain a watchful eye over me. I will leave County Hall under the cloak of darkness, I will garage the Z4 and drive via the longest route possible to avoid Hampton View. I am somewhere between defeat and exhaustion, but I still have my dignity; I'll not give in to these occupying forces.

* * *

The world started to become pasteurised once we had national not local newspapers. Once national events became important, local flavour went out of the window. Then everything else followed. Radio, television, theatre, food. Hotels too. So Patrice and I used a Travelodge. At the time they were still new enough not to have become sad; they had novelty value, given that they were cheaper than a seaside B&B that would probably smell of stale tobacco. They were also perfectly anonymous. A step up or down form Hagley Road.

Everything went smoothly. I met her in the pub/restaurant next door. It had 'Fayre' in the name, but the food looked limp, uninterested, defeated by the effort of keeping itself on the plate. Synthetic and pasteurised. The waiting staff had a similar approach. As a kid I was taught that communism was evil, that in Warsaw, Cracow and Budapest staff were surly, impersonal, disinterested. Then the Berlin wall crumbled and we began to realise that it wasn't the political system that made people who served unimaginative food surly or disinterested, it was a symptom of the futility of the roles they performed. For the

122

purpose of our rendezvous, the restaurant, with its synthetic food, emotional neutrality and air of desperation suited our needs perfectly. I remember glancing around, wondering if all the other people in the place, at least those minus kids, were simply meeting for an illicit Saturday afternoon fuck? Mondeo man finds an outlet for Mondeo sex?

Patrice did her best to make the event seem OK. She genuinely looked pleased to see me and I suppose, if I thought about it, I was happy seeing her. Not delirious, just happy – a sexual happiness.

"You're looking great," she said, the g and the r rolling off her tongue as if she was auditioning for a bit part in a Latin soap opera.

"Thanks," I said, my economy with words doing little to disguise the fact that this was transactional. Food-room-sex-leave.

"You look good too," I responded. And the conversation bobbled along without any sense of real warmth or passion in much the same way as over my Ploughman's lunch and over Patrice's 'Seafood delights platter'. If the sea really was as delightful as the dish suggested, I thanked my lucky stars I was not an amphibian. ? — Fish !

So no coffee, no dessert. A quick walk across the car park to our room. Passionate kissing, fumbled belts, hands in underwear, two bodies moving together in lust, loud shouts, orgasms – although I was convinced that Patrice sometimes faked, something Alyson never ever did – then a few moments of lying in silence before we would start again. I would nuzzle Patrice or she would start stroking my penis and off we would go, like tube trains moving between stations.

At a quarter to five, I turned the TV on and watched final score. I discovered we had won 2-3 with a last gasp late winner from Bob Taylor and then I showered and got dressed.

"I have to go," I said. I had left Patrice sleeping, her dark hair wildly strewn across the pillow.

She propped herself up on her elbow. She was naked on top of the bed.

"Oh can't we just have one more go?"

She was like a child at a fairground, enjoying the rides, never wanting to get off.

"Next time," I said, and kissed her on her cheek.

"Next time? Great! So there is going to be a next time?"

Stupid question. "If you're up for it." I said, like we were discussing whether or not we would go to see a movie or spend an hour ice skating.

"That's great," said Patrice, using her Latino 'great' yet again.

I mumbled a few farewells, gathered my things together, checked myself in the mirror for love bites or any other incriminating signs, smiled weakly at Patrice and then left.

I'd arranged with Al that I would drop the car home and come and meet her at Joy's. I had about three hours to get word perfect about what happened at the match. Luckily at services on the M6, I managed to bump into a few Baggies fans, insisted on a blow-by-blow account and persuaded one of them to let me have his programme. My alibi was complete.

* * *

I wake with a jolt. I have fallen asleep in a big rocking chair that sits in the bay window at Stockwell cottage. My neck has cricked and the glass of whisky I was holding has spilt across the polished wooden floor. It looks like I have been visited by a yet to be house-trained puppy.

Three days now. Three days when I haven't called her or spoken to her. Is it over? Are we finished? Do 50 year old men

124

'finish' anyway? I thought that's what teenagers did?

Tomorrow is Good Friday. I'm supposed to be taking Kalpna to Birmingham to see West Brom play on Saturday and then we're going to Stratford-upon-Avon to see 'Macbeth'. That was part of the deal. Football for me, Shakespeare for her. I hate Shakespeare. I am convinced that he wrote, secure in the knowledge that one day hearing aids would not be able to cope with the false rhythms of the iambic pentameter, or whatever it is. And Kalpna is so like Lady Macbeth. It is creepy. Who am I? Banquo's ghost? No idea, no idea whatsoever. *? pure ambition*

Then I notice that there is a knocking sound coming from downstairs.

I pad down the stairs into the hallway, look through the leaded glass pane on the front door and see Alpha on the other side.

I open the door to her.

She steps back. "Hi," she says softly. "What's the matter?"

I'm still a bit bleary-eyed but invite her in. She doesn't step forward.

"No, she says. "Look, I can't stay. I just want you to know that Mum is really upset. She doesn't know what she's done wrong or anything. Please call her, Mark."

"OK." I nod. "OK – I'll call her."

"Promise?" says Alpha.

"Yeah, of course," I respond.

"Tonight? Please?" She looks at me with big, sincere, bovine eyes, which melt any resistance I have. I realise she has learnt all her mum's skills of manipulation so quickly.

"OK!" I say.

Alpha smiles.

"Hey," she says changing her tone, "love the new car! Can I have a go some time?" Her smile is really wide, she is one of the loveliest kids I know.

"Maybe," I say.

"Maybe yes?" she asks.

"Let's see if things can be sorted out with your mum. Then 'maybe yes'."

"Cool," she says.

She walks down the path and then turns back, I haven't yet closed the door

"You know," Alpha says, "I think my Mum's in love with you."

She moves on quickly, but she has sewn the seeds that will mean that I will call her mum, that I will drag myself back to the sexual frontline and that, despite my better judgement, I will be sat in a theatre in Stratford –upon- Avon on Saturday night, trying to work out what the fuck Macduff is saying.

* * *

Dinner at Joy's was always a tedious affair. When I arrived, I knew the night was going to be even harder as she had invited Reeta and Kat, a gay couple who were so PC that you daren't even ask them to pass the salt for fear of offending the memory of Ghandi. As soon as I arrived, they were like a hawk with its prey.

"So how was your afternoon with the English Defence League?" Reeta started.

"Sorry?!" I said, knowing exactly where the conversation was heading.

"You know, football – full of fascist thugs innit?" Reeta responded.

Then I had to listen about how she had been reading in some ultra-left, ultra-hip independent rag that the EDL were targeting football fans in Birmingham. QED anybody in Birmingham who followed football was a hooligan.

"Pretty simplistic stuff isn't it Reeta?" I mused, "and surely it doesn't work in other contexts?"

Kat, who wasn't the brightest of people at the best of times, and whose dull senses had been dulled further by several glasses of wine, tried to be clever.

"What – like all those white people who went to South Africa under apartheid weren't racists? All the right-wing miners who read The Sun didn't deserve what they got? Yeah?"

"So we are all colonialist then Kat? Supporting the war in Iraq? Funding the bombing of the Bennies on the Falkland Islands?"

"No, but," I could see Kat struggling for words so I put her out of her misery.

"Look Kat, you pay taxes under the Tories, you fund their warped policies and ideas, but that doesn't make you a Tory, does it?"

Joy decided to step in. "Come on, no need to fight on my birthday, hey?"

I went to say more but Al reached across, placed her hand on top of mine and squeezed it gently. She looked into my eyes and smiled at me, a sort of cute smile that made her glasses move ever so slightly on her nose. Then she leant across and kissed me. It was a message. 'Look I know that these people are tossers, just relax.'

So the meal plodded along whilst I listened to the drivel that passed for conversation emitting from Kat and Reeta. It seemed that there was no subject they didn't posses an offensive half-baked opinion on and no matter that they didn't feel qualified to pass judgement about.

We'd got to the cheeseboard and the memories of my afternoon of passion had begun to fade. So I was taken aback by Joy's next comment.

"Bet you were glad to get out of the rain at the end of the game?" she said.

Fuck! Had it rained? I couldn't remember if the pavements were wet when I came out of the Travelodge.

"To be honest, it was such a cracking game that the weather didn't really matter." Hopefully this would do the trick.

"Just that Kevin, my brother, was at the game too. He said he was drenched by the end of it." Joy looked at me, tilted her head to one side; she was more than inquisitive.

"He was probably protected by his bobble hat,eh Mark?" Reeta chirped in.

Al giggled. Whilst I was insulted by Reeta's snide comments, it gave me a hook out of the quagmire. Then by accident another occurred.

I waved my hand towards my head. "Oh that and the swastika," but just as I came to the middle of what I was trying to say, I knocked a glass of wine over, spilling it on to Al. She leapt up.

"Mark! For fuck's sake!"

The wine was well on the way to staining what I knew was one of her favourite tops.

She leapt up from the table and rushed to the bathroom, intent on saving the said favourite item. *it.*

She had hardly walked a few paces before she was pulling the top off over her head, her breast now exposed for all to see. *gone!, Already*

"Mmm, I'd rather have those than the cheese" said Reeta.

"Stop it" said Joy playfully.

By now, her and Al had disappeared in the bathroom. Kat meanwhile had left the table to get some kitchen paper leaving me and Reeta at the table.

"Who's a lucky boy then, eh Mark? But I think there'll be no pudding for you tonight – if you get my meaning."

This really wasn't the place and I'd had enough of her snide remarks, her leering at Alyson. Mustering all my wit and creative passion, I responded.

"Oh fuck off Reeta, OK?"

She put her hands up in mock self-defence but I'd made the point.

Joy returned.

"No real damage, that stain will easily come out Mark. You can go and see the patient if you want."

We both wandered towards the bathroom. Halfway down the hallway, Joy grabbed me by the wrist, putting her face close to mine.

"By the way – my brother came back with a sunburnt nose." Her tone was aggressive, threatening, said just at the limits of my hearing. "It was a glorious August afternoon. OK? So just for future reference, get your fucking facts straight before you tell lies! Remember – you're not the only one who loves Al."

I was taken aback. What did Joy know? What was her game?

I pushed the bathroom door open.

"Here's the perpetrator of the crime, come to apologise for his misdemeanours, haven't you Mark?"

The look in Joy's eyes told me that she had my number. Her choice of words told me she was on my case.

Al just smiled weakly.

"Come here, you mad, clumsy arse." She was still naked from the waist up. She kissed me and gave me a hug. She had her back to Joy.

Joy looked at me and mouthed 'I'm watching you.'

Al and I pulled apart. As we did so Joy tossed Al a black t-shirt that she pulled on. She kissed me again.

"Shall we go back and have cheese, you can bring the bath just in case you want to slosh coffee over me later, huh?" Al teased.

"Actually, I need to pee," I said.

I was left alone in the bathroom. I slid the lock shut, turned the big light off and turned a shaving mirror light on above the sink. The nausea was pacing through me. It took about 30 seconds and then I vomited.

I quickly cleaned up the mess, sprayed air freshener to remove the smell of sick and splashed my face with water.

I felt cold, cold to Al who I loved and to Patrice who I was using. And chilled that I was being watched. This was becoming messier and messier. I hate the effects of bright sunshine. I have skin that turns crimson rather than tans, no matter how much sunblock I slap on. There and then, surrounded by the scent of pine air freshener and vomit, water dripping down my face, I glanced at my nose. It was pale, not even freckled, and never had I wished more for that sense of heat, that want for skin to peel from an honest sunburnt nose.

* * *

I can't remember if it was Harold Wilson or Jim Callaghan who had introduced it but I remember that the media hated the idea of the May Day bank holiday. It was as if the 'Daily Telegraph' imagined that Callaghan would stand in Trafalgar Square whilst hammer and sickle-clad soldiers marched through the London Streets. Equally, the tabloids loved the fact that it always rained on the May Day bank holiday, thus proving the folly of having a public holiday to celebrate workers rights and solidarity. I think it also tends to always rain at Easter, and sometimes snows. But nobody seems to talk about the chocolate-munching holiday being abandoned on the grounds of climatic inconvenience. A more paranoid mind might link the profitability of the confectionary industry with the advertising revenue received in the tabloid press for Easter eggs. Whereas what did May-Day give the press barons? Just an excuse to gripe about the decline of civilisation as we know it.

In a way that is gloriously European, Giovanni has always celebrated the May Day holiday. This is at odds with his personal politics, and certainly is at odds with Jane's world view which sometimes made Thatcherism seem like a limp-wristed liberal credo, but his commitment to May Day as a holiday was never in question. We have escaped together over to The Ship while Jane bathes Matty and gets him ready for bed. It feels really good to have Geo here; a point of reference in what still is a predominantly alien peoplescape. That is, with the exception of Jim, who greets Geo like a long-lost relative and then bores us both silly about a holiday he had in Amalfi in 1986. "Lovely people" he keeps saying to Geo as if he is deaf. But then it's not malicious and we eventually manage to struggle to a seat in the window that overlooks the harbour wall.

"Is it?" asks Geo, gesticulating to the painted wording on the harbour wall.

I look where he is pointing. 'Dead Slow' is written in huge white letters at the entrance to the harbour.

"Maybe," I say. "Yeah, quite often really."

"You alright matey, you seem very quiet?" Geo enquires.

"Yeah, I guess so." This, as always, is a signal to him that he can push the inquisition further.

"Go on?" he looks at me gently, inquisitively. So I begin to explain my predicament about Kalpna. I leave out some of the arse-clenching details but give Geo enough information to know that I find it all weird. I lose track of how long I have been talking for and then realise we've both drained our pints and we've been sat, quietly chatting, for the best part of half an hour.

Geo rises to get another couple of drinks.

"To be honest," he says, "I don't see what the problem is. I know things in the bedroom weren't great with you and Al. Now you've got a horny doctor, you seem to be complaining. Why's the grass always less yellow on the other side of the fence, Mark?"

It's a bastard of a point – why I can love and hate the guy in equal proportions – and goes to the core of our friendship. He returns from the bar with two more pints. We sit in silence for a few moments.

"You were the same in the band," he says. "You were never happy that we were making money from it – you wanted fame, fortune, success."

I laughed. "I just wanted to get fucked," I said.

Geo won't let this pass. "Rubbish! You wanted success, you wanted to play the NEC, Wembley Stadium, everywhere. But yeah – you also wanted to get fucked!"

"Live in the moment," he says, "accept everything for what it is. It may just be great sex, it may be a bit at the edge of things, but ask yourself – what else is there to do here?"

He has a point. I look out into the harbour. A few gulls are ripping apart an old bread wrapper that has blown onto the harbour wall, couples are walking hand in hand in the greyness of an early May afternoon, but it is hardly pulsating, not quite downtown New York, not even downtown Newquay most of the time. Sure you can take an open-top sports car for a spin, you can sit and admire the aesthetic, but beyond that, something has to fill the period between working and not working.

"You finished lecturing me?" I ask.

"Yeah," he says in a friendly but resigned way. "Just get it all in perspective mate."

Perspective? Me? Now that is funny!

* * *

September came. Always my favourite month really. I love the warmth of English September days; the remnants of summer linger, but as the nights close in there is a promise of the romance of early winter. Your team are normally still in all the cup competitions, even if you're bottom of the table there is still time to dump your manager or hit a run of form and make the play offs. In September, the pattern of life begins to settle down.

Al liked September too. She always wanted to be in the countryside in September. She loved walking in the Malvern Hills or going down to Hay-on-Wye or just 'being' in September. I think she also liked the fact that once the football season had got into its rhythm I gave her Saturday afternoons to do what she wanted whilst I went to the match.

After my day trip to Crewe I became worried, so that that particular September was underpinned by a sense of tension. I increasingly avoided discussing Joy with Al. For instance Al and Joy would, before my trip to Crewe, regularly try to drag me out for a Friday night balti. One Wednesday evening, we were sat on the sofa and Al raised the balti option with me.

"Hey! You fancy a balti this weekend, hmm?" she'd say running her fingers through my hair, something that always melted me. She continued, "There's someone on at Ronnie Scott's on Friday that Joy want to see and she reckoned the three of us could hack along."

I feigned disinterest.

"Can we see how things are on Friday?"

"Why?" Al asked with a giggle. "Do you think you'll get a better offer?" She then kissed me on my head. She was being playful – I always loved her playfulness. Not that I deserved it, but I loved it anyway.

"A better offer than a balti with Joy? Well I might fancy catching my bollocks in the fridge door, you know?"

She punches me, again playfully, but her expression has changed a bit. "Aw – come on!" she protests, "anyway you can trap your bollocks in the fridge door anytime!"

But we never ever did get to go for a curry with Joy because things never seemed to fall that way.

Yet Al was becoming increasingly affectionate. She wasn't pulling away to the other side of the bed anymore when I hugged her and she had even started kissing me in bed. Not passionately but gently, tenderly.

One Sunday afternoon, I was in the bathroom having a late shave. I was stood in a pair of boxer shorts in front of the mirror just finishing off when Al wandered in to run herself a bath. She too was only in a pair of panties and seemed OK. We'd done a usual Sunday morning thing of reading the papers in bed, that sort of thing, but were getting ready to go to the botanical gardens or something. As she sat on the edge of the bath, humming along to something or other on the radio, she started to reach over to me and stroked the small of my back.

"Careful," I said "You don't want me to cut myself."

"Hmm," she said in a sort of dreamy way.

Then she reached forward and put her hand into my boxer shorts, trying to find my penis. I gasped because Al had not done anything remotely like this since the abortion.

"Face me," she said quietly.

So I did. Then she proceeded to remove my penis from my boxer shorts and gently started kissing it, moving my foreskin back so should could place light kisses on the helmet and along the base of its shaft.

"Touch me," she said gently. So I reached down and began to stroke her naked breasts, feeling the nipples stiffen to my touch.

"No," she said, and I thought she wanted to stop, "touch my clit."

She still had hold of my penis, rubbing the foreskin backwards and forwards as I slid my fingers into her panties. She was very, very wet. She gasped as my finger slid into her then stood up and kissed me on the mouth.

By now her panties were off and before we knew it my penis was nudging against her pussy lips, looking for a way in.

"Wait," she said. She turned the bath off, took me by the hand, led me to the bedroom, pushed me onto the bed and reached for a pack of condoms. Within moments she was on top of me, moving up and down, making all the sounds that I hadn't heard in such a long time.

It took neither of us very long to come but come we did. And then we both cried and kissed and hugged and just held each other again.

She turned my face to her so I could see her. She had a huge smile.

But she spoke slowly, through happy tears.

"I've been wanting to do that for so long. So long, Mark – thank you."

And she buried her face into my shoulder laughing and crying at the same time.

I hugged her tightly. I kissed her. I manoeuvred myself and began to lick her pussy, which despite the smell of rubber I really needed to do. Again she seemed to come very quickly; she was very turned on.

And then I couldn't stop crying. I just kept crying and saying, "Thank you – I love you so much," and in the end she just put her finger on my lips and said, "It's OK, I know Mark, I know." Then I fell into a deep, deep sleep. When I woke, Al was standing over me with a cup of tea in her hand and stroking my hair.

"God" I mumbled "what time is it?"

She smiled. "Six," she said.

I groaned "Oh! What about the botanical gardens, our Sunday?"

"We can go next week," she said gently and handed me a cup of tea, "here."

I took the tea from her, propped myself on my pillows and smiled back.

September. Mellow fruits, mellow love. The memory of the bitter taste of trips to Crewe fading. Then kissing Al. Making love to Al, holding Al after we had both come. And now sat in a darkening room in mid-September drinking tea whilst the woman I love smiles at me. No wonder I love September so much.

* * *

We are back in the kitchen at Drake House. Jayne is preparing Matty's tea. Matty is wide-eyed and excited by not being in Bristol, occasionally interrupting the grown-up conversation with a few babbles in sign language, to remind us, he is here. For the major part he is busy with a book while an early evening May Day shower hits against the window in concert with the tabloid media's efforts to put a dampener on events. Alpha will be here in an hour so that three of us can go to Kalpna's for dinner. I'm tense about this. I wonder if Geo will blurt something out about how weird I'm finding the sexual stuff and already half regret the discussion at The Ship.

"Mark, Matty keeps using a sign that we haven't seen – do you know what it means?"

I think 'this is a daft question, my signing is bloody awful really,' but do my best to help.

"I'll have a go – what is the sign?"

Jayne interrupts Matty from his colouring, something that is not greeted with the happiest of faces as he was in the process of crayoning a sheep a rather vivid green, is this kid on drugs?

Jayne signs to Matty "Show Mark, sign new, Mummy don't know."

Matty smiles.

He makes a sign like a light going on.

Jayne turns to me?

"Well?"

I sign to Matty

"Ah – flash? – Yes?"

Matty nods.

"Good sign" I continue "Like for lightning or camera."

"Or bathroom at seaside" Matty signs.

I thought I'd misunderstood what he said.

"Bathroom?" I ask.

Matty nods "Flash!"

"Flash?" says Jane. "Hmm,that's odd. So why does he keep making it when we're having a bath?"

This was strange.

"How long's he been doing it?" I ask "I mean it might be a new sign they've taught him at school and he's just over using it."

"Like when you first learn to say fuck or piss?" her husband interjects.

"You can always be relied upon to lower the tone of the conversation, Geo" Jane says, a bit harshly in my view. Jane turns to me.

"He's only been doing it for the past few days, since we got here."

Odd. Very odd.

"Beyond me," I say "You know, kids are never entirely logical are they?".

"Nor are men," says Jane, throwing a glance at Geo.

Matty interrupts us.

"Green sheep good?" he wants approval for his psychedelic artwork.

"Not many green sheep around here," I sign.

Matty giggles.

"Green cows?" he asks

"No, only boring black and white cows."

He picks up a red crayon and starts colouring a cow in the picture. This kid has anarchist tendencies, no doubt about it.

I glance outside, leaving Matty to his psychedelic, disturbing crayoning. It has stopped raining, outside the kitchen window, early evening sunshine was speckling the town with warm hues and hints of the summer to come. I realise how much I miss the vantage point of Drake House and how much I long to be back here. I start wondering what it would cost to buy but know that Wilma Mapp would be unlikely to sell, particularly to me. It's too big anyway and too far from Exeter.

Jayne takes the crayon off Matty, plops a plate of pasta onto the table and makes the sign to eat to Matty.

Matty makes an exaggerated sigh, offers me the crayon. I decline.

"No," I sign, "Finish it with Alpha later," but I have to fingerspell Alpha for him.

"Who?" signs Matty, looking very interested.

"Babysitter" I sign back.

Matty nods. I am sure he is working it all out in his head. 'There's a babysitter coming and Uncle Mark says I can crayon with her. I mean I'd rather have some devilment with her, maybe watch cartoons even, but if it makes Uncle Mark happy then why not.' The kid seems old beyond his years, I assure you.

Eventually I decide to pop upstairs and get ready. By the time I come back down, the kitchen is clean again. Matty is sat like an angel in the lounge, Alpha is arriving and Geo and Jayne are both looking very smart – as they always do – stood in the hallway.

"Hi Mark," says Alpha and comes and kisses me on the cheek.

"She never did that to me," says Geo to Jane.

Alpha gives him a dirty look and I laugh.

"Everybody gets used to Geo eventually," I explain to her.

She's not interested. She has spotted Matty and introduces herself by a combination of gesture and mime. Matty seems delighted and runs across the lounge to get his less than idyllic rural scene for joint completion with the pretty babysitter with big eyes and a fun smile.

Jayne checks Alp is OK and then we leave together.

Matty waves to me as I'm going. He points upstairs and makes a questioning 'flash' sign. *(careful reader!, P139-143 audience expectation)*

What is it with this kid?

* * *

Why do couples do it? I mean, why do they become couples? Aren't we brought up to be independently minded or is conditioning so great that we're forced into joint decisions, joint mistakes, joint holidays and eventually monogrammed matching towelling dressing gowns? What drives the human spirit, that which has journeyed across the globe in search of new lands, that which has discovered electricity or split the atom, moved from the invention of the motor car to space exploration, to decide that bliss is in fact having someone to wake up next to in bed and make a cup of tea for? I have no answer to these questions. None whatsoever.

But once the blockade of sexual activity was lifted, Al and I began the next phase of our journey to joined-at-the-hipness. Over time, we had both begun to earn more money. Al was now a full-time Physio at Sutton Coldfield and I was earning a good salary. The John Major era was giving way to the dawn of the smiling imbecile, also known as Tony Blair, and it was clear that property owning was the way forward. So after a period of time, the decision to buy somewhere wasn't just a possibility, it became a certainty.

We managed to find one of the few Victorian properties on the Edgbaston-Moseley border that was not gentrified and well within our price range. It required, in estate agents term's 'some superficial updating work'. If you were given the details of Stonehenge, an estate agent would probably use the same words. So you know you would be faced with more than a plastering job and putting up new shelves. The potential of the new place was amazing. There was even a massive 120-foot garden that was probably home to several lost tribes of ancient Briton and also contained the sleeping knights of the Round Table. Yet we both loved it, loved the fact that here was a project we could get our teeth into. A property that would become our mark on the world and a property that we could technically get away with calling Edgbaston even if locals knew Massie Road as Moseley. South Edgbaston, maybe?

Everything happened so quickly and there seemed to be a period of constant negotiations between mortgage brokers, estate agents and solicitors. I seemed to be handling most of the calls about this and my working day focussed more on property dealing than managing my team. In the middle of all this, I got yet another phone call.

"Mark Garvey," I barked, convinced that it would be some

other incompetent professional involved in the house purchase industry.

"Hi," the quiet but familiar voice said, "Long time no speak huh? How are you?"

Patrice and I hadn't spoken, not since Crewe. She was just a part of my past I wanted to escape.

"Oh hi Patrice," I said, as flatly and without emotion as I could. Sensing my lack of commitment to the conversation she moved into probing mode.

"Is now not a good time? I mean I could call back later?"

I was silent. I must have sat with the phone against my ear, wondering what to say for a good 30 or 40 seconds, a symphony of silence for a telephone call already so short.

"You still there?" she asked, the 'r' of the 'there' rolling through the phone like distant thunder.

"Yep," I said. It was too firm a yep, almost a snap.

"Well look," and then she paused, "can we meet? I mean there's a game at Tranmere Rovers and there are quite a few nice places to stay in Liverpool."

And as sharply as the previous affirmative came my negative.

"No way," I said "No."

"No?!" she said, like it was some great insult.

"That's right" I said, determined to keep the conversation to a world record of minimum words possible. Any commentary team would have noticed this as a personal best.

'Oh and the boy from Birmingham does it again. A whole conversation using only two-word responses. Just where does he manage to get it from?' the commentary would run.

"But you said there would be another time, a next time."

"Well – not now."

"Not now – in the future do you mean?" Patrice asked. I could sense the pleading in the tone.

"Not now, never," I said quietly.

"Oh well couldn't we?"

I just put the phone down. There was no point.

'Fantastic – he finishes on a silent, incomplete sentence. The crowd's going wild. Oh and it's a 6.0 from the Russian judge! 5.9 from everybody else! So different, so unlike Garvey's previous style!'

But there is no commentary team. Nothing. The phone rings again.

"Mr Garvey, it's Mike Warburton here of Warburton, Challoner and Delaney."

It had been a skirmish. I was back in the safe territory of incompetent estate agents and expensive solicitors. Perhaps I had escaped the troubles in the North of Ireland too?

* * *

Alpha is crying. Sobbing big sobs. Meanwhile Matty is stood, looking a bit bewildered.

"I think we should call the police," Says Geo, he's trying hard to control his anger but it is totally understandable.

Dinner had been going really well. Kalpna and Jane were getting on famously, Geo was obviously smitten too and I was being given the 5-star treatment by Kalpna. So a good evening was well underway. We had just sat down to our main course when the phone rang. Kalpna decided to leave it on the answer machine which is how we heard Alpha's voice sobbing down the phone.

"Hi…it's me, are you all there. Can you pick up…please! Pick up! Pick the fucking phone up!"

Kalpna ran across to the phone and Geo and Jane seemed to freeze. He told me in the car that he thought something terrible had happened to Matty, so the fact that it hadn't was a relief.

Not much of a relief under the circumstances, but a relief anyway.

I hadn't even heard the message clearly until Alpha started to swear. So I listened to it again whilst everybody grabbed jackets and turned ovens off. At this point, none of us knew exactly what the problem was, other than that Matty and Alp were OK, but she was totally freaking out about something that had happened. The drive between Hampton View and Drake normally took a couple of minutes. That evening, with Geo driving, we managed it in about 45 seconds.

It took about 5 minutes to establish what the problem was. It had started when Matty had got up to use the loo and had come downstairs to Alpha making the flash sign. He dragged her back upstairs; Alpha hadn't a clue what was going on. She watched Matty stand over the loo to have a pee and then it happened.

From the piping in the corner there was a flash, similar to that which you get from a camera.

At first Alpha thought she had imagined it, but Matty made the flash sign and sure enough she knew. The very thought had made Alpha's stomach cramp. She sent Matty to his room for a moment whilst she investigated but as she moved across the bathroom floor in the direction where the flash came from, the thing started flashing away.

Geo had been up to investigate after hearing, between massive sobs, a tear-punctuated version of the story. He had found, lodged behind a flat, black, Perspex glass screen that covered the end of the bathroom plumbing, a small camera. It wasn't clear how this was working, but the implications were obvious. Somebody had been taking photos. First of Matty and then of Alpha. Geo was now insisting that the police be called

Kalpna was the first to respond.

"What are the police going to do?"

"Investigate the pervert who put the thing there!" said Jane, as if Kalpna had taken all leave of her senses. I too thought Geo was right. This made no sense whatsoever, but keeping it away from the police also seemed bizarre.

"Jane's right," I said quietly to Kalpna. But she seemed tense. Perhaps she just had an instinctive disliking of the police but it struck me that they really were the only people that could get to the bottom of this.

Alpha began to cry again.

"Oh Mum, I just want to go home." I mouthed to Kalpna 'shock'.

Jane turned to Alpha. "It must be horrible for you. Go on go home."

"Won't the police want a statement from her?" says Geo. But Jane gives him another one of her looks, less sharp, but one which indicates 'give the kid a break'.

Alpha seems to sob even more after Giovanni's comment but her mum is already leading her to the door.

"We'll walk back up to Hampton view," she says.

Jane interrupts.

"Can I come with you? I mean, God knows how many more of those things there are around the place. I certainly don't want Matty to risk any more photos."

Kalpna nods, understandingly.

Jane sweeps Matty up into her arms. He is rubbing his eyes with the back of his knuckles, a sign that once again sleep is catching up with him. A few whispers between Jane and Geo takes place. Geo tenderly kisses Matty on the head and smiles at him weakly. He signs, puzzled and a bit distressed.

"Matty bad??"

I sign to him "No! Matty Good. Flash bad. Go stay with Aunty Kalpna."

Matty doesn't seem entirely convinced by any of this but

144

then nor would I be if nobody had bothered to explain to me what was going on. Then Geo hands Jane the car keys.

"We'll walk back up," he explains to Jane, and then, almost for confirmation, he turns away and speaks to me. "We could be here a while – it's best that Jane has the car."

As they leave I pick up the phone in the hallway and dial 999. I ask for the police, explain the situation and then we wait.

I join Geo in the kitchen. He has poured two large whiskies, straight. He offers me one as I enter.

"Grim, grim stuff," he says.

I nod firmly, not sure if he is referring to the whisky or the events of the evening. I sip from the glass, tasting it as it slides across my tongue. Indeed it is grim, in every sense.

I look out of the window across the town of Hope Cove. It has suddenly become less of a picture postcard and much, much more sinister, more threatening. I glance towards the top end of the town and see on the horizon the flashing blue light of an approaching police car making its way towards Drake. I am filled with a sense of foreboding. A deep sense of unease. I know that something has changed that will forever alter my relationship with Drake House, Hope Cove and many of the people who I thought I could trust. Grim, in every sense.

* * *

I'm not sure whose idea the party was. I think it was Al's. Initially it was planned as a break from the tedium of renovating the house. We had both failed to realise how long it would take to get even the simplest things done, like having a wall plastered. Winter was drawing in, and the central heating radiators all weren't giving seemed to not give off enough heat and we had gradually begun to realise that maybe we had taken on something more than we could afford. Al was miserable and I was miserable.

I'd also become concerned about my job for the first time in ages. Maybe it was a symptom of moving from tenant to homeowner status, but a planned re-organisation – resulting from the retirement of an existing AD – had all of us worried. There were sleepless nights, long fractious team meetings, dreaming of the possibilities for the future and then realising that the future could be awful – bloody awful.

So at the time the party seemed a good idea. I went mad with invitations – everyone from casual support workers through to Geoff. Then there were friends from far and wide, with people like Geo mixed in. Add to this the combination of half the Physiotherapists in a 50-mile radius, more Oz exiles than there were Australians in Sydney and the combination was set for a wild and fantastic evening.

On the afternoon of the party, Joy came over to help sort out the food. She argued with us about food fascism when we told her that everything was going to be veggie.

"That's so unfair!" she whinged. "Like, you know, people have needs!"

"Not in my home. They're guests. Full stop."

Al, sensing a row brewing, moved us on.

"Come on you two – huh? And Joy, Mark is right – this is our home, not a public conference."

It was the first time I had seen Al ever disagree with Joy in front of me and it felt like a small but significant victory.

"Whatever!" said Joy, dismissing the affair with a wave of a hand but a look that suggested she wasn't really in agreement with us.

This seemed to inflame Al even more.

"Whatever?! Whatever! Hey, you don't have to stay you know. But if you are – show some fucking respect!"

146

Now I was blown over. Al was becoming a tiger with Joy. Needless to say, Joy was given an incentive that may have explained her behaviour later that night.

By party time, we were at that point of frenzy that only comes when the party is your own. That dawning realisation that this was a stupid idea, that we needed more drink, that we didn't know who the fuck was coming, and that Al and I were both already a tiny bit pissed. Everybody seems to occupy this space. Psychologists must have a name for it but I think I would call it pre-event-whose-stupid-dumb-ass-idea-was-this-syndrome. The only cure for this is alcohol, so that when the invited but unwanted guest arrive you are so happy, or pissed that they will mistake this for genuine evidence that you are in fact pleased you invited them, when you were secretly hoping they would be killed in a motorway pile up whilst en route.

By midnight this was all forgotten. The place was rocking. From the disco in the basement to the debauchery taking place in various rooms, everything was fantastic. Geo, unaccompanied by Jane, was having a whale of a time – flirting with care workers, talking about politics, telling jokes and so on. At one point, Geoff and I were arguing about the Baggies and what was needed for the remainder of the season to get promotion when he just stopped.

"Fuck it!" he said.

"What???"

"Nah, look I'm sorry, I can't say."

"No, go on."

"I want you as AD."

I blinked, wiped the froth of the top of the new bottle of Czech Bud I had just opened, thought 'he's pissed' but checked anyway.

"You're taking the piss huh?"

"Fuck off I'm not! The leader wants you for it, the boss sees your strengths and I think they're all right. Come on. Do it."

"Seriously?" It was all too surreal, being encouraged to move up to the next stage of my career whilst pissed, the smell of spliffs wafting down the hallway and the odd person passing in various states of undress. Life shouldn't happen this way.

I was about to respond when Joy brushed between us.

"You two still arguing about West Brom?" she asked.

This inspired Geoff to start chanting. "Baggies! Bageeees!" he started yelling.

"Ask him about the Crewe game," she said.

Geoff missed the point and started rambling on about Bob Taylor and what have you. Joy moved on, throwing a look at me that immediately told me she was here to cause trouble.

Before I could follow her, I was interrupted by Geo.

"Fantastic party matey!" he said "All these women!"

By the time I'd introduced Geoff to Geo – and Geo had explained that, no, he was in fact English but had no interest in the Baggies – Joy had taken cover back in the undergrowth of the party.

I had a need to go and find Al to make sure that nothing had already been said and then my alcohol-pickled brain couldn't remember if my liberal hospitality had included stuttering Keith of the non-trip to Crewe. Fuck!!! Was he here? Was he downstairs somewhere?

"Geoff," I said in a half panic, "you haven't seen Keith have you?"

"K-K-K-Keith," he responded unnecessarily, "N-N-O!"

I didn't need this playground humour but left him laughing at his own bad taste joke, whilst Geo looked on, none the wiser.

I spent an hour looking high and low for a person at a party who I may or may not have invited. I found various people in various states but none had seen Keith. I even interrupted

Gemma in mid-coitus to ask her if she'd seen him.

"What!!" she asked, making no attempt to stop with whoever was underneath her.

"Keith!" I asked

"Fuck off Mark! Can't you see I'm busy?" I was amazed. We could have been arguing over photocopying and I made a mental note that at some point I should get to know Gemma better. But not now, there was too much at stake.

Becoming more sober as time went on, I realised that he probably wasn't about. Things were getting calmer, anyway. I ~~still~~ hadn't run into either Al or Joy. Eventually I made my way ~~back~~ down to the music and the cellar. Everything was mellow, ~~less frantic~~. A chill-out album was playing and a few people were doing slowies together. I noticed Reeta dancing with a new conquest, a bigger more rotund woman than Kat had been. Reeta smiled at me and gestured with her thumb across to the corner.

The light was dim in that part of the room. I thought I could make out Joy and I thought she was snogging somebody. Somebody in a black t-shirt, somebody in a tight miniskirt, just the sort of thing Al was planning to wear. And then Joy pulled back and I blinked.

How long do these things take to register? The bass notes of the music playing seemed to be all I could register and then Joy, turning to look over her shoulder as Al buried her hands in her face. Joy smiled, a vicious nasty smile at me, and mouthed one word.

I guess I stood there for only a few seconds but ~~for a moment~~ it felt like the world was falling apart. Here was the woman I loved kissing somebody else and that somebody else ~~seemed to~~ looked like she not only knew what she was doing but knew what the woman I loved liked.

~~It was the word that confirmed~~ Something had taken place

149

that shifted ~~and moved~~ the ground from under my feet. ~~Now I was trapped~~ It was like she was mouthing ~~to me~~ 'take it or leave it'. I was a hostage, a hostage to everything.

It was an easy word to lip read. It needed no context.

'Crewe.'

* * *

It's 3.30 in the morning. Geo and I are leaving Drake House (and making our way back to my place.) I feel the cool breeze blowing against me ~~as I turn the lock in the door.~~

The police officer with us, Detective Sergeant Mellon, waits as we close the house up.

"None of this is good, Mr Garvey," he says, his local accent rolling the words from his mouth, making it sound like a folk song.

I nod. It has been a long night. The police have managed to work out that the camera is radio controlled but need to do further tests to work out from where. They're not sure if there is a link to a mobile phone and in turn to the internet, which makes the whole thing even more chilling.

Geo and I have both been as co-operative as possible. They want to interview Jane, Alpha and Kalpna in the morning and are going to leave one officer on site all night. We agree that we'll all meet back here at 11am – together with those of us who have yet to make statements.

The past few hours have been chaotic and disturbing. I understand that the police are only doing their job ~~in these circumstances~~, but Geo is less co-operative. He hasn't enjoyed ~~some of the~~ questions which have hinted that the police haven't ruled us out of the equation. ~~They're only doing their job but~~ It is a horrible, nasty, ~~and~~ sickening situation. Worse still, Geo is worried about how many photos of his child could have made

150

their way onto the world wide web for sickos everywhere to... it just doesn't bear thinking about in any depth.

We start the walk back up the hill to my place.

"This is a nightmare," Geo says quietly.

I am tired of talking. I have grown tired of the concentration of lipreading in such stressful circumstances so I just grunt in agreement.

"My son. *My* son. You know Mark, as a parent you have huge fears. You worry about them dying, you worry about them getting hurt, you worry about them getting abused but this somehow seems worse. So much worse."

I can sense his frustration that I am not responding but no words can describe or compensate for what is happening. In the end I stop and just hug him.

Something strange happens then. For the first time since I've known him, Geo is crying. He is sobbing. He's seen me cry many times. In fact when Al and I were finally splitting up he seemed to see me crying more often than anything else. But Geo crying is a new one.

"Giovanni, Giovanni mate. Come on. We'll sort it all out."

"Poor Matty," he says. "If only we had paid attention to the sign-language. I just feel we're out of our depth now. How can he ever trust us? How, Mark?!"

I know he's tired and I know that he's upset.

"Mate, don't talk such bollocks. You and Jane are perfect parents for Matty. Anyway, he need never know about this – not all the details."

"But he's a witness. He spotted the camera. Won't he have to appear in court?"

Already Geo is racing ahead of himself. Court? I know from experience that we would have to have someone to charge. Bringing this to a hearing could take years.

151

"Cross that bridge when we get there mate."

We eventually get to my home. There are messages on the answerphone from Kalpna and Jane. I phone Kalpna back, explain that we're at my place and that we all need to talk in the morning. Then at the end of the conversation I make a mistake.

She is just about to put the phone down.

"It's been a long night," she says. "Get some sleep."

"I know – I am really tired."

"Sleep well then," she says, and pauses.

"Kal," I say softly, "I love you."

She doesn't respond.

"Go to sleep," she says, "and sleep well."

Eventually we put the phone down. I am so angry with myself because I know I really don't love this woman and hate the fact that I have learnt nothing from the past. I am using the phrase as an emotional shorthand. It doesn't mean I love her at all. It means I need her and I hate myself for needing her and being needy. In the middle of all this mess, all this chaos, I reach for those three words, 'I love you,' like an alcoholic turning to the bottle for comfort. Surely it's not true, surely I can't make the same stupid mistakes again and again.

By now I'm too tired to even reason with myself. I climb the stairs to bed, pull back the duvet cover and hope that sleep will take me away from the frustrations of my own empty words and gestures.

* * *

I have often wondered if I am a coward. I know I am a pacifist and could never take up arms, I know that given the choice I walk away from physical violence. I will argue with people, I will stand my ground over arguments, but I will never use

152

violence. I know that some things are wrong and some things are right and I probably know that I would never have been the kid in Tiananmen Square standing in front of a Chinese tank, risking my life for everything I believed in, because ~~I know that~~ I would just not have it in me to do that. I am not even sure that if I was a firefighter at the Twin Towers I would have found reasons not to go back into the burning building and rescue colleagues. Maybe I would have explained that there was some dry cleaning I needed to pick up. And I certainly would never have jumped from the upper floors as the building burned. Then again, maybe there is a confusion. Exceptional courage is not the same as cowardice, is it? Who knows?

~~After the party~~ I did not confront Al about her kissing incident with Joy. I knew that to do so would risk all sorts of things ~~and I wasn't going to put whatever those things were at risk.~~ I reasoned ~~in my own mind~~ that for Al it was the drink, or that she had given in to Joy's amorous advances in a moment of confusion. I saw her as a victim, not as a perpetrator ~~of the events.~~ Not Al.

Joy was a different matter and I knew that she was bribing me. I struggled for days with what to do, wondering if Joy's snogging equated to a 1-1 score draw for my indiscretion with Patrice. No way. I may have pulled a goal back, but Al's act was merely a freekick in a dangerous position. The best I could hope for was a red card and a lengthy ban. The possibility of being shipped out of Al's life altogether nagged. I also couldn't be certain that Joy hadn't given Al at least a hint, an idea, that the guy she was with, the man that I still assumed she loved, was a rat, a git, a cunt, a twat, a bastard, a shit. I knew that my own words would never be as accurate or hurtful as the ones that Joy could use herself so I gave up trying to find contemptuous ways to describe my own acts.

~~Whatever happened,~~ we seemed in the few days after the party to both avoid discussing what had happened and yet to unconsciously acknowledge that something had 'happened'. A strange atmosphere existed between us. We were loving but cautious. Not sexual but not cold. Al seemed to do all the things she normally did, talk to me with her same warmth and love, but it was like a beat was being skipped. Then I realised the difference. There was an absence of future planning from our conversation. Everything was in the moment whereas previously one of the key features about our conversations together was our ability to project positive futures. Simple things; the great weekend we were going to have, the good film that was on TV that night, the next game at the Baggies I was looking forward to. This stopped. No forward projection and it was strange and unsettling. 'Is this how things are when they're over?' was a thought the recurred time and time again.

I was having strange dreams too. Dreams in which Joy would be stood by the bed with a knife. She would slice the knife across my wrists, just drawing blood, allowing me to bleed slowly. Then as I lay there bleeding, she would kiss Al everywhere she could. I would wake with a start and an enormous erection; the combination of terror and girl-on-girl sex confusing me and my penis in equal measure.

Towards the end of the week after the party, I bumped into Geoff again, at a member's briefing for Social Services Committee.

"Great, great party," Geoff said, grinning broadly.

"Thanks," I smiled, wondering what was going through his mind.

"Your mate Giovanni is a nice bloke too," he said with enthusiasm. "Seemed to have an encyclopaedic knowledge about your life. Your ex-girlfriends, favourite food, you name it, he seemed to know it." I made a mental note to call Geo – what had he told Geoff?

"Yeah," I said "Geo is a diamond."

Geoff lowered his tone. "And you haven't forgotten about the AD post have you?"

'So he wasn't pissed,' I thought, 'he meant it.'

Geoff continued, "I've persuaded HR to only advertise that one internally. It will go to advert on Friday, closing date's in two weeks. You have to apply, OK Mark?" He looked at me, making sure that I could see he was being serious.

"Great," I said "If you think I've got what it takes, I'll go for it."

"To borrow a phrase from Geo – you are definitely Champions League material on this one – just like Gemma."

Fuck! Fucking Geo! Why had he given away the Premier League stuff to Geoff? Anyway ,Gemma was only Premier League, never Champions League.

Before we could carry on, the Chair was calling the meeting to order. Despite Geo's indiscretions, it seemed that I was still a frontrunner.

I was keen to get home to tell Al the news. I reckoned that this might help to move things to a new stage. However, I got home to find Al sat in the living room in tears. She'd been crying for some time.

"What's the matter?" I asked.

She reached across the sofa to an airmail envelope, her mum's unmistakable handwriting on the front.

"Dad," she said quietly.

"What? What's wrong?" I asked.

"He's not been well for a bit, but now he knows. He's had test It's crap, Mark!"

I sat down beside her, held her in my arms and rocked her gently for a moment. She continued to cry.

"I'm being punished, aren't I? I'm being punished for the termination, for my lack of passion towards you? For the Joy thing?"

She was losing it. Genuinely losing it.

"Call your mum," I said. "Now. You'll feel better once you've spoken to her. Go on – I'll make tea. It'll be breakfast time over there."

"But it costs so much, and – "

I held my hand up. "Just call," I said. "I'll make some tea."

By the time I returned with two steaming mugs of tea, she was on the phone, talking to her mum. I could tell her mum was crying and that Al was really pulling herself together to keep talking to her. This was good therapy, it allowed Al not to feel sorry for herself and to think about what her mum was going through. Eventually, after 15 minutes, Al hung up.

We sat silently for a moment.

"I'm sorry I lost it," she eventually said. "I just don't know how to deal with it. Cancer? What the fuck did my dad do to deserve that?" She smiled. She was trying to make an ironic joke.

I kissed her on her forehead. "Come on. It's early doors yet, they get these things early enough, you know."

Al started to rant again. I just hugged her, stroking her dark hair as I held her. "It's OK sweetheart, it's absolutely OK. Everything will work out."

And it was. I mean, not about her dad – that was horrible news. But it was good that she had acknowledged the thing with Joy at the party. But she was all over the place, despite having got a grip on things.

"I'd go home for a bit, but we can't afford it," she said, "and I need to be with you."

This gave me the chance to tell her about my discussions with Geoff. She seemed genuinely pleased.

"That's great," she said, "that's really great." She smiled and kissed me. It was a gentle kiss, but passionate nonetheless.

"Look," I explained. "If I get this, why don't you go home

for Christmas. The extra money from the new job would mean that I could more or less pay for your flight out of my salary."

She really did kiss me then.

"Ah Mark, you know that would be brilliant! Do you really think I could?"

"Let's see," I said.

And we'd moved on again. We were talking about the future and planning and putting whatever had happened at the party behind us. It felt good, really good to have Al back. Maybe I had done nothing brave, nothing courageous, but I had done something just as important. I had been generous. Maybe generosity was my strength not courage? What I didn't realise was that my willingness to pay for Al to go home would be tested, much sooner than I thought.

* * *

It's 10.45 and I am on the phone to Kalpna.

"What do you mean you're not coming? This isn't meeting for a coffee, it's a criminal investigation."

Geo and Jane are sat at the breakfast table drinking coffee. Matty is colouring his pictures. He seems to have sensed there is a problem but he is more or less back to his normal self.

"Look, Alpha will be there. I'm just not feeling well. I only came back with you anyway. It's not like I lived there like you ever did and I just drove you home."

I can't believe this. She's a doctor for God's sake. She must understand how these things work.

"They'll need all of us to make statements."

She gets cross. "I didn't say I wouldn't make a statement. I will. But not today. I'm really not very well at all."

'God!' I think. 'like we have a choice about these things.'

Our conversation is interrupted by a knock on the door. I make my apologies and hang up.

At the same time Jane has crossed into the hall. I think I can hear Peter Holland's voice at the front door.

Sure enough, in a couple of moments Peter is stood in front of me.

I'd explained the basics to him in an early morning phone call but I didn't expect him to come down.

"Hello," he says. He isn't acting his normal jolly self. He's being deadly serious. "Have they arrived yet?"

I shake my head, indicating 'no', and then spend the next few moments introducing him to Geo, Jane and Matty.

"Have you got a solicitor involved?" Peter asks. This idea throws me as I really hadn't considered this. Geo interrupts.

"Why on earth do *we* need solicitors?!"

Peter sighs.

"Look," he says, "at the moment you have to accept that you are both at risk here." He looks at me for a moment like 'come on Mark – put your professional brain into gear – be objective.'

"Like we would install this kind of thing!? It's outrageous to suggest that!" Geo is really getting worked up again.

Peter raises his hands to calm Geo.

"Listen my friend, this is not me being awkward but think it through. Objectively. In the worse case scenario, you could both end up being charged. Worse still, somebody could decide that Matty here is 'at risk' and who knows where that would end. I just want you both to get the right advice." He turns to me.

"Mark, I've taken the liberty of asking my solicitor to attend. County will cover the costs but it is important that you have somebody with you during any questioning."

I glance out of the corner of my eye and catch Jane's

expression. She is ashen. The horror of all this is beginning to stack up for her.

Then there are the implications for me. I can see the headlines: 'Director of Social Services in paedophilia photo scandal.' Coming on the back of the Birmingham bollocks, this will not be good.

We are interrupted as, simultaneously, Alpha and Peter's solicitor, Colin Knapp, arrive. Alpha immediately crosses to give Matty a hug, which is returned by a huge smile from Matty. But Alpha's eyes look dead; she doesn't look like she is dealing with this well.

Mr Knapp takes us into the lounge. The sun glints off the sea; it is a beautiful morning for once, but the day is darker than many I have ever known. Colin explains he will accompany us both during our interviews and monitor the police line of questioning. If they raise suggestive or leading questions, he will object on our behalf. They have already agreed to give him the notes from their interviews with us from the night before. The important thing is that we remain calm and that we give as truthful an account as possible.

"Let's get some coffee brewed; it's going to be a long morning."

Knapp leaves Geo and I in the lounge. He looks close to tears, just like Jane.

"Come on matey – it will be fine", I say to him.

"Peter – he's done the right thing getting his solicitor involved."

"Yeah – he's a good guy." I say, slowly nodding positively.

"Mark – we're all good guys here – let's not forget that."

We both stand and bear-hug each other. It's like a scene from a mafia movie. And the thought runs through my mind 'am I a good guy? How could I allow all thi:s to happen?'

Before I can shake off the stupidity of the thought, Jane appears. The police have arrived.

* * *

I probably should've shown her the door straight away, but I'd had a couple of glasses of wine and really wasn't in the mood for a fight.

Al had been gone for two days. Christmas was approaching and we had made a desperate attempt to get the house into a decent state so that I would at least be comfortable whilst she was away. We talked about me joining her but even with the promotion it was pushing the boat out for us both to go to Oz.

I had been sat in the kitchen with a bottle of wine and watching the end of a Premiership game on TV. The kitchen was now the nerve centre of the house, partly because it was finished, partly because the Aga gave off warmth that always made it cosy, ~~and~~ also because Al and I ~~seemed to~~ revolved ourselves around talking and food. Maybe it was also a hangover from the size of the place in Edgbaston. We had grown so used to one-and-a-bit room-living that we didn't know how to properly use all this other extra space.

But now Joy was sat at the table opposite me.

"You heard from her since she landed?"

With the question, my mind was cast back to that first Christmas – the scene at Perth airport, the happiness. And maybe all those feelings were current because we'd already had one phone call and ~~I'd had an~~ email from her while ~~when~~ she waited for a connecting flight in Singapore, so it felt a bit like the past was alive again.

Joy ~~by now~~ had pulled up a chair and was pouring herself a glass of wine.

"Going to be a quiet Christmas for you then?" she probed.

Instead of responding, I resorted to sarcasm. "Help yourself by the way," I said flatly.

Joy continued, oblivious.

"Are you going to spend it with anyone, anyone special?" She wasn't even trying to disguise the insinuation behind what she was saying.

'Bollocks!' I thought, 'let's wind her up.'

"Well, I have a few options and, you know, something about mice playing and cats being away."

She raised an eyebrow, but no more.

"Be mad of you to fool around – fooling around means you may end up with people who you can't trust."

I wondered how much she really knew and what were her sources anyway. I mean she was such a bullshitter that her complaints about my journey to Crewe could have been an educated guess.

She drained her wine glass.

"More," she said insistently.

I poured her some more and we sat in silence for a while. On the TV screen, the commentators were in post match analysis mode, wearing stupid Father Christmas hats and trying to be as jovial as possible. Joy and I, on the other hand, were sat, showing no interest in their brave attempts to cheer us.

"I don't understand," she said "why anyone would want anybody other than Al, myself."

I wouldn't be drawn into the conversation. I was determined not to say anything that would incriminate me myself.

"I mean, she's perfect isn't she? Great looks, great figure, great personality. You'd either have to be very stupid or very greedy to want something more." As she spoke the words I sensed that this was more than an off-the-cuff conversation – this had been rehearsed.

"Well," I said quietly, "I love Al. That's where it starts and that's where it ends."

"To the exclusion of all others?" Joy's question coincided with another draining of her wine glass. "More," she said, putting the glass down in front of me.

"Yes," I said firmly.

Joy began to giggle.

"I do a nice Belfast accent you know, I've got cousins over there."

'Where the fuck is this conversation going?' I wondered.

Joy continued, "But you never really have fancied me, have you?"

I looked at her. Joy wasn't unattractive. She wasn't conventionally attractive either; her blonde hair neither well styled nor grown long. She had a body disproportionate to the size of her face, her breasts and thighs being heavy like ripe fruit, and her face slim and angular. I'd never really thought of her sexually before.

"I think you've had too much too drink," I told her.

"Why don't you fancy me?" she asked. "I mean me, you, Al – think about it."

"Up!" I said, losing my temper now. "Come on, just get out!"

She stood but it was obvious that she was already quite pissed.

"Fuck," she said, "I can't drive like this – can I stay?"

"No – you should've thought about that before you decided to drink so much."

"And you always think about the consequences of your actions, hmm? Even when you're watching that pathetic football team of yours! Even when you're fucking other people? Maybe Al should know about some of the things you do."

I grabbed her by her arm tightly.

"Hey! Bondage is one of the things I don't do."

I pulled her close towards me.

"Keep your fucking nose out Joy! OK?" I was nose to nose with her.

"I'll keep putting my tongue in though, hey? You ought to try it – you'd like my tongue."

"Just go!" I yelled.

By this point she had wriggled free and had started to climb the stairs towards the bedroom.

"I'm going to bed," she said. "If you like, I'll phone Al now to check if that's OK, Oh and to ask her if she has ever heard of Patrice – but I'm sure you don't want me to do that Mark, so be a good boy and let me stay."

I was furious but she had me trapped.

"Do what you fucking like," I yelled after her and returned to the kitchen, slamming the door and turning the volume of the TV up.

I'd been sat there fuming for maybe 10 or 15 minutes when Joy threw open the kitchen door. She had Al's dressing gown on.

"Turn that down – I can't sleep!" she yelled.

I was really pissed off now.

"Who said you could wear that?!" I said, pointing at the dressing gown.

"I'll take it off then," she said. As she did so she revealed her naked self to me. My eyes, despite my anger, were drawn to how erect her nipples were and the lack of hair down below.

"1970, good year for nipples in this area," she said.

"Put the dressing gown back on!" I said.

"But you just told me to take it off." She was stood there stroking her breasts, making the nipples stand out even more. "You ought to try these in your mouth – you'll love them. Al does!"

It was all getting too much. I pushed past her, stormed upstairs and shut myself in the bedroom. Surely she was teasing me, with her comments about her breasts and Al's like for her nipples. It was then that I noticed that Joy's clothes were on this side of the door. A few moments later she knocked.

"I'm going – can I come in and get my clothes?" she shouted from the other side of the door.

I'm not sure what happened after that. I know when I opened the door she was naked. I know that I didn't do anything. I know that I woke up the following morning and she was next to me and that my penis was sore. Lesser detectives would probably be able to piece together some of what probably happened. How about Al?

* * *

Three days have passed. Geo, Jane and Matty have gone back to Bristol early. To be honest, I think Jane is mentally exhausted by it all. Matty cried when he left because he wanted to spend more time with Alpha and wanted to do the paddling that he had been promised before they arrived.

I'd booked the week off anyway so I haven't been into work. I am feeling cheated, though, and Kalpna has taken to her bed again. Apparently she has made a minimal, factual statement to the police but that's as far as it goes.

DCI Mellon has also met with me a couple of times. He has ruled Geo out of any wrongdoing but by implication has not ruled me out of the equation. We had a conversation about whether or not I had ever seen any flashes when I rented the place. I can't really recall any but everything seems so bizarre.

In these situations, there's nothing much I can do. The past few days have been punctuated by phone calls from Geo, meetings with Mellon – who Geo and I now refer to as PC Fruit, and me furtively interrogating every possible person in Hope Cove who may have some link with the property. I spent yesterday in The Ship, even wore my hearing aids, just to see if I could pick up any gossip from Jim. Yet I know I am not cut out to be a spy. When I am furtive, I'm actually dodgy looking, what I take to be a casual glance is probably much nearer to an interrogative stare. A couple of tourists in the pub, nearly got physical with me when they thought I was making eyes at their partners. All too dangerous – all proving that I never had a chance of a career with MI6, no matter how much I convinced myself.

Jim nods to me.

"What *are* you playing at Mark, disturbing the peace like that?"

'Just trying to be discrete Jim,' I say. He laughs loudly, sardonically.

"Well keep practicising eh?'

I decide to leave The Ship. Maybe it is not the best place for me to be.

Alpha is also taking things badly. She came to see me this morning.

"I feel shit," she said, and for once she looked it, "and I miss Matty – he made me all broody."

I smile at this. "Well if it's any consolation, he misses you too. According to Jane he keeps on asking when he can come back and see you."

"I can't wait to go back to Bristol because Jane has said I can babysit him." For the first time in a few days, she genuinely looks happy at the prospect. "He's helping me realise that I really want to do something about rights when I finally get to be a shit hot barrister or lawyer or whatever." She seems to mean it. But I know that at 19 she is just a kid exploring her ideals and doubtless she'll end up doing corporate property law or copyright stuff.

"Where do you think this will end, Mark?" she asks me, looking earnest and frightened.

"Who knows?" I respond. "PC Fruit has hinted that they are on to something but we'll just have to wait and see."

"I heard Jim say that they have questioned Wilma Mapp," Alpha informs me.

"Really?!" This is genuinely news to me. I'd not really thought about her role in this. "Maybe there is a God!" I say.

Alpha laughs. "Don't be mean." She smiles. It's good to see her smiling. She's been so down for so long that her smiles are worth the wait.

So now Alpha has left. I sit making mental notes and I try to consider all the possible people who could have done this. Past visitors to the house? Someone with regular access? Wilma Mapp? I find myself persuading me *concluding* that the only possible person who can have done this is the highland beastie herself and I am shocked at how satisfying I find the prospect.

In a different life, with perfect hearing – whatever that is – maybe I would have made a great detective. I recognise it's one of those dreams, like wondering if I really could've been a top class rally driver or if, instead of giving up after one visit to the air training corps, that I could've flown Concorde. Still, if I'm moving in this direction, hopefully PC Fruit and his basket of companions will also be treading the same beat.

* * *

Those

That three-week period whilst Al was gone became a torment. I was totally confused about what had happened between myself *me* and Joy and she didn't show her face again, or her breasts come to that, in the entire period Al was away.

On the other side of the globe, things weren't good either.

Al's dad had taken a turn for the worse and ~~the early signs were~~ ~~that~~ the cancer was spreading. I really felt for him, ~~I remember~~ wondering why all the shitty people in the world tend to get nothing. But they end up being shitty, which is a cancer in its own right if you're a mugger, a drug dealer or some other form of low-life that exploits other people. ~~Plus~~ Al wasn't taking it well, and her mum was having even bigger problems keeping up with things.

I got a phone call from her on New Year's Eve.

"Hi," she said, flat and down. "Why is life so fucking crap sometimes? You know, I'm here and the sun is shining and the days are hot but all I can see is my dad dying in front of me, ~~Mark? And~~ I don't want to celebrate the turning of the page on the calendar because I know that this year could be the year, well more than likely *will* be the year my dad dies."

I didn't really know how to respond to this. I guess I had been lucky and unlucky in that both my parents were dead by the time I was 21. When these things happen early in your life, you know that death is all part of the living game. But Al had never experienced this before, so.

"I know – it stinks. Do you want me to come out and join you?" I asked.

Al hesitated. "Erm, no I don't think so." There was something about the hesitation that was familiar. "You know, old friends and family are here and that's kind of nice. You've got work anyway."

She seemed keen to move the conversation on. "How's Joy, have you seen her since she got drunk with you?"

I almost dropped the phone. How did she know about this? Al continued:

"I got an e-mail from her and she said she'd been a bit of an arse. I mean, I said to her 'Joy you're always a big fuckin' arse so don't worry."

I wondered what else the email had said.

"I'll talk to you about that when you get back." I genuinely just wanted to tell the truth, Yet confessing to not knowing what had happened between me and her best friend struck me as being a little inappropriate.

And At the end of conversations like this, I felt so far away and so lost to her. It didn't help that Christmas and New Year in England were colder than I could remember. There seemed to be no sign of sun whatsoever, just cold, grey days when the temperature never climbed much above freezing and there wasn't even the prospect of snow to paint out the grey and leave the world clean and purified.

I drifted through life. Spent New Year's Day at the Hawthorns and then drove down to Bristol for a drinks party with Jane, Geo and a bunch of thespians, all friends of Geo.

Late in the party, pissed on too much punch and mixing my drinks, I 'fessed up to Jane. She was appalled.

"You slept with who?!" she said loud enough for people around us to glance in our direction. And being drunk, I had forgotten that Jane didn't posses Geo's tolerance of my amorous crusades.

"You're a fucking idiot then aren't you! I thought you loved Al???"

I did, I did. I kept trying to explain to Jane that it was a mistake and an error but she would have none of it.

"You sleep with her best friend and then expect forgiveness? Isn't there still a bit of the Catholic faith left in you, Mark?"

Before I could answer Geo had intervened. Our argument had got louder and I think Geo had a sense that his best mate was being beaten into a verbal pulp by a woman half his size and twice as wise.

I ended up in bed, crying myself to sleep in pity of my own idiocy and lack of knowledge. I really didn't know if I had even had sex with Joy, I just knew I didn't know – which in itself was bad enough. And I always have a fear that the way you are on the first day of a new year shapes the way you are for the rest of it. So here I was, crying my eyes out and confused about what I had and hadn't done. Worse still, I also knew that I had to confront Al about some of the things Joy had said to me. So not only was I worried about how she would react to the episode with Joy, I was also worried about an emerging agenda that pushed us deeper in to the mire.

I returned to Birmingham, more worried [anxious] than ever by [about] the future and my ability to keep the wolves at bay. There was Joy and there was Jane. But these things come in threes. And sure enough there in the early new year's post was an envelope with a Belfast postmark, addressed to Al and I, curiously with Al's name first on the envelope.

I opened it. A simple message.

'Happy New Year Al & Mark – Al – make the most of him while you have him – Patrice Hardy.'

I was disgusted. Mostly I was disgusted by the formality – a declaration. I was also disgusted by myself – how did I allow this mess to develop? How could I put so much at risk?

A new year loomed with war on three fronts. I was tempted to raise the white flag there and then. Why [The fact] I didn't might in my own personal history be described as 'the miracle of South Edgbaston'. My own little Dunkirk. But we always forget the first victim in war that makes the harshest of realities easy [easier] to bear.

* * *

We came up on Thursday. Kalpna had decided that there really was no point in us staying in the oppressive atmosphere that had developed in Hope Cove. Plus, she had argued, we hadn't actually had a weekend away together yet. Not surprisingly I suppose, given that in reality we hadn't know each other for that long. Still, in the past I may well have thought about marriage, by now whereas I now know in my head that this is about sex. It's a pity my heart tries to convince itself otherwise.

The sunlight glistens on the lake in St James' Park. I keep admonishing myself for not knowing the names of the different water fowl that peck at the bread cast on the surface by spring tourists. It is a warm day, a really good day so far.

We spent the morning over at the Tate Modern, a building that always takes my breath away and reminds me that good can come out of chaos no matter what happens. The art itself is not the point. In the Tate Modern, you go to see the transformation of a derelict building and the posturing of the empty lives that seem to assume adults who can draw like Matty are talented. Kalpna was none too impressed by the pretensions, or the people trying to pass themselves off as Bohemian but who probably made a living work as advertising sales staff, accountants and junior civil servants. Hardly the most alternative of lifestyles.

Now the relief of the park, the warmth of the mid-May sunshine is helping to lift us again. I ponder how strange it is that living in all the beauty that is Hope Cove, I feel stressed, whereas the hustle and bustle that is London makes me so much more relaxed. Also, I have been quieter here. For instance, for the past few minutes we have been wandering around the lake, lost in our own thoughts, not talking to each other but gently holding hands. Occasionally Kalpna breaks off and wanders to the side of the path to admire a plant or a strange, designer-looking duck. Yet most of the time we just seem to be enjoying the moment, allowing the day to pass as the tourists wander by or civil servants make their way between the park and the pen-pushers that run Government.

Despite the beauty of it all, I am aware that there is an underlying tension between Kal and I. Our conversation flows easily until we begin to discuss the incidents at Drake House. Not just the camera, but also her unwillingness to meet the police. I have been perplexed by this for days but Kalpna immediately responds with an excuse. It came up over lunch.

"Come on Mark, we're meant to be here to escape all that nonsense." She is not angry, just calm.

"But we need to."

She interrupts me. "We need to celebrate the fact that we are in a city where you and I pass for normal. A white male with an Indian woman. At home, I often think that we're seen as a cultural sideshow. Something to entertain the natives."

I swallow the hook. "Oh, come on Kal, it's not that bad is it?"

And skilfully she changes the conversation to the advantages and disadvantages of Metropolitan life. So we never did get to discuss Hope.

I wonder if all of this is simply what Kalpna says it is – a break from the frontline. I've never really escaped from a crisis before, well not one like this anyway. So I'm struggling, I'm struggling between trusting her and accepting she is right, or doubting her and wondering why I doubt her. Not a good recipe in anyone's book.

These musings are interrupted by Kalpna. She places her arm around my waist.

"I need to go back to the hotel," she says softly.

"Why?" I ask – suspecting she may not be feeling well or some other similar something reason.

"I want you to make love to me – I want to play with our toys."

The toys are a reference to a couple of stupid vibrators we

171

bought as we wandered through Soho yesterday. Last night I would have nothing to do with them, much to Kalpna's disappointment.

"It's a beautiful day, can't we go back later?" I ask.

"No. I want to go back now, by taxi. I want to start in the back of a taxi."

This is bloody silly. It will cost us a fortune to get back to the Aldwych at this time on a Friday.

"We could walk – at least then we'd get a win-win."

"I want a fuck-fuck. Now."

Before I can stop her, Kalpna is wandering out through the gates and hailing a cab on the Mall. I toy with the idea of not joining her, but ~~toying with ideas and not having sex are just different things~~. I can toy with ideas on my own; the same can't be said about sex.

In the back of the cab, she starts stroking me through my trousers, kissing me, encouraging me to do the same. I feel sorry for the cab driver who looks totally disinterested. I want to engage him in conversation rather than engage Kal in sex. As all these ideas are racing around in my head, Kal's mobile rings.

She holds up a hand – like I was making the running, ~~anyway~~ – and speaks to the mobile.

"Hello Alpha," a pause, "who?" another pause, "when?!" Kalpna runs her hand through her hair, something I notice that she does when she is either stressed or turned on. "OK, I'll tell him." She listens again. "We were. Until this. OK – bye."

She puts the phone back in her bag, her mood has changed. She seems totally cold – in an instance.

"What?!" I ask, perplexed by the hot and cold nature of her passion.

"They've arrested Wilma."

"Wilma who?" I ask not even thinking.

"Mapp! Wilma Mapp, of course!" She snaps at me.

I am struck first by the change in mood and then pleased that DCI Mellon may have got his ~~man~~ wo.

"Mapp! I knew it – I knew it!"

"Quite the little Sherlock, aren't you?!" Kalpna says dismissively.

By now the taxi has arrived at the hotel. I get out to pay. I turn to Kalpna. "We'll order champagne I think!"

She slams the cab door behind her. "Oi!" yells the cabbie, "they're tough but they're not that bloody tough."

"I'm just so not in the mood now Mark!" She wanders into the hotel without settling up with the less than happy cabby.

By the time ~~my back is turned~~ he's paid, Kalpna has disappeared up to ~~her~~ me room. Then my mobile vibrates in my pocket.

I fish it out and read the text. It is from my mystery sender.

'1 down 1 2 go!'

The cab pulls off, life moves on and I am left wondering what on earth the world is doing to me.   — Victim

*   *   *   yuk

It would be fair to say that I pondered what to do about the Joy-Patrice-Jane axis for several days. I seemed trapped between three very strong but very different forces. Each one had the ability to seal my fate but each one required a different tactic.

There was, I decided, no point in hoping that Geo would sort the Jane scenario out. Geo was a good guy, a really decent bloke, but he knew better than try and cover up lies for me to Jane. It took me a while to understand it, but one of Jane's great strengths is that she takes no shit – from anybody. So she has to come to her own conclusions about the way forward. The best I could hope for was that Geo would at least keep Jane at a distance ~~from the battlefield~~ until I had resolved war on the other two fronts. Yet I knew that this was only a delaying tactic – sooner or later, they would meet, and then what?

I contemplated all sorts of ways of dealing with Patrice. The simplest one was to have her murdered. I can't believe now that I even contemplated this but I found a few dodgy internet sites were there was a suggestion that the going rate for a former IRA assassin was about £5K – the cost of a holiday for a lifetime's peace? Struck me as ~~being~~ a good deal. Yet the more I thought about it, the more I recognised the risk I ~~faced~~. Imagine getting caught! How the hell would I explain it all to Al? Oh, and where would I actually get £5K from? I suspected hired assassins were unlikely to take Access cards and was doubtful that the Co-Op Bank's ethical policy would ~~ignore~~ accept a request for a loan to hire a killer. Along the way, the morality of it all got lost. So in the end it wasn't a moral imperative, just the fact that I didn't have the bollocks to do it. So there was no solution that I could come up with that would work. Still, she was a long way from us in Belfast. All I had to do was get up every morning and intercept the post, make sure Al never answered the phone and well it would be easy...Hmm – I remained unconvinced.

Joy caused me even more difficulties. I tried phoning her a couple of times but got no response. The fact that she had already mentioned some of this to Al made me wonder if she hadn't gone down the route of her own pre-emptive strike. I toyed with the idea of finding a male lover for Joy so that, at the very least, she would have a sexual distraction from Al. And maybe when she was ~~happily~~ regularly getting her brains fucked out she would mellow. Or Al would be so disgusted by the betrayal that she would realise it was all ridiculous, that Joy was using her to fulfil a sick fantasy and that the only person whose nipples deserved licking was me! ~~Then again, just how likely was~~

it? Who? Maybe I could persuade her to go for the rugged silent type, maybe the former IRA assassin would agree that she 'wasn't bad' and I could persuade him to drag her across to the north of Ireland, never to be seen again? All these maybes had one effect. They just drove me round and around in circles until I realised that there was no solution to Joy.

I sank in to depression. Called in to work sick, dug out old photos of me and Al and realised that all was doomed. I sensed there would be no more free and easy days with her, no more scenes like so many of those in the pile of pictures I looked at. Al kissing me; Al holding hands with me; Al smiling, holding a pebble discovered on a beach. None of this would survive the landing of a plane from Perth.

Then it occurred to me, that there was one option I hadn't considered. It was an option that didn't require too much rehearsal or too much thinking about but a great deal of courage. Compared to murdering Patrice and all the other stupid options I was considering, this one would also leave me with a shred of dignity.

"So that's why I'm telling you all of this," I said to Al the Saturday morning after she arrived back. "I want you to know the truth."

She stared at me blankly for a few minutes.

"Let me get this straight. You're being bribed by a woman you know from Northern Ireland who claims to have slept with you?"

"That's about it, yep," I nodded solemnly.

"OK," Al continued "and Joy?"

"Tried to seduce me while you were away and claimed that you and she were lovers."

Al nodded slowly to herself. 'No' she seemed to be thinking, 'none of this is making any sense.'

"Did you believe her?" Al asked.

"I thought she was trying to wind me up – you know, after the party thing – I kind of thought that she had something on you."

Al nodded again, disbelievingly. Given that I had spent the previous 20 minutes explaining all of this in my own words, I had expected her to be a bit more agitated. There was no sign of that.

Eventually she turned to me.

"Mark, I love you. I only want you."

She was looking at me with a steady, calm gaze.

She smiled, held out her arms.

"Come on, we can't sort all this out. Let's just get things moving again." She crossed the room and hugged me.

I knew I didn't deserve this. I really knew it. And I had told Al a version of the truth, but not the truth. So Patrice was claiming to have slept with me, even though we actually had. Joy had seduced me, or at least I claimed she tried to and thus was able to sow enough doubt in Al's mind about her own friend's motives. I hadn't linked the two, and when Joy did, I was able to pass it off as me having confided in her when she came around at Christmas, thus turning defeat into victory because now Joy was showing herself to be somebody who couldn't be trusted, even when a nice guy like me was seeking advice from her best friend.

They say that all is fair in love and war and that in war truth is the first victim. I managed to win a famous victory with versions of the truth, but then forgot. It is easy to win battles; winning wars is much harder.

* * *

I look at it. Tangled, almost hard to recognise. There are elements

176

of what you would call a car, but ~~these are random elements as if~~ drawn by somebody who had a memory blockage and then ~~decided to~~ stick together the bits they could remember ~~from a car~~ in an abstract way.

On the seat there is broken glass and a stain. I take the stain to be blood which immediately starts me off wanting to cry again.

Ryan Davis is alongside me.

"Not good is it Mr Garvey?"

He seems to be a master of stating the bloody obvious. I nod agreement ~~with~~ him.

It is all too shocking. We returned on Sunday evening ~~back~~ to Hope Cove. As we left the train at Plymouth to collect Kalpna's car, we were met by the leader of the Council – Lance Somerton. He looked pale, his face drawn. I knew immediately something was wrong.

He took me to one side and briefly explained what had happened. Peter had left County Hall on Friday evening, a bit earlier than usual, partly because I wasn't around for our usual chat. He'd got his car to the huge roundabout just before the M5 junction when – well nobody was exactly sure what happened next and the police were still trying to find out ~~what had happened~~. Peter was in a coma, not expected to survive.

I was due at the garage to get my identical Z4 serviced that Monday morning. It seemed ridiculous not to take a look at the wreckage that was Peter's Z4. I am struck by how mangled and tangled the whole thing is and wonder how anyone could survive this.

"The thing is," says Davis, "~~is that~~ yours has got better airbags than his. You'd probably survive something like this."

I want to slap him for the insensitivity of the comment but we're interrupted as Anna joins us. She's as upset as anyone as she spent time covering a maternity leave as Peter's PA. You only have to see them chat to know that there is real affection between them. Now we're both left hoping against hope for such a solid, decent guy.

"Oh, is this it?" she asks, her eyes huge with the horror of it.

"'Fraid so" I say, and we are stood silently, three people contemplating the meaning of life and death, confronted by a sculpture made by modern man and his lifestyle.

Anna's phone rings. She steps away from Davis and I, speaks quietly into the phone and turns her back to me.

"Yes, yes," she says softly. Initially she appears to be OK but then shifts her position and speaks more quietly, leaving me and Davis continuing our silent contemplation.

Eventually Anna turns, tears are streaming down her face, her shoulders rise and she drops her handbag, which crashes to the floor, spilling cosmetics, car keys and a picture of Dom and Liam. I move to hold her to try and comfort her, but I know. Peter is dead.

* * *

We seem to despise politicians these days. They're either corrupt or incompetent and sometimes both. Yet the contempt in which we hold those we elect is never the same as the way we judge ourselves is it? Yet maybe we behave in the same way.

You can imagine the relief a politician feels when he or she gets away with a half truth. 'I've done it and they believe me.' Onwards and upwards. You might be selling arms to a country you're not meant to sell arms to, or lying about weapons of mass destruction or claiming that crime has fallen when it's gone up and dogs are now officially cuter, smarter and fart less. But the public bite on these lies and you move on, knowing that the next lie is also going to be swallowed.

When we get away with lies, when we know we have told only a half truth that has been totally believed, we all become politicians. Politicians are, of course, the most public embodiment of successful liars. Yet look at recent history. Peter Sutcliffe? Ian Huntley? Osama Bin Laden?

I never did accept Patrice's invitation to see Tranmere play. We won anyway. But nor did I go to the games at Bristol, Loftus Road or Fulham. I had match day programmes and match day souvenirs. Not the scent of Bovril, the misery of defeat or the joy of a winning goal. Those games remind me of the softness of Patrice's breast, the frantic pace of our love-making and the sense that once we succeed in convincing those who trust us most that we have not lied, all other lies become so much easier.

* * *

Life is always an outside broadcast with hearing aids, even the new digital ones. You get unwanted background noise or the sound of the wind rustling against the microphones. You may think that it's good to hear the wind, but when you don't normally hear the wind it's just an irritant.

I have been stood for 15 minutes or so in my raincoat in a cemetery that looks down on to Dartington and the river beyond. It is an unpredictable day, where the sun is replaced by rain at the blink of an eyelid and when cold becomes hot and hot becomes cold far too quickly. We are nearing the end of the priest's eulogy at the graveside, and he has scattered the first crumbs of soil onto the coffin, indicating that Peter's body will soon be buried and sealed. I have attended a number of funerals and I have only recently understood the finality of all of this. Occasionally words are drowned out by the buffeting of the wind so that it seems that the vicar has decided to recite the ceremony in staccato, giving the impression that he has never done this before and can't quite remember recently learned lines, like a bad actor.

I glance across at Chloe, Peter's wife, and wonder at what point she ceases to be thus and becomes Peter's widow? She appears brave and strong but Flo has told me that her cousin, who lives next door to her, has been kept awake by her crying and wails of anguish. It seems so sad.

The earth is piled onto the coffin and some of his children drop flowers onto the fresh soil, posies, apparently Peter's favourite, – and we are nearing the end of the ceremony. Chloe looks up and catches my eye. She smiles a weak smile at me and mouths 'Alright?' I'm touched that in the middle of her own grief she finds time to care about other people. I so want to be positive for her but the best I can do is shrug my shoulders and look away. I make a rule of never crying at funerals but this rule is being tested to the hilt today.

There are a few councillors stood at the graveside. You can almost tell which party they represent by the way they are approaching the ceremony. The Tories seem to have gathered to honour a war hero – one or two who served in the last war have even turned out wearing medals. The Liberals on the other hand could be off to a business meeting, their tones are grey, and they seem to be using The Guardian as shelter from the occasional showers. Fortunately the one token Labour member attending is old Labour. He pays his respects without fuss, gently but respectfully. Peter always confessed to being a Labour voter, but he was very old Labour, pro-nationalisation, anti-American and much more that would now be seen as outlandish and self-indulgent. But he once said to me 'there's nothing outlandish about removing fear from ordinary people's lives.' And in the end he held them all in contempt because each one of them in their own way was simply trying to say, 'look at me and fuck the rest of you'.

Eventually the mix of family and colleagues melt away. Anna has driven me here today, partly because she knew Peter well but also out of respect. It somehow wouldn't have been right to turn up in an identical Z4 as the living embodiment of that which could still be.

As we make our way to the cars that will take us to the inevitable buffet of vol-au-vents and sausage rolls, Lance Somerton approaches me and takes me again to one side.

"Mark, I need to talk to you about the acting role."

This seems to me immediately disrespectful in the circumstances. The last thing I want to discuss is real work.

"Can't it wait?" I ask, and glance in the direction of Chloe, indicating how inappropriate I find the whole business.

"The work of the county has to go on, Mark. It's a nasty situation but you know as well as I do that we can't just stop everything over one death."

I stop walking so that we are further back from the rest of the funeral party.

"So?" I ask.

"Look, you've obvious talent, you know you have and…"

As he speaks, I start to wonder, 'is he going to ask me to act up? Am I to be the Chief Executive?'

Lance continues. "We know that you can meet the role, but.."

And like the Americans say, everything before 'but' is bollocks.

"I've asked Henry Peterson if he'll act up until we can organise a proper recruitment process and then-"

I stop listening. Henry Peterson! He is so old school! The joke around County Hall is that he still writes his ledgers in

181

quill and ink. He's known as a safe pair of hands and what have you but he is more like a plodding, predictable donkey.

I listen to Lance again.

"With the allegations from Birmingham still around, and this latest incident at Hope Cove, well you'll understand we just can't take that kind of risk."

Now I'm angry. How can he justify my guilt by association in both instances, how can he decide that my professional ability is in question over unsubstantiated claims and sordid spying by Scottish landladies? I want to push him over in the mud, I want to tell him to stuff his pathetic County Hall Chief Executive job, but I don't.

Instead I walk silently, briskly, away, wanting to be away from this narrow-minded, mean-spirited bigot and alongside people I respect. Eventually I catch up with Chloe and gently touch her arm.

She turns and faces me, her eyes still moist from graveside tears.

"Mark," she says, by way of recognition. But she says my name gently, almost coaxing me.

"Chloe," I begin, "I just want you to know he was the best person I ever worked with. The nicest, the warmest and the most able. I feel so privileged to have known your husband."

And she smiles gently at me.

"Oh Mark. He adored you, Mark. He never stopped talking about you, you know. I am sure he was convinced he'd found a successor."

Just for a moment we stand there, looking at each other. The wind continues to blow and chaff at the microphones of my hearing aids, but Chloe and I are left in silence together. I break my rule. I start to cry. Then it's a wrap. The OB unit in my head is calling to us, the sound man has finished. The location filming at the cemetery is over and we can all go back to our trailers until the next time we are required to mourn the passing of the people we love. As the credits roll, I understand that without Peter at my side life has just become much harder- so much harder.

P. 79

CHAPTER ~~3~~ 4

I had an uncle who had done something similar before. My Uncle Tom, who thought he had defeated cancer, decided to make a trip back to England and loved every moment of his visit. He celebrated life and died 24 hours after returning to his home in San Diego, having said farewell to all his childhood places.

Of course, I never mentioned any of this to Al, who was really excited about seeing her dad again but also worried about how well he would actually be. Her mood was childlike though, as if her dad represented Christmas.

Superficially, the house was finished. Since Al came back from Perth, we had covered up all the duff jobs and papered over the cracks. We seemed to have developed a real ability to do this to both our physical environment and our relationship. She was still seeing Joy but now never invited me to go out with them. I am not sure how this made me feel but I was just pleased to have Al in my life. Have her all to myself. She was still as loving but her passion was waning. I put this down to the stress of the situation with her dad and there were times when she looked fragile, childlike, a little girl a long way from home who just seemed lost. Still I loved her, still I wanted her, and still I battled against the lust that was conquering me more than my love, pushing me away from fidelity.

But in late April, Al and I drove down, in what was a new Volvo Estate at the time, to pick Al's mum and dad up from Heathrow. We waited in the arrivals hall at Terminal 4. Al excited but tense, I just wanting her to be OK. Eventually through the crowds we saw her mum making her way forward but we couldn't see her dad. Then a double check and we both noticed at the same time Al's mum pushing a thin, drawn man in a wheelchair, a bad copy of the man Al's dad had been. Instantly Al buried her head in my shoulder; she wanted to cry, I could sense her anguish.

"No Al, don't do this to him," I said firmly. "He wants you to be pleased to see him."

And she managed within a few seconds to pull it all back together and to smile to her mum and wave. Then she rushed over to the wheelchair and in an effort that would've been embarrassing to any disability rights activist, hug her dad and the wheelchair in one big embrace.

I reached her mum and took the heavy bags off her. She smiled and kissed me gently on the cheek and then her dad started.

"And what about me Garvey, eh? Don't I get a bloody peck on the cheek?" The little drawn man had lost none of his larger-than-life personality.

"There I was, hoping that you being ill would make you less gobby," I said, deciding to confront the situation head-on.

"Now I like that Mo," he said turning to Al's mum. "Our Mark here comes straight to the point, no nonsense, I'm ill." He turns to me. "I'm sick to bloody death of everybody pretending there's nothing wrong with me, like going around in this underpowered XR2i is some sort of fashion statement." He banged the side of the wheelchair as he made his point.

Al giggled and I just smiled.

Eventually we were in the car. I had expected Al's parents to be tired on the journey back to Brum. Whilst Mo slept, her dad seemed wide awake and kept up a running commentary about everything on the journey. Some of it was funny, some of it was offensive but I heard it as a humorous requiem recited solo by a dying man. A man who seemed genuinely pleased to be back in the country where he was from.

They were only staying for three weeks, the most the Doctors would allow him to be away from Perth for, but it was a fantastic three weeks. By judicious use of flexi-time and home working we managed to contrive it so that there were only a couple of days when Al's parents were left alone. Even then, her dad's brothers managed to travel down from the north-west and spend time with him. Al loved it and I too was genuinely happy. Me and her dad still got on so well, even when we disagreed. He was incredulous at most things, none more so than the way football had changed. One afternoon he got talking about his other great love, Everton.

"How come," he said one afternoon, sat in the garden drinking chilled water – beer was out of bounds – "that Everton do worse in cup competitions these days than Tran-bloody-mere Rovers?" and his rant, entertaining, at times misty-eyed, lasted a full hour about the failures at Goodison. So I kept quiet, and on the penultimate Friday of his stay asked him if I could do something special with him the following day, just me and him.

"Eh, I'm not going to one of those bloody lapdancing clubs Mark. Too risky in my condition."

But I promised him it wasn't a lapdancing club and that whilst Al and Mo were going shopping he and I were doing something much more entertaining.

So I found myself with a man in a car beside himself with joy at 2.20 that Saturday afternoon. It had taken some doing, not least to arrange the access, but having met with his brother and his nephew in the Baltic an hour before, we then made our way to Goodison to see Everton play. It was like taking a child to a

Christmas grotto. His eyes bright, excited by the sheer pleasure of not just being in a football ground but being at Goodison, being back amongst his own tribe for what we both knew would probably be the last time.

Then at 5.15, after a dull 0-0 bore draw for me, but a festival of athletics for him, we started the journey back. For the first time in ages he was quiet, silent. He had the back of his head to me as he looked out of the window at the other cars taking fans home from the game; at a changed Liverpool city centre, so different to when he was a kid, and at all the things in the world that were now so much more important because they were slipping from his grasp by the second.

He turned to me, and his lip trembling, his face filled with tears.

"You're fucking marvellous, do you know? I had my doubts, I honestly did, but for you to do this"

And then he gazed away again because men of his generation were not meant to show gratitude or emotion like this, they were meant to be tough, hard men who took life and death in their stride.

"The airport," I said and he quickly looked across anxiously.

"No, not yet, I've got a few more days yet haven't I?" I sensed the panic of a man who honestly thought that was his next destination.

"No, no," I said, smiling "Of course we're not going there now."

He looked immediately relieved.

"Well bloody what then?!"

I laughed.

"I wanted to find a way of thanking you for that first Christmas, I wanted to try and make you as happy as you made Al then."

> & me

We both smiled, reflecting the scene ~~in our own minds~~ privately. And then he was back, no time for emotion or sentimentality.

"Tell you something, that referee was bloody awful – that was deffo a penalty when Jeffers was brought down in the box, don't you think so?"

So it continued. Subsequently I may not have lived up to his estimation of me. I mean, if he met me now he would probably kick the shit out of me rather than sing my praises, but despite screwing around, despite being an arse and a half and probably ruining his daughter's life, I hope that in a small way that day in Liverpool repaid a little of the debt I will always owe him.

* * *

The third time. It's just as scary.

This hurts, this really hurts and I am feeling faint.

The worse thing is the stench, the horrible smell of rubber in my nostrils. Add to this the pain that I am feeling and it is less than fun, no matter how you describe it. It's every time now, too and the abuse gets worse and worse. Since London she only calls me 'Fucking Sherlock!' and there is an anger to what happens that never has any tenderness.

Those toys that we bought in London have come in useful too. I have been sat here for about fifteen minutes and now Kalpna is dragging me forward by my hair. My hands are tied behind my back and she pushes me flat onto my stomach. I'm worried I'll choke but just when I think I am going to my air passage opens up.

Now she is probing at me with a very large dildo. She has smeared my arse with some sort of lubricant and I can feel the tip touching against the rim of my anus.

Kalpna pulls me back upright so I am sat squat on my knees. I can't sit fully back because to do so would involve me being penetrated fully, and this is painful enough.

I hear the front door slam downstairs.

"Shut the fuck up and say nothing, OK?" Kalpna hisses at me.

I hear her unlock the bedroom door and can't make out if she's locked it again. I so do not want Alpha to see me like this.

Outside on the landing I can hear Alpha and her Mum talking but can't make out everything that is being said.

"He's..;long...;sleeping....;Yes....shower,....OK."

Then Alpha responds – loudly.

"So we're not going to the Cinema tonight?"

I hear footsteps walking away, the conversation becomes indistinguishable.

Eventually I hear the door unlock and can tell by the perfume that Kalpna is back in the room.

She kneels down beside me. Her voice is aggressive but quiet.

"I'm going to unlock you now Mark. Clean yourself up and in 10 minutes' time come downstairs, do you understand?"

I hum a yes. As I do so she has reached for my penis and begun to rub me hard, to erection.

I hear Alpha call. "We'll be down in a minute, just leave us alone."

She continues to rub me whilst she is talking and despite myself I end up ejaculating onto my naked thigh.

Eventually my hands are untied.

"You've got 10 minutes. Get a fucking move on and make sure you clear up this horrible mess."

As she passes me she kicks me in the stomach, winding me. She shuts the door on the way out.

I am left terrified, huddled on the floor. Eventually I stop crying, pull the mask off and keep gasping as I now breathe easily.

Love? This surely cannot be love? I want to stop but on several occasions she has taken photos of me. She even has an envelope in her bedside cabinet with the council leader's address on. She claims that the envelope contains photos of me. I can not test this, I daren't test this. The thought keeps recurring: 'since Peter died life has not been easy at County Hall.' The memory of Peter's kindness, Peter's gentleness increases my agitation, the clashing of his tender heart against the thuggish behaviour of Kalpna.

Orwell talked about a future where there was a boot continuously stamping into a face. He simply failed to see that it isn't totalitarianism that catches us but lust. It is the same boot, casting us in the same trap and dreaming of any possible escape.

Then I sit bolt upright. I am drenched. I am alone in my own bedroom. There is no dildo, there is no rubber mask and this is the third time this has happened. I am no longer smiling after Kalpna; I am sobbing, crying, and disturbed – hoping that these nightmares stop.

* * *

To begin with, in our first season back, it was just occasional. Three occasions to be accurate. We met in London a couple of times and then in Bristol. Oddly, Patrice seemed not to mind that I had decided to take up where we left off.

Once, in London, we did talk about it.

'I always knew you'd come back you know, I mean the sex was just too good for us both wasn't it?'

And I hated her accuracy, hated her being so bloody spot on. I would leave our liaisons and return to Massie Road, feeling great and terrible. This was like a blood sport where I was dodging Al's ability to catch the scent and, at the same time, having much more fun than the fox ever could. It wasn't serious anyway, just something I did on the occasional Saturday afternoon when time would allow, a bit like trainspotting, a secret hobby. I often imagined including it in conversations when hobbies or past times came up.

'What did you do this weekend, go to the match?' a colleague might ask.

'No, I did a spot of illicit fucking actually'

'Really? What an interesting hobby!'

'Yes, I tried wind surfing but didn't like it. Kept falling off, getting wet, you know?'

'Oh – wind surfing is a drag.'

'Quite. This way I get to keep warm but still get some exercise in. Keeps the abs beautifully flat.'

'Is it expensive?'

'Well, you know. Hire of a room, decent bottle of plonk, petrol getting there and back, programmes.'

'What? They sell programmes for it?'

And then I would have to explain the gory details, the deceit, the lying, being a two-faced bastard.

Sometimes I wonder. When does the human spirit decide to up the ante? When do we reach a point where we are not just content with being a bit deceitful, we have to become really deceitful? It must be like being a magician who can do card tricks. After a while you grow bored with the audience gasping at you always being able to pick their card out from the pile. So you learn something new and before you know it, not only can you produce random bouquets of flowers from up your sleeve but you've also learnt how to cut someone in two. Course, you worry the first time you do it but you get the blade in the right place and you saw away, knowing that after you have done it once there is no gore or blood. Just the satisfaction of knowing, just for a little while, that you're amazing yourself as well as other people.

My trick was to cut me in two using a football fixture list. And low and behold the great Garvey, he returns each time unscathed to the arms of a trusting Australian lover. She kisses and loves him and worships him because he is quirky; she doesn't really understand about this silly football thing. Anyway, whilst he's going to the match, there is no chance, no chance whatsoever, that he will find you learning tricks from another book, is there?

Sometimes we forget that by standing in the spotlight we give people space to hide in the shadows. Sawing yourself in half is nothing in the glare of the houselights; real talent is doing it in the shadows at the edge of the stage.

* * *

I am in Bristol, on a Tuesday morning, the day after the Whit Bank Holiday weekend. I am looking after Matty for a few hours, who is on half-term break from school. At the moment he is just the person I need to be with.

He has been wanting to talk for a few minutes. He makes a sign. It is like he is drawing two big saucers surrounded by straw.

"What?" I ask

And then he finger spells A-L-P-A.

"Alpha?" I ask – and he does the two circles and straw sign and I realise that he has created a handle for Alpha. I check this with him and he nods emphatically. It's quite a good handle.

"What about Alpha?" I ask.

"Married?" he asks.

"No," I say.

"Alpha marry me?"

I smile. The kid's chasing older women now and I wonder whether or not this kid could be mine. He has good taste in woman.

"You too young," I sign.

Matty lets out a deep sigh.

"Love Alpha," he says.

"Look for girl own age," I sign "When you're 16, she'll be old and wrinkled, she'll be at least 38!"

Matty looks horrified at this prospect, but then maybe when I was 6 I too never worked these things through.

"Uncle Mark marry Alpha's mum?" Matty asks.

I shrug.

"Marry Alpha?"

I laugh. "Too young," I sign, "and I'd break your heart."

Matty giggles but we're interrupted by Geo. He enters carrying two big bags of shopping. He is putting a 'brave face' on 'the situation.' He signs to Matty "Don't listen to Uncle Mark, he's bad influence."

Matty is genuinely amused by this and signs back what Geo has said.

"Bollocks!" I sign and Matty laughs hysterically, thrilled that a grown- up has used such a rude sign.

"You alright matey?" he asks as he moves in to the open-plan Kitchen area beyond the table that Matty and I have been sat at.

"So-So," I say. Not exactly sure what it means.

"So what are you going to do? Short term, I mean."

I really don't know the answer to that one. I've never been suspended before and this is the first week when it will click in properly.

"Oh, I'll amuse myself. Hang out here for a couple of more days, lay low for a little while longer if I can."

Geo is more than accommodating. He repeats a mantra that I've heard many times, that I'm welcome to stay as long as I like, and besides it's good for Matty having me around.

"Maybe that's my future career," I jest, "as a childminder?"

I listen as Geo admonishes me for my negative thinking but I have a sense of things slipping away.

The meeting with Henry Peterson and Lance Somerton is still fresh in my mind. Neither had been friendly, both incredibly business-like, and I swear Peterson was taking a perverse pleasure in it all. 'The status quo can not continue,' where the exact words that Lance had used, and yet I was totally uncertain about what the status quo amounted to. Essentially two things seemed to be happening. Firstly, members were panicking at the mess that was unravelling around the 'Drake House Scandal' as it was becoming known, and also some of the old farts that ran County Hall were using this as a way of clipping my wings, reining me in. Now that Peter was gone, I was left as a sole progressive in the management team. The rest were happy to return to the old days of whipping stools and birching if staff failed to record their flexi-time accurately and if Marks & Spencer's blue suits were not seen as the order of the day. So scores were also being settled by people too cowardly to discuss the pace of change.

It felt like Birmingham all over again, only this time I was so new in the place that I didn't have the support or a track record to protect me, or Peter to keep the local narrow – minded and talentless pen – pushers at bay.

Flo and Anna had agreed to keep in regular contact. Both were angry at the way I was being treated, but were powerless to do much about it. Flo in particular shocked me.

"They can't do this to you Mark, they just can't!' She seemed so angered by it all that she could hardly speak. So whilst I expect most of the calls in the interim to be from Anna it was, in fact, Flo who called to keep my spirits up and to keep me informed about the gossip.

In times of crises, I returned to those I trusted most, so once again I gathered my sails in and set a course for the harbour that was always safe, always a place where I could be protected from the ranging torrents even if the addition of a 6-year-old signing kid removed some of the tranquillity. Strangely, Kalpna did not offer the same protection, the same sense of security. In a way, I sensed that she really wasn't that interested, which depressed me and annoyed me in equal amounts.

Now I don't know what to do. I don't want to go back to Hope Cove but nor do I want to hang around in Bristol. I feel like I am in purgatory, waiting for life to happen, unable to control my fate.

* * *

"Like you're the only one allowed to have a career?" Al asked, arching her right eyebrow at me.

"I'm not saying that," I said, "I just don't think it's the right move for you."

"But, like, you didn't even check with me about your career change, yeah? You just assumed I'd be OK about it all because you're a man."

That was unfair because it was far too accurate. I was being made to feel guilty for my success and until now we'd never really argued about career choices. I assumed that being a physiotherapist was all she ever wanted, so her desire to move to a new hospital for promotion came as a surprise more than anything. Al had never struck me as ambitious but then to be honest she'd never really talked about work, well not until recently anyway.

"You know I've exhausted the possibilities in this job," she said, "and there's a limit to how exciting seeing the same people every day can be. I've got to the top of my grade and I want a bit more. Is that a problem?" She stroked my hair the way she did sometimes, a conciliatory gesture she would use as a sub-text. 'Hey,' she was really saying, 'I still love you, you know.'

"I mean, I'll still have your dinner on the table, iron all your shirts and let you join the golf club if you want to. We can even buy a caravan if that would make things better, huh?"

I knew she was taking the pee over her last point. Despite progress, we shared most things equally, or at least from a man's perspective I think we did. Al was probably still the centre forward when it came to hoovering and cleaning the bathroom, but this was a genetic thing. Men just don't know how to cream cleanse sinks; woman seemed to do it better.

"Come on," I said, "there's no need for that. I just didn't realise that you weren't happy with what you're doing."

This irritated Al. "Not happy with what I'm doing? Who said that? I just want to go further, earn a bit more. You know I've seen what's happened to my mum. When dad goes, what will she have?"

She also had a point. Al had been pensive since her Mum and Dad had gone back. I knew she was unsettled like something was eating at her. She was clear she wanted her life to be different to her mum's.

"I've been talking to Martin about it and – "

I sighed. A long deep sigh.

"Why do you always do that?!" Al protested.

"What?!" I asked.

"That sigh, like a dog farting, whenever I mention Martin."

'Do I?' I thought. 'Well, it's because he is an over-fond, over promoted arse and you seem to think he's a god.'

"Haven't really noticed it," I said, lying in a fairly clumsy way.

"Maybe you need new hearing aids." she said.

That hurt because one of the things in the rule book we had established was no nasty comments about my hearing. It's not that I was hypersensitive to it; it just wasn't fair.

Al continued regardless "Because then you'd know how irritating that noise is."

Like a summer shower on a hot day, this comment seemed to signify a change, a time to pack away the comfortable deckchairs of our conversation, gather up the picnic rug of warmth that was spread between us and run for the shelter of the barbed comments, which were so much easier to trade than caring for each other.

So a civilised discussion turned into a less than civilised argument, and then became a full-blown row. Not, it had to be said, the first of our stormy encounters since her parents had left. I found myself downstairs watching old videos of West Brom games whilst Al took a book and a bad mood to bed with her. And that's when, I think, as a form of vengeance I started a new affair. That was certainly the first night of this new affair.

This, compared to fucking Patrice, was much easier to arrange. This could be done from the comfort of my own front room while Al slept. This involved me and my right hand and late night porn channels through our cable subscription. I have no idea if Al ever knew about what was taking place on these occasions, but surely some mornings she must have seen the tell-tale signs. A pair of my boxer shorts left crumpled on the living room floor, a tissue left on the sofa, curtains drawn that would normally be left open and a slight cheesy smell emanating from my penis in the morning.

Looking back though, what was I playing at? What was either of us playing at, really? As time went on, the number of nocturnal sessions spent in front of the TV late night increased, the number of illicit bonks with Patrice also increased and then I decided that if I could get away with all of this then where were the boundaries?

Oh, and she got the job.

* * *

The tape recorder starts again.

I am sat with Colin Knapp and DCI Mellon in an interview room in Exeter police station.

"Is my client actually being charged with anything?" Knapp asks Mellon.

"No Mr Knapp," and then a long silence, "he's helping us with our enquries."

The silence hangs in the air again between us.

"Let's try again Mr Garvey," and Mellon goes back to the same line of questioning he pursued yesterday.

"You rented Drake House for how long?" Off we go.

He simply will not believe my reasons for renting a place so far from Exeter as if choice and nostalgia can never be reason enough.

Then he starts a new line of questioning which is low, disgusting and makes me want to place a house brick through his forehead.

"And your relationship with Alpha?"

"What about it?" I ask, doing nothing to disguise my irritation or disdain.

"She's a little on the young side for you, isn't she?"

"She's my partners daughter!" – This is unbelievable!

"Well, that's not in doubt. Thing is a number of people claim to have seen you in close, intimate situations. Just before Valentine's night in The Ship, for example."

Knapp protests to this line of questioning, arguing that it has nothing to do with the case.

"Other than," Mellon interrupts, "the device we discovered had been taking pictures of her."

"I mean, you have a reputation, Mr Garvey." Mellon sits back waiting for a reaction.

"A reputation?!"

"We know about Birmingham and the allegations made against you when you left."

Knapp protests again. I nod in disbelief and I now wish I was back in the recurring nightmare that is rubber masks and bondage.

* * *

Patrice was an occasional fixture but one that was often difficult to arrange. There were complications with her being in Belfast and me in Birmingham and there was little opportunity to meet outside of the football season.

I'm not sure when I started wondering about something more local but I suspect it was shortly after Al's mum and dad had gone back. To be honest, there was no reason for me to do this. Al was passionate with me, occasionally distant, but the relationship was satisfactory in most respects. OK, we were arguing more, and yes I was spending frequent periods after midnight wanking in front of moderately soft porn, but things between Al and I were OK. I still loved her too, which seemed strange because I knew that doing what I was doing was a pretty poor way to demonstrate that you loved someone.

My eye was roving though. I had become more interested in blondes. I suspect this was because Patrice and Alyson were both dark brunettes and so blonde was like a frothy latte rather than my usual double espresso. Also, late night porn seemed to feature an unbelievable number of blondes, not all of whom were, admittedly, natural blondes, but half the thrill was finding this out as their panties were removed.

In my new role as AD, there were undoubted opportunities but there is a difference between equality of opportunity and doing something about it. I tended to take the view that I really shouldn't get involved directly with people I work with. But then there was a residential away-day for myself and my middle and senior managers. I think it was residential because people wanted an excuse to get to know each other, or maybe they just wanted to get pissed.

The business of the day was conducted without much incident, although I noticed Gemma, she of the party bonking fame who had worked her way up to team leader, was being particularly friendly towards me. Friendlier than anybody else. At all previous away days, there had been very little glamour, so Gemma represented a change – a latte in a sea of espresso. Then at dinner there was the a game we played, at my behest, where I encouraged the 14 of us to talk about what would be in our personal room 101s. Well Most people mentioned the usual stuff, Cheryl Crow, people in 10-items-only check out queues with 12 items, toilets you have to pay for and so on. Gemma's list was saucier and included vibrator batteries, men who were bad at oral sex and then more run-of-the-mill stuff. But she changed the tone and gave me a look at the end of her list which I took to mean 'geddit? Keep up Mark.'

So we all retired to the bar and I ~~really was going to go.~~ I mean, I honestly intended to stay for one drink but as I had just bought the first round, other people insisted on buying drinks for me. Gemma sat across from me but she was keen to keep making eye contact. In the end there was me, her and Simon Pickering, a new day services manager who also seemed to have a keen interest in 'Gems' as she had now insisted on being ~~referred to.~~ called

If I had have been wise, I would have left our Gems to gain a more intimate knowledge of the problems of day centre provision, but wisdom was not an agenda item. So instead, and Gems later confessed to using the same tactic, we just let Simon drink himself to a stupour. In the end the three of us made our way upstairs and Simon, falling and stumbling, was left in a heap face down on his bed. For him, too, the 'wisdom' thing would have to come under AOB in a future meeting.

This left me and Gems.

"Fancy a coffee?" I asked her.

"A fuck would be nicer!" she said.

And that's where it started.

We were discreet and she was careful to make sure she left my room at 6am ~~and deliberately~~ feigned a hangover so that she could keep out of the group's way. 'Very good,' I thought, 'very discreet.'

And at the end of the second day, I asked if anybody needed a lift back in the Edgbaston direction and bang on ~~queue~~ cue Gemma stuck her cute little hand up and said 'if it wasn't too much' trouble, etc, ~~that she would take me up on the offer.~~ Then, instead of going to Birmingham, we drove out towards the Cotswolds, wandered down a footpath and once again had sex, but this time in the open air.

So in the space of 18 hours we had bonked twice. I wish I could tell you I felt terrible about it, but I didn't. Compared to Patrice, Gems was much nicer, a better, smarter all-rounder. A natural blonde as well, which kind of made the whole thing so much more justifiable in my own self-justifying mind.

Unlike Patrice, Gems was a nice kid. Despite her sexually ferocious appetite she was actually decent too, fundamentally decent. Like all decent people, she didn't want to be treated indecently. Yet I knew that even half decent people stood no chance with me. I often wonder now if a conversation about day centre management, getting bored about the detail of incontinence pads and pressure sores, and eyes glazing over with her new colleague, would have been the better option.

* * *

I am shaking as DCI Mellon speaks to me.

I thought I was going to be charged, but this is somehow worse.

I have been called back to the police station and advised that Mr Knapp needn't be present. However I insisted on Colin joining me because I was losing my trust in the entire judicial process.

I still haven't been back at work for about 6 weeks, so the trip to the police station has broken the monotony of endless days filled with walking on the beach or taking endless digital photos of driftwood just to see if I could come up with something creative. I have taken to keeping myself to myself because the line of questioning PC Fruit pursued last time made me realise that far from being a quiet sleepy community, Hope Cove is more like an old iron curtain totalitarian state. You can never be certain who is watching you, who is going to link some perfectly innocent act to something much more sinister.

I can feel my lunch, some hummus and salad, giving serious thought to leaving via the same route it has come in. Eventually I manage to speak.

"Are you sure?" I ask, my hand trembling.

"Pretty much so, yes."

"But who would do a thing like that?"

Mellon nods negatively. "The point is" he says "we think Peter wasn't actually the person who they intended to kill."

"But he was murdered?" In saying the word it changes all of the circumstances of Peter's death.

"Yes. And We just think that they wanted you, not him.".

I think he's joking for a moment, but quickly realise that this is no joking matter.

"Who would want to murder me?" I ask

"Well – we think that's what we have to find out. You got any ideas?"

My mind races. I've made enemies in life, but none that would actually kill me. I don't even think anybody disliked me that much, with the exception of a few of my past lovers.

"Nobody hates West Brom fans that much," I say, knowing the joke is inappropriate but trying to use humour as a way out.

"The good news," Mellon announces, "is that you are not now a suspect in relation to the Hope Cove incident."

"Great!" I say, "not a crime suspect but a potential murder victim! Perhaps we should order champagne?!"

Colin Knapp speaks.

"So in Peter's case, how do you know it's murder?"

Mellon explains at length that there is evidence enough. His car was in A1 condition, the crash scene investigation revealed that there had been no attempt made by the driver of the horsebox to actually prevent the accident, and a large amount of money had been transferred into the horsebox owner's bank account 24 hours earlier.

"Plus," says Mellon, "we later discovered details of your car registration, approximate timings for when you left County Hall each day and other information that shows foul play was involved, all in the glove compartment of the vehicle that collided with Mr Holland. Hardly a professional job, but there you go."

"We'll be making a formal announcement later today. We are also giving you police protection, for the short term at least. I'm sorry, Mr Garvey."

Knapp and I stand. Mellon offers me a hand to shake. He is now not my tormentor but my protector. So I reach across and shake it, although I don't know why. Is it a handshake to give my consent to being a murder victim? Will he give me a form to complete and a bonus subscription to a gardening magazine as part of Devon and Cornwall's special offer on murder victims?

Eventually we get outside to the car park.

"I'll drive," says Knapp.

So once again I am left feeling that my life is incidental and wondering why he won't let me drive. It is only when I get home that I see that my face is smeared with tears, tears of self-pity, and I know; once again, I am not a hero.

* * *

Football teaches us many things, not least of which is the fact that results are not a foregone conclusion. Your team may be a goal up with 90 seconds to go, but a lapse of concentration at the back, a dodgy decision by a referee and you are left defeated, blown away, by life's unfairness. Remember the European Championships in 2004. England a goal up against France. Then in the dying seconds it was 1-1 and before you could blink England were 2-1 down. That feeling, this isn't fair, this can't be happening. It was though and it did. Those people who knock the beautiful game really don't understand that football is life.

In Hollywood movies, happy endings are happy endings,

but not in life. In life, you get the good news that your partner's dad appears to have beaten the cancer. And you celebrate, you dance on the streets of your life at how bloody amazing these results are. For a few days you go around grinning, happy, there is a god, there is a god!

Then it's 3 months later. In the middle of the night a telephone rings. You don't hear it but you feel your partner get out of bed, you see the landing light go on and you wonder what is happening. Then you hear a distant crying that grows into a rising wail, which becomes so loud you worry that the person who you still love most is injured. You move out of bed and down the stairs and you see her in her T-shirt, emblazoned with 'Never give up' and a cartoon of a woman leaping and you know that something is wrong.

She passes you the phone, and sobs *sobbing* and so you, in your bleary-eyed, sleep-disturbed and turgid brain know that something is wrong but you can't sense what it is. The faintness of the telephone line suggest the call isn't local and then you hear Mo crying at the end of the phone and she's saying:

"He's dead, Mark! He's dead, and Patrick too."

So you look across to the linesman, you look across to the referee as events on the pitch unfold but they won't have it. 'I thought we had this one sewn up,' you think, and you're angry because you had already celebrated the victory, but now it's like the world is ending. Because people who survive cancer are not meant to die on a rugby sevens holiday, they're not meant to be splattered across the pavement with their son in the heat of a Balinese night, they're not supposed to be victims in some mad war conducted by people who meant nothing to them. They were just enjoying the fact that one of them wasn't dying and the other enjoyed his rugby. The grief and the anger hit you at the same time, and there's too much detail to take it in straight away.

Eventually you put the phone down, you hold the sobbing life that you love so much next to your chest, and you try to comfort her even though she keeps repeating;

"He'd survived it! He'd survived it!" and she continues to cry in her anguish.

There's nothing you can do. It's a truth, and you're crying too because there was love and you cared and you were happy that such a great person had been given a new lease.

So it's worse than the worst possible defeat and it's the same. There is no God, there is no justice, just you and the person you love mourning another one of life's horrible defeats. And for one moment you wish, a tiny part of you demands, that life should be more like it is in the movies and less like that you have seen when high tackles fly in, when the referee misses the obvious penalty, when offside is onside and when defeat is snatched from the jaws of victory in the mud and the rain on a football pitch.

* * *

This is exhausting.

I am awake. Kalpna is lying next to me, we are at Hampton View. For the past few days I have been too worried to stay at my own place. If they knew about my car, they must know about where I live. At Kalpna's, I have agreed to no police protection. I think I am safe whilst I am here.

I have woken every night for the past week at exactly 3.33 am. Like clockwork I am awake, almost wide awake, each morning at this time. My mind immediately goes to the list of people who may or may not want me dead. I have been racking my brains every night for two weeks and it gets no easier; it gets harder.

It is amazing what I can remember. I can remember kids as a

teenager who may hold a grudge against me, people like Steve Niblock, a guy whose girlfriend I nicked for one summer in 1978. Surely nobody would want to kill me over that? Then there are professional rivals, people who I have disciplined, people who I have failed to appoint to jobs. Again there is no one who I can imagine to be so aggrieved that they would remove my right to exist.

The endless churning over about who may want me dead is exhausting and is a constant. So far the only people not on the list are members of my family and West Brom's current first team. Even then I am worried that some of the posts I have left in internet chatrooms about certain player's performances are coming back to haunt me. Surely Jason Koumas wouldn't take a contract out on me? I mean in some games he just wasn't there, but that's no reason to shoot the messenger is it?

The more obvious suspects just don't bear thinking about. I haven't seen Patrice in over two years, I've had no romantic links with Gems either and none of the short flings I had just before moving here ended on anything other than amicable terms.

Kalpna rolls against me. She senses I am awake.

"Go to sleep Mark," she mumbles. That's all she does; she doesn't touch me, or comfort me physically, just tells me to go to sleep. I just can't turn my head off from these churning thoughts.

I glance at the clock; I've been lying awake for about 40 minutes now. I slip out of bed and go downstairs, I wonder if I'm hungry and go in to the kitchen. Before I turn on the light I notice something moving in the garden. Is it a person? Do they know I'm here? I drop to the floor and crawl along on my belly towards the kitchen sink. From this angle I can see nothing and without my hearing aids I will hear nothing too. I slowly ease my way up against the edge of the sink that looks out into the garden. Outside the moonlight illuminates the long lawn but there is nothing where I thought I saw the movement.

I am crouched down with my eyes peering across the top of the sink. Suddenly the kitchen light switches on. 'They're in here!' I think. 'This is it!' I pick up the first thing that comes to hand (on the draining board) – an egg whisk – I wonder exactly how I am going to defend myself with it. Then quickly I turn around.

Alpha is wetting herself with laughter.

"Mark?! What on earth are you doing?!" She can hardly breathe.

"Turn the light out!" I yell. "They're in the garden!"

She is still giggling but does as she is told.

She comes and squats beside me and looks over the sink top. She is trying hard not to laugh.

"Are you qualified to use an egg whisk in self defence? I thought you had to have years of training to use one of those properly?"

"Shsss!" I hiss. "Look, there they are!"

Alpha takes it more seriously for a moment.

She looks to where I am thinking and sure enough there is movement, just near to the bin store.

"Cunning," says Alpha.

"Shsss," I demand.

"I mean, that disguise is so like a real fox you could be forgiven for thinking it is actually one, don't you think?"

I squint my eyes. I look carefully, then breathe a sigh of relief. It is indeed a fox.

Alpha is laughing uncontrollably now but then she sees the real fear in my eyes, the real worry.

She strokes the side of my face.

"Come on," she says. "I'll make you some hot milk and you

can go back to bed. But watch what you're doing with that egg whisk, you could lose a bollock to that thing."

It's only then that I realise that I am, indeed, naked from the waist downward. I cup my hand around my groin and just manage to conceal my penis.

"Bit late for that!" says Alpha, "just go and get a dressing gown or something."

I go back upstairs,walking like a man who has decided to let his pet hamster sleep in his crotch. In the bathroom, I take my dressing gown off the back door and slip it on. Kalpna has not stirred. I poke my head around the bedroom door and she is sleeping, unperturbed by my absence, unaware of the way we have repelled an attack by a bloodthirsty fox in the middle of a summer's night.

This really is exhausting.

* * *

It was a shock, but I guess I had to deal with it.

"But I want to pay my respects" I said.

"Yeah, but it's just a family thing. That's what Dad wanted."

She looked at me and she seemed to have her mind made up.

"So I wait here and you tell me all about it in what – three week's time?"

"Er, no, it'll be longer – probably six weeks."

"You're going for six weeks?!"

"Do I need your permission?"

"And you don't want me there with you? Not even at the end?"

"Look, Mark." She was becoming irritated, "I've got things to sort out with my mum, there's paperwork around dad's business and there's only really me to do it."

This felt all wrong.

"Couldn't I help? I mean, I'm sure I could deal with some of the administrative stuff for you."

"It's a kind offer, but no, no thanks."

'No, no thanks.' Are we lovers or in a professional meeting here? I wondered.

Then the bombshell.

"Er and," she paused, "well, you and Joy wouldn't get on that well together in Perth."

"What?!" I thought I had heard what she said but I needed her to say it again because I was hoping I had misheard it.

"You're taking Joy?!"

"No, Joy's coming with me. There's a difference."

"The difference being?" She could see my anger and see my frustration mounting.

"Well Mark, the difference is that she won't complain about the number of home games she'll miss and maybe she'll listen to people rather than telling them what to do."

This was big and getting bigger by the second.

"So you'd rather have Joy with you than me? Is that what it boils down to?"

Al sighed. It was followed by a long silence.

The she spoke gently. "Come on, I need you to support me on this."

But I was in no mood for supporting, I really wasn't.

"And this," I said hooking my fingers around the word 'this', "is exactly what? You know I think I have a right to know."

"You know what it's about, so let's just not go too far into it shall we?"

I wanted clarity though I wanted to know exactly what was going on.

"Look," she said, "Joy has been a real help recently, whereas I don't think you've been there for me."

This was un-fucking-believable.

"So the period we've been together doesn't count? The period we've known each other for is less important than Joy's recent support."

"Mark don't be a fucking arse! OK? Just don't!"

I felt stupid. I felt really, really, stupid and I wanted to hit Al but knew I couldn't do that. In the end I just turned. I picked up my jacket, picked up my car keys, slammed the front door harder than I have ever slammed a door in my life and got in the car and drove.

I drove like a madman, through red on amber lights, overtook on the inside lane of the M5, carved caravans up, flashed cars out of the way in the fast lane and never once seemed to drive at much below 95. Eventually I turned off the motorway and drove in to mid-Wales.

I made one call on my mobile. Gems answered on the first ring.

"Hello Mark, this is a surprise." Her tone was friendly.

"Look, I, erm need to see you. Can you come and meet me?"

"Sure, where are you?"

"Erm, Abergavenny."

"What? In Wales?"

"Yes."

"I'm in the centre of the Bullring at the moment. It will take me a while to get there."

She was unfazed, calm. To her credit she arrived by about 9pm – just in time for dinner.

Later we were in bed. I was filling her in on what had happened with Al. Gemma had a way of talking that made you feel like she was really thinking about what she was saying. Not that she was intense; just engaged. Brushing her blonde bobbed hair back off her neck, she turned to me.

"I'd leave her if I were you," Gem advised. "It's clear things aren't going to get any better, so why prolong the agony."

This was new territory for me. Leave Al? Like, end the relationship?

Surely not? Al had been a fixture in my life for so long that she was part of living. It was as if Gems was suggesting I should consider having my legs amputated because I had, once or twice, tripped over. I remembered too that everyone carries an agenda, no matter how virtuous they seem. So Gems' observations came from a person who seemed to be quite enjoying having a sort of relationship with me and maybe who hoped, one way or another, to develop things between us. She wasn't neutral, she was a player in this piece and her perspective possibly reflected this.

Yet the doubts remained and a fitful night's sleep, interrupted by moments of passion, left me thinking this one through more and more so that by morning I had, for the first time, begun to contemplate life after Alyson.

* * *

This is a new game.

I am sat on the bed and I am blindfolded. Kalpna is being very gentle to me, there is only occasional pain, which she sometimes apologises for. She moves my feet, spreads my legs out wide and then masturbates me so that I am hard. Then she moves from the bed and I hear a clicking, the clicking of a camera.

She comes back to the bed again, kisses me on my mouth, places my hands on her buttocks and again I hear the whirring of a motor on a camera's shutter drive.

Eventually she straddles me, I feel her thighs either side of my legs and as she places the tip of my penis against the lips of her vagina the camera starts clicking again, it must be on some electronic timing device because the shutter seems to be taking a photo every 10 or 15 seconds.

Each time I try to touch her, or try to remove my blindfold, she stops me. She places my palms flat on the mattress and continues to make love to me. Occasionally her nipple is placed in my mouth for a few moments and I kiss or nibble it gently.

Her breathing eventually quickens. She eventually comes, pushing my head back away from her. More clicks, more photographs being taken. Then she stops.

I feel her move off me. There are sounds in the room. I go to speak.

"Can I – "

But I am interrupted by Kalpna.

"Quiet Mark, I'll sort you out in a moment."

A few minutes pass. I sense my erection subsiding. There are no more photographs being taken. The bedroom door opens, the bedroom door closes. I sense I am alone but know better than to move from the position I have been left in. After a few moments I am aware that she is back in the room, perhaps she went to pee or check that the house was still empty.

Eventually the blindfold is removed. It takes me a moment and I don't have my glasses on, but eventually I can focus on Kalpna. She is wearing a grey, pleated skirt, her hair is up in two bunches and she has a white blouse on. She also has knee-length socks on. She looks like an adolescent schoolgirl.

"Was that good for you?" I ask, amused at the fantasy that she is indulging in.

She just places a finger to her lips.

Slowly she takes off the blouse, under which she is naked,

removes the skirt, under which there is no underwear, removes her socks and is naked beside me on the bed.

We start to make love again. This is nearer to her usual, harsher style.

"Come on Sherlock," she says, "get yourself to work."

Then she is biting me and pinching my buttocks, scratching at my chest – anything that might cause me a little discomfort. I look over her shoulder and notice that there is nothing where I thought the camera should be. I don't have time to weigh this one up much because soon she is coming and I too have reached orgasm.

We both flop onto the bed. Her breathing and my breathing are all that fills the room. I listen, I can feel my heart beating and I wonder if perhaps I am getting a little too old for these games. Kalpna drifts off to a post-orgasmic sleep.

I look at the ceiling. Physically that was fun but I find it all deeply unsettling and decide that we may have reached a point where these games either have to stop or have to be explained. I know I am between a rock and a hard place. To question them could mean that there is nothing, but to continue with them seems like I am indulging in something if not sordid then certainly bizarre.

I reach across and stroke the small of Kalpna's naked back. We need to talk. But these discussions can wait, for now, for a little while longer because I can sense a new erection forming.

* * *

People who know me will tell you the time to worry is not when I am ranting or raving, something I do a fair bit, or even in what would pass for a foul mood. The time to worry is when I am quiet and uncommunicative, because then I have withdrawn my willingness to give another person time. There can be lots of reasons for this. Sometimes, at work, it's because I know that I am dealing with idiots and the kindest words I can use are silence. At other times it's because I know that I really am angry. So silence becomes a defence mechanism to stop the axe that is my tongue from striking out and harming people when harm is the last thing I intend to give. Then there is the silence that is necessary because words fail to explain the loss or pain that I am feeling.

I stayed away for several days. Three nights in Abergavenny. It felt like 30 nights, because even when you have spent 24 hours in the place you realise that each day simply repeats itself. You name it, it doesn't happen there. Gem left me on Sunday and I phoned in sick to work. I also sent a text message to Al.

'Away. Pls don't call.'

That was it. Normally I would put a kiss on a text message. Normally I would say I was missing her. On this one I kept it to the shortest and briefest. I could have called her but silence seemed, for whatever reason, the best response.

After I checked out of the hotel in mid-Wales I wondered what to do. I had no desire to see Al, or even to be in the same house as her. I thought about fleeing across the Irish Sea to Belfast. Then again I also knew I really couldn't face Patrice.

Eventually I moved back to my default position and phoned Geo. There was no reply at home so I tried his mobile.

"Matey! Where are you?!!" he responded as soon as he picked up the phone. 'So Al has sent a telecommunications search party out,' I thought.

"Erm, at the moment I'm in a layby somewhere south of Ross-on-Wye."

"Al's called. She's really worried about you. Is everything OK?"

I nearly made a sarcastic response to his last comment. 'Think it through Italian man,' I thought, 'my partner doesn't know where I am, I am calling you at mid-morning on a work day, does this sound like the behaviour of a man who is *not* in crisis?'

Instead I resorted to the use of 'fine' as a code.

"Look, I'm fine honestly, it would just be good to meet up.'

"Do you want to come to Manchester?" he asked.

Then I remembered, he had got a role in 'Uncle Vanya' that was at the Exchange, he was starting rehearsals this week. 'Oh, bloody Manchester!' I thought.

So I pointed the car north, deciding to use A roads rather than motorways. I really didn't want to use the M5 and M6 route because I knew I would be tempted to take the easy option and drive home. If I went home, I reckoned I would not have got to the bottom of what was going on for me.

Later than evening, after a tedious journey stuck behind slow lorries and caravans, I sat with Geo in a pub in central Manchester. Manchester itself seemed to be a city that was winning the peace, with post-war construction creating a sense of a city rising from the ashes. Just a pity nobody had told the locals that the war had ended more than 50 years ago.

Outside the rain was lashing down, creating small rivers and mini seas all around.

"It's the start of the monsoon season," the barman said to me as I got our drinks in.

"Really?" I said as he handed me my change.

"Oh aye," he said, smiling. "Last years ended yesterday." He chuckled at his own joke.

Finally Geo and I were sat in the relative quiet of a corner of the pub that overlooked the canal. It was a long conversation, one that really didn't get into our stride until the second or third pint. Until then Geo enthused about what a friendly and fun city

Manchester was and spent a bit of time bitching about the people he was working with – former soap opera stars and b-list celebrities who had found themselves cast in roles that were just beyond their acting abilities. He was convinced the run would be performed in front of half empty houses and get appalling reviews.

Eventually we got to Al and me. I explained about not going to her dad's funeral and the fact that she was taking Joy with her.

"I think it's over," I said, and I could sense the tears welling up inside of me as I said those words to someone other than myself for the first time.

"Don't be daft," he said, "You're just pissed off with her."

It seemed a fair point but there was something deeper.

"If I love her, why do I keep shagging around?"

"That's only Patrice," he said gently, "old times, that sort of thing."

Then I explained about Gemma. That now, it wasn't just Patrice, it was also Gemma, and that I felt like a cunt.

"Well you are being an arse, I mean it's bloody risky seeing one other woman, but seeing two? Don't you get them confused, mate?"

Yet Geo's tone still wasn't serious and even though we talked things through, I think his take on things was that I was just confused, angry and that as soon as I saw Al again, in fact the sooner I saw Al again, the sooner it would be that I could start to set things right.

"But drop Gemma and Patrice," he added at the end. "Concentrate on the woman you love."

I left Manchester the following morning, having slept on the floor at Geo's digs in Chorlton. Just before I left, my mobile rang. It was a withheld number, so it could have been work. I answered.

"Hi, it's me," said Al.

There was silence.

"You there?" she asked.

"I'm here, yes."

"Look," she said "I'm going tomorrow, will you be back before I go? I mean, we have to talk Mark."

"I'm heading back now," I said.

"So can we talk? I mean when you get back."

"OK," I said. "OK, we'll talk."

So as I approached Birmingham I had run through what we needed to talk through and what needed to be said. There was still the possibility that we could salvage stuff and I was feeling optimistic.

I got home maybe about lunchtime. I was struck by how tidy the house was. Then again, whereas I did silence when I was upset, Al did cleaning. I'd seen her go through the house like a crack cleaning force in the past when I had done things to upset her – if only she could hire herself out in Kabul or Baghdad when she was like this. Yet the signs were that she'd been upset too.

In the spare room, Al's bags were packed, ready for the trip. I thought to myself that if things were really serious maybe she wouldn't have gone.

Mid-afternoon, my phone rang again.

"Er, it's me again," said Al.

"Yep," I responded, determined not to get drawn into a long conversation.

"I'm going to meet Joy for an early evening drink but I won't be back late. OK?"

This just wasn't true to form. An early evening drink with Joy was never just an early evening drink. Usually early evening for Joy was 2 am and a late night was some time at around about 6 in the morning.

"Aren't we meant to be talking?" I said, "and you are going to have a fair bit of time to *chat* with Joy."

"Look, don't Mark, OK – and I promise I'll be back later."

The conversation ended. I busied myself with paying bills and catching up on Baggies e-mails. Then 8 became 9 and 9 soon became 11. I tried ringing her mobile a couple of times but just got her voicemail.

Eventually, at about midnight, the harshness of a hard floor in Chorlton caught up with me. I decided that bed was the best place for me. I opened our bedroom door and looked at the bed. Al's books were on one side, my collection of football programmes and holiday brochures on the floor next to my side of the bed. Sleeping here felt inappropriate. Al would, no matter what state she was in, eventually sleep in here.

I went up to the attic, set up the futon and went downstairs.

I scrawled a note for her that I left on the dining room table.

'Al, you're obviously busy. I've gone to bed (in attic). Please do not disturb me (I underlined 'please' three or four times). Give my love to your mum, hope the trip goes well. Mark."

No kisses, no emotions, nothing.

I climbed the stairs, closed the attic door behind me and pulled the quilt high around my neck. For a while I lay there, wondering if I could hear sounds coming from downstairs. Maybe she would come back, maybe she would apologise. Instead nothing. Just me in a house, alone, without Alyson.

* * *

CHAPTER 5

She looks tired and a bit drawn as she stands in the dock. I have avoided making eye contact with her, instead listened carefully to everything that has gone on. The courtroom is not how you imagine it, certainly not like in the movies. It is not packed to the rafters with members of the third estate, nor is it as adversarial as I thought it would be. A barrister for CPS, her defence counsel. It's a preliminary hearing. She is being charged under the Sex Offences Act. The clerk of the court reads out the charges and to each one she responds.

"Not guilty." It is the same steady tone.

Geo decided he wanted to attend court and I came along to support him. It was a convoluted affair, getting the courts agreement to allow us to attend. We are both witnesses in the case. Eventually, however, under strict conditions, they said we could come.

This hearing lasts all of 20 minutes. I gain no satisfaction from seeing her there in the court. I am sad. Sad that all these potential lives – the police found images of over 200 children in her possession – have been somehow harmed by a woman of her kind.

Eventually a full committal date is established, bail is refused and Wilma Mapp is lead down to spend the next few months on remand until a full trial hearing can be established, probably not until the new year.

It has been hard getting to this point, particularly for Jane and Geo. The police, as of yet, have not been able to establish if the images of Matty have been sold on to the internet or simply didn't go beyond the initial image-capturing stage. Jane's not been too bad, considering, but Geo has fluctuated between rage and depression. I just think the sooner the whole business is over the better.

On our way out, PC Fruit nods to us. Geo returns the nod. The exchanges of men conducting grim business in grim circumstances.

Then we're out into the bright sunshine of an October day, the sun at it's highest point in the sky, the air still warm.

"OK Matey?" Geo asks brightly, but the brightness disguises what I know to be a sense of hurt. He is upset by the whole process and when my mate is upset I'm upset too.

"Yeah, come on, let's go and meet Alpha."

We wander through the city centre and eventually push our way into an Italian eatery-cum-bar next to the Old Vic, Renato's. It is an old haunt where I used to hang out with Geo and Jane in when he first came down to Bristol to train as an actor. The walls are festooned with the pictures of cast, past and present, who have appeared at the theatre next door. By day it loses some of its bohemian air, whereas my memory of it by night is something akin to a modern 'Moulin Rouge', but maybe time has deceived us all; maybe it was just an eatery popular with thespians. Surprisingly Alpha has never been here before. I thought about this and realised that compared to my alcohol-driven days as a student, now they really do read for a degree, think about their career and ambitions and generally start the rat race very young. What sort of rat race are we creating here where, by the time kids are 21, they have already worked out their pension plans? But showing Alpha this place may help to distract detract her from her ambition for a few hours, so lunch with her is a treat, in every sense of the word.

She waves to us as we approach the table and smiles brightly, a smile that puts the ugliness of the past few hours long behind us.

I lean across and kiss her as I reach the table and then she stands and gives Geo a kiss too.

"Hello," she says, "how was it?" The bright smile is being replaced by an immediate look of concern.

"A few more kisses from you will help," says Geo. Alpha smiles.

"You keep the worst company Mark!" but she is teasing Geo. Over the past few months, Jane and he have got to know her much better. Perhaps it's wise if she is, after all, going to be their future daughter- in-law, if Matty has his way. Her regular babysitting has done little to repel Matty's romantic ambitions, but I seriously think the pair of them are smitten with each other for very different reasons.

"I've got your post," says Alpha, and hands me a range of envelopes, including one from Pat Quinn's office. I've been in Bristol all weekend, having dragged Geo along to see Bristol City snatch a stuffy 3-0 victory over West Brom. I drop the envelopes into the inside of my jacket pocket but the envelope from Quinn seems to be calling me.

Our pizzas arrive and during the meal one of the waiters wanders across. Geo stands and shakes his hand, making an occasion of the simplest encounter in the way he always does so well. He chats in fluent Italian to the older waiter who is serving us. He gestures to me and then to Alpha. The waiter, who looks on the old side of 150, takes Alpha's hand and kisses the back of it.

"*Enchate*," he says and Alpha giggles.

"Do you remember Marco," he says to our waiter. He clearly doesn't but nods anyway, smiles and shakes my hand too.

"*Lo studente?*" he asks Alpha.

"Si!" says Alpha and I am impressed by even this short exchange. The waiter smiles "And you're friend of Giovanni?"

Alpha nods.

"OK, you come with your friends, get a bit drunk, and next time you get free pizza. OK?"

Alpha smiles; she has been brought into the broader Italian family that is part of Geo's community in Bristol.

We chat over our lunch. Geo is full of gossip about various thespians on the wall and a few wild evenings we have spent in here. He deliberately tries to embarrass me by telling Alpha about all my failed attempts to chat women up here, about drunken arguments with their boyfriends who more often than not seemed to be only a few feet away and evenings when, due to squandering our money early on, we would literally sing and play for our supper.

Finally, coffee arrives. I have to move my chair to let the waitress pass. She manages to push my jacket off the back of my chair and in so doing causes the envelopes to spill out onto the floor. The letter from Pat Quinn is looking up at me again.

"I think that post wants to be opened," says Alpha.

So I turn my attention to the mail while she and Geo chat and flirt over coffee. I deal with credit card bills first, no shocks, just a bit of ouch when I realise how much debt I am running up. Then I slide my finger under the flap of the letter from Pat Quinn.

I pull the contents out. A letter and a cheque. I skim read the letter and look slowly at the cheque.

I read the letter again, making sure I have taken everything in and then again look at the cheque, making sure I didn't misread the amount.

"You OK?" says Alpha.

"Sorry?" I say, lost in the moment. [*handwritten: repeats*]

[*handwritten: Alpha*] Apla says it slowly. [*handwritten: Alpha says, slowly*] "Are you alright," she says, emphasising each word.

I don't reply. Instead I turn to Geo.

"Geo what's the waiter's name?"

"Oh, it's er." He ponders for a moment and then clicks his fingers as he remembers, "Giuseppe."

I call the waiter over, whisper into his ear. He smiles benevolently and nods.

It is my favourite drink, at once decadent and refreshing and I smile as Giuseppe removes the gold foil from around the neck of the bottle and eases the cork from the bottle.

"Champagne?!" Alpha comments, "Free pizza, champagne, a girl could get used to this." There is just the tiniest hint of sarcasm behind this comment which I ignore.

So I simply place the cheque – for £50K – onto the table.

"Fuck!" says Geo.

We raise our glasses to Pat Quinn. The bollocks is settled.

* * *

When I was a kid, not that I'm not now, the summer holidays were a magical period. A whole 6 weeks of nothing to do, maybe a family holiday in the middle to Hope Cove, but nothing else. No school, no having to be at places at a given time, just time to be away, to be me. The excitement and anticipation at the start was unbelievable. I would have time for me, no teachers nagging, no parents complaining about homework that had to be done, nothing. As time went on, summer holidays became more complicated, so that they meant girlfriends, teenage hangovers or camping holidays to Cornwall with 'the lads'. Then as a student there was the time in the band with Geo, but by then summer holidays had become longer, more complicated, fraught with rows about musical styles and whether or not my lyrics were too deep and meaningful (as if the line 'Jean Paul and Simone were right, there's no point in this pointless life' was anything other than shallow and meaningless). Yet the figure of '6 weeks' still had a charm. Like Christmas Eve or the first Saturday of the football season, it conjured up romantic notions, hope, and dreams that could be, adventures to come and unfulfilled, glorious promise.

6 weeks as an adult was a different matter. Particularly 6 weeks when you were confused, uncertain and still more than angry about things. Those 6 weeks when Al went home for her dad's funeral were the opposite of the carefree joy experienced as a child, even if they ran from the start of the football season to mid-September. They were a crap 6 weeks, a detestable 6 weeks; 6 weeks spent in an emotional wilderness where the future was just a question mark.

Then other things changed too. All through the closed season I hadn't heard from Patrice and in the end I actually called her.

"Oh, hi stranger," she said.

"I thought it was the other way around," I responded. So we chatted about nothing much – the summer, work, nothing of consequence for the first few minutes.

"So when are you coming over?" I asked, growing bored with Patrice's description of her new 4X4 that seemed to be her pride and joy.

"I'm over for a conference in York in September," she said. I was struck that York was one of the few English place names that she couldn't make more exotic, and sort of disappointed by that.

"What about coming over to meet up?" I said. Then, in what I think is commonly known as 'a turn up for the books,' she went quiet.

"You still there?" I eventually asked.

225

"Look, erm, Mark," she said, "I don't think it's a good idea that we meet up. You know, not in the way that we were."

I thought about this and, almost childlike, decided to probe her a bit more.

"Why's that then?"

"Well, I suppose you were going to find out anyway," then another long pause.

"Yes?" I said, a long yes.

"You see, I've started seeing somebody properly and I really don't think it's a good idea that we -"

This was annoying.

"Hang on," I said, "I've been seeing somebody *properly* in all the time we've known each other!"

"Och," she said, "just because it was OK by you doesn't mean it's OK by me now, does it?"

I was stunned. Patrice Hardy taking the moral high ground, having made all the running down to the depths of the moral valleys?

Patrice continued. "You know Mark, it was lots of fun – I'm not saying it wasn't – I just think we should move on. Don't you think so?"

I thought 'a casual throwaway sentence said by a ~~causal~~ casual throwaway lover' and ~~I think~~ the conversation petered out.

"We could always meet for a coffee sometime," she suggested. 'Coffee' I thought 'was never high on the list of things I enjoyed doing with you.' Yet rather than have a row I decided that there was no point.

"Hey, whatever," I responded, the 'whatever' said in the American way that had become so trendy and so loaded with meaning.

So the conversation ended and with it the strange, sordid, state of affairs that had sustained Patrice and me.

Al and I had also had a few phone calls, fractious conversations on crackling lines. The first one was made from Singapore Airport. She started telling me how much she missed me and how sorry she was about having 'goofed' the night before and stayed out so late. I reflected the word back to her.

"Goofed?" I said.

"Yeah," she responded. "I feel such an idiot."

"Al, I think 'Goofed' is an understatement. How about 'fucked up?' Even that doesn't really hit the mark, but it will do for starters."

"Well, you know, I just was out late and like I've been out late before, I mean what's like the big deal?"

The conversation deteriorated from that high point. I tried to explain to her that 'goofing' and not coming home but staying out with your female lover, friend or whatever were somewhat different and then she started to get cross with me, suggested I was being too possessive and at the point just before her language was about to offend the customs of locals in Singapore, her money fortunately ran out.

We spoke again but our opening movement set the tone for most of the conversations across the next 6 weeks.

In the middle of Al's absence, I decided that I really did need some company. Gemma and I hadn't seen each other since Abergavenny – well, accept in meetings at work. So when I called I wasn't expecting the sort of response I got from her, which was very, very cool.

"What's the matter?" I asked after we had agreed to meet up and to have dinner the following night.

"I'll tell you tomorrow," she said.

I tried to probe her a bit more but, no, she wouldn't budge on it.

"Mark," she said firmly, "tomorrow. OK?"

When the tomorrow eventually arrived, she was a changed woman. She refused to touch my hand, wouldn't let me kiss her on the lips and just seemed to be behaving like the ice maiden.

Towards the end of the meal, in a nice Indian restaurant near to the Mailbox, she eventually told me the problem.

"I was at a conference last week," she said.

"Really? Any good?" I responded.

"Well, I met somebody you know."

"Oh, who?" I felt reasonably relaxed. I had a profile, so by this point in my career, lots of people knew me or knew of me.

"Guy called Dermott," she said "Mike Dermott."

"Oh he's a wanker!" I said, a bit too loudly, because a couple at the neighbouring table pulled a face.

"Yes," she said, "he talked highly of you too." She continued, "and, is it, Patrice?"

She let the name hang in the air for a while.

'You bastard, Dermott' I thought, and I knew that I was blushing at the very mention of Patrice's name.

I looked down at the table, studying the intricate patterns my meal had made on the starch white linen tablecloth.

"Sounds very sordid." Gems eventually said.

"It was," I said, deciding to tell the truth-'was' being the operative word.

"Really?" said Gems. She looked at me and held me with a fixed, impressionless,gaze. "Dermott said you were encouraging her to meet up with you quite recently."

I shrugged my shoulders. It was a fair cop.

"Look, Mark," she started, "you know I knew about Al and I thought 'well things come to an end and maybe I'm just lucky' but to be honest I now just think you're -" then she stopped. "Oh I don't know."

A waiter was passing the table. Gems reached for him.

"Excuse me," she said, "we're in a hurry, could we just have the bill?"

He looked to me, because only a few moments earlier we just seemed like a couple having dinner, not saying much to each other, but then we were like millions of other couples who passed through the place. I offered no resistance, just nodded in a resigned way and smiled at him when he brought the bill a few moments later.

Gemma looked at it, reached into her purse and fished a £10 note out.

"You can see to the rest. As far as I'm concerned, we're only ever work colleagues now, got it?"

With that, she got up and left. I swear that the couple at the neighbouring table, who I now realised had purchased tickets for our conversation, applauded her parting lines. Doubtless they were pleased that the loud, uncouth guy was being written out of the pretty blonde girl's lovelife.

I thought about being cool, about ordering another Kingfisher beer and sitting amongst the ruins of a perfectly good meal, but to be honest I knew that the simplest thing to do was to get up and go. A decent woman had been struck by my indecency and I now wanted to leave the scene of my humiliation.

The second three weeks dragged. I saw Gems in meetings and she was perfectly decent in the way that perfectly decent people are. We just didn't speak about anything personal after that, well not for a while anyway. As for Al, we had a few more fractious phone calls, the odd emails, but nothing to suggest that her return to Birmingham would result in our lives being perfect again.

I realised how empty my life was becoming when on a Tuesday night, with nothing to do after work, and the rain falling hard enough for Noah to consider building a second ark, *were?*

I went to watch a reserve game. West Brom was playing Walsall. The fixture was attended by a few hundred people, all watching like perverts at some sort of warped fetish party. Looking around the crowd, I was struck by the fact that you didn't see people like this during daylight hours. They were like rusted clones of the rest of society; amazingly well informed about who was who on both teams, abusive to the referee but, oddly, occupying a world where they were king. Not one of them seemed to have any ambition or hope left in them, not one pair of clean shoes, none NHS glasses, jeans bought anywhere other than Primark. They looked like they had been placed into a virtual reality of what life could be like and seemed, more worryingly, to know this.

When I was a kid, the world seemed to open up for 6 weeks of glorious summer. How strange it is that the adult world so twists the potential we all once possessed.

* * *

I am crossing the car park. It has been a late social services committee and it is getting dark. I think I must be getting older because I am convinced that my twilight vision isn't what it used to be. I must at some point get myself to an optician.

I climb into the car and as I turn the ignition in the switch the radio turns on. Radio 5 and a preview of a game between Arsenal and Everton is being mentioned. I think how much Al's dad would've enjoyed hearing the commentary on that one but decide I would like silence. I punch the front of the radio and the green electronic display fades. Just me, the car and silence.

It's been good being back at work. I've gradually managed to claw back a tiny amount of the ground lost to Henry Peterson. Even the leader has changed his tone a little now that the bollocks has been cleared up. Anna and I, with Flo's help, are slowly allowing Henry and Lance to make their mistakes, and then seizing on every opportunity that we can to make capital out of it. It's not aggressive, but it is effective and slowly Peterson is being undermined by his own conservatism, much to our satisfaction.

I am looking forward to dinner. Kalpna has promised to cook me an Indian meal. She rarely does this, but when she does I am always overwhelmed by the quality of what she produces and wish that she would do it more often. Her daal is to die for, her bombay aloo a feast in itself and she makes better stuffed kulcha than I have ever tasted anywhere else.

Soon I am driving down country lanes, heading back towards Hope. It's a warm evening; the evenings always appear warmer here. Even though we are in the last week of October, it feels balmy; summer is not a distant memory yet, it's still gently present.

I hit a straight bit of road about 10 minutes from home and put my foot down. I'm enjoying the sense of speed, the sense of power as I drive. Then from nowhere a car appears behind me. It's flashing its lights at me, and I wonder for a moment if it's the police. I slow to pull over but he just slows too. So I think 'bollocks – some farming fuckwit – let him wait.' I indicate again, accelerate off and think I have lost him.

Then, a few moments later, it's behind me, very close – too close – on my bumper. Again, I slow to let it pass. It slows and stays behind me. What is it? A Range Rover? The lights are high enough for it to be a Range Rover, it could even be a small van. I am just trying to work this out when bang! It knocks against my bumper, there is a sound of metal twisting -a horrible noise. I am struggling to control the car as it slips and slides across the narrow lane. I can taste the fear on my tongue now as I just manage to keep control. Then, crash! I scrape a drystone wall and lose a wing mirror.

'What the fuck is this?' I think. I can feel the panic rising in me. I have to do something. What? What?! I throw my headlamps and fog lamps on at the same time. This causes my tormentor to slow. Seizing the moment, I accelerate away. I'm twisting and skidding along the lanes, but so is the vehicle behind me.

I feel sweat forming, on my brow, on the small of my back. My stomach churns and I feel so stupid, why did I have to drive the Z4 today?

We hit another straight stretch of road. I accelerate, using the gears to increase the space between the two of us. But whoever is driving behind me is skilled; they have no problem keeping up. 65, 75, God knows what speed we're doing. I can smell the tyres burning; I'm scared, really really scared. I can't concentrate fully on the road, Peter's name is all I can really think of. Yet I'm keeping one eye fixed on my mirror. I need to make sure they don't ram me again. But no matter what I do, braking, accelerating, skidding through corners, they stay behind me.

Then another bang as it hits me again. This time I have less luck. There is a horrible sound of metal hitting stone as I bounce around on the slippery road surface. I grimace. One of my headlamps has now gone. The road ahead is less well lit. But I know I need to keep driving.

I start yelling.

"Fuck off! Fuck off, you bastard! Fuck off!"

He's still there, on my tail, threatening.

We must be a mile out of Hope Cove now and the 4X4 or car or whatever the lump of shit is it is still waiting to make its move. Then in the road ahead of me I see a light. Somebody is leading two horses down the narrow lane just above the top of the village. I can see that the horses are panicking, getting friskier by the second, flustered by the roar of the engines as we approaching them. They're startled, unsettled. I see one of the horses rear, kicking out its forelegs. Then the horse bolts forward!

I'm aware of crashing, I feel glass cutting into my arms. I glance momentarily in my mirror. The 4X4 has gone. I catch the shape of a horse, struggling in the middle of the road. Then I am spinning, the car is turning over in the air. There is smell of burnt rubber, and petrol, I can smell petrol too. I think about the Indian meal I'll miss, wonder about death, hope that the pain that is burning through my arm won't last too long. Hope Cove looks strange from mid-air; it's upside down.

Then everything is black.

* * *

The first thing that struck me was her hair. Gone was the long shoulder-length of dark black that had previously framed her bespectacled face, softening her features and highlighting her killer smile. Then there was a tattoo, carved at the top of the shoulder of her right arm, a wheel-like shape with Indian influences, like a growth, a cancer.

We were meeting on neutral territory, away from Massie Road and all the baggage associated with it. We had chosen early evening, dusk in fact, in Stratford-upon-Avon. We were in a pub, something with duck in the title, near to the RSC. There were a few early evening punters, the men sipping pints of English ale, the women content with their dry white wines, port and lemons or what have you. In no way were any of these people local, all were here for the evening performance of *Twelth Night*. It was probably all they could do to resist dressing in Elizabethan garb and singing 'hey-diddy-diddy' nonsense.

I am not sure what role I was cast in that evening. The Fool? Orisino? I think Al had wandered in from another comedy too, possibly *The Taming of the Shrew* or maybe a lost character from *A Midsummer Night's Dream*. Either way she seemed discordant, out of place with the people around her.

She smiled at me as she sat down.

"Hi," she said, softly, her tone friendly but her body stiff, her movements restrained, hardly concealing the underlying tension.

"Can I get you a drink?" I asked.

"Erm, yeah," she responded "a pint of bitter".

I raised an eyebrow

"Bitter? Have you gone into the building trade then?"

She just smiled but as I glanced across from the bar I noticed that she had also put on more than a few pounds. 'Not surprising,' I thought, if her favourite tipple was now a pint.

Eventually I came back with two pints and a couple of packets of crisps. We sat in silence for a few seconds. Neither of us touched the crisps but they sat there like a pair of forlorn children. Unwanted. Things we had because we couldn't think of anything better to spend our money on. In the silence, I realised that there was so much we could have said, and yet so much that seemed superfluous.

"You've lost a bit of weight," she said quietly.

"Yeah," I responded, "I've tried to cut down a bit, worried about becoming a fat blob."

She smiled

"50 will look good on you," she said.

"I'm not complaining. Some people in the past never got to be this old."

She smiled. Then there was a silence between us. It was an OK sort of silence, not uncomfortable – the silences that people who have shared lots of noise can tolerate.

Eventually Al spoke.

"So what are we going to do?" Al said. "Me and you?"

Despite the fact that we had not moved forward in the intervening 3 months, I had no answer to this question.

"I honestly don't know." As I said this I looked deep into her eyes because I really was clueless about this one.

The simple solution was to part company. Sell the house, split the proceeds, and move on. But simple is never easy. I knew I really wasn't in the right frame of mind to do this.

"In a way," said Al, "I'd like to come back and live with you."

I nodded to myself. This sounded good but maybe it was because it represented a sort of shelter in the past.

"Is that possible?" I asked.

And with a look that was from a million years before, she once again placed her top teeth on her bottom lip and nibbled them sexily, before responding.

"I think it's worth an effort, don't you?" she asked.

I did, but a bit of my pride was getting in my way.

"Is it that simple? I mean, don't you think an apology is in order?"

"No," she said, "it's just what happened, what else can I say? You played your part, I played mine."

So despite myself I found my own little demons not wanting to give way. I'm not sure if it was pride, or stubbornness or just stupidity, but it meant that that evening we resolved nothing.

We met four more times, turning our quest for reconciliation into a test match series. Finally, with our futures finely balanced at 2-2, we met for a decider, just before Halloween, at The Lost Weekend.

I must admit I was losing my stomach for the battle. I think I was picking up from Al that life with Joy, whatever was going on there, was not going too well. So whilst I sliced her opening attack away to the boundaries, I was clueless once she brought on her spin bowling.

She began crying.

"Mark," she said "how clear do I have to make it? I really and truly love you. More than anybody else on the entire planet! I mean, what the hell do I have to do to get the message across?"

I swung at this delivery but I got nowhere near to the ball, she cleaned-bowled me with a slow paced emotional delivery that distracted me from the aggressive game I'd been playing. After that one, my innings collapsed. She could do anything and when she took the crease she just went for it.

"What happened to the lovers we were?" she asked, scoring an easy 6. "Is this the person you planned to become?" 4. "So unforgiving? So Mean?" Two 6s there.

I was in disarray by the end of this onslaught. It was left to my tail-enders to try and hold out.

"I'm really confused," I said. "I want things to be better than this."

"I love you," she insisted.

Whack! This was pointless; I couldn't do anything in these circumstances.

I looked at the scoreboard; the series was lost, that much was clear.

"OK," I finally said. "Let's see how it goes."

Soon the umpire was pulling up the wickets. The slow motion replays were flashed up on the big screen. It was all over.

For the time being.

* * *

I can smell shit. I have an overwhelming stench of crap around me and I wonder if this is what hell is like? All I can sense is pain and a feeling that I may have crapped in my own trousers. I'm too hot as well.

There is a harsh, plastic taste in my mouth. I'm confused. Where has this come from? My throat also feels raw and I gradually become aware that my eyes are closed. I try to open them but it seems like it's a tremendous effort to do so. I am aware that there is artificial light beyond my eyelids but I can't work out where I am. I can also hear a voice, indistinct, but it is definitely a human voice somewhere and the words are coming across in staccato. In between the words I become aware of a steady beeping noise. Where do I know that noise from? I recognise it, but what is it?

These sensations come and go. It sometimes feels like hours before I can make out any changes and then lots of things happen in seconds. Then a new sensation. Something moves me to the side, I am definitely lying on my side and somebody is touching my buttocks. Water, I feel water splashed against my buttocks then I have my genitals rubbed with something damp and then I am left alone. It's not unpleasant but it's disorientating. Then it all stops again.

Time is passing. I am aware of time passing. And for a long period there are no new sensations. Occasionally the smell of crap is stronger than at other times, and I am also hot. The pain – is it subsiding or am I just getting used to it? This really is confusing. And why do I keep hearing the 'Muffin the Mule' song' running through my head? That stupid woman who was with him, what was her name? And was Muffin a 'he,' anyway? This is hard work.

Was I asleep? I notice my eyelids don't feel as heavy as they did, they're a bit lighter. They're definitely getting easier to move. I move them. The light gets brighter but then I have to shut the eye I've opened.

Wait. Somebody is saying my name now.

"Mark, Mark can you hear me?"

I recognise that voice. Who is it? It's a woman, but who? My mum? No, she's dead. I know she's dead.

Somebody is touching my arm too, I think, and the same voice is saying my name.

"Mark, Mark are you awake?"

Gentle touches down my arm. This is quite nice actually.

Then another voice, another woman.

"Good," it says, "he's getting stronger, that's a good sign."

Is it? Who's getting stronger? Me? I couldn't get any weaker.

Then silence again for a long time. Ages. Soon I can feel the nice touches on my arm and I'm not hearing the Muffin song quite so often. I keep getting flashes of a horse though, a big horse, a grey mare, caught in a road. What's that about?

Woah! Both my eyes are open, how did that happen? They're just open and it's not hurting. I can see a face too, it's close but it's looking at me. Smiling? Who is it?

"You've been having a bit of a lie-in, haven't you?"

I think I smile but I can't detect any movement for the moment. Then I know that the smiling face is my niece, Jenny. What's she doing here?

Then another face. Ooh. Pretty. I know this one too.

"Hello you!" it's saying, "you never did lend me your car, eh?"

Alpha. I don't remember ever introducing them to each other. How come they know each other?

Then somebody in a nurse's uniform. Pretty, very tasty actually.

"Give us a moment, I just need to do some checks, you can come back in a few minutes."

She looks down at me.

"Hello Mr Garvey? Do you know where you are?"

What the fuck am I meant to say to that?

"You're in the hospital, at Heavitree."

Am I? Oh, OK.

"You've been very poorly but you're going to be OK. Well you won't be playing for West Brom this season, but there's no long-term serious damage, not that we can work out."

I wonder what she meant about no serious damage, long term?

means

"Now," she says. "Let's see about making you a bit more comfortable."

I feel her remove the plastic thing from my mouth and as she takes it away I notice it's a ventilation device. Ah! That makes sense. But my mouth feels sore.

"Suck this," she says and passes me a beaker with a straw in it.

God that's good, just water but it feels so good.

"Your niece is here, and your nephew and, is it Alpha?"

Bloody hell, they're holding a family reunion in my honour?

Then Don, my nephew, is at the bed. He's smiling at me.

"Hello Mark," he's says. "She was a cutie, wasn't she?"

Then the waterworks open, I don't know why but I cry and cry. As I do so the pain increases in my arm, in my hip and then, then, it all comes flooding back. The car, the field, the horse. Oh, God, what did I do?

I speak "The horse?" I say through the tears and Jenny puts her face close to mine.

"Later, later. Just get better."

"I couldn't."

Jenny puts her finger to her lips, shushing me.

"Just sleep, take it easy, come on." She strokes my arm again.

I can remember now. The fire brigade, an ambulance. I can remember bits of it. I can remember the horse, a grey mare, it crying in anguish, I could hear it from inside the Z4.

"Is it dead? Is it dead?!"

Alpha places her face in front of mine.

"Sleep Mark, like Jenny says."

So I close my eyes. I feel the pain, I feel my arm aching, I feel helpless. And I just wish somebody would tell me about the horse.

* * *

By nature I am not a revolutionary. I can be radical at times, think outside the box, but I am the last to ring in the changes overnight. I'm too cautious and if I ever led a revolution it would be one that considered all the options, checked how things were going, if everyone was OK with the direction and then, once we all agreed, move forward, but not until I'd slept on it.

The strength of gradualisms is that it allows change to take place at a pace we feel comfortable with. Maybe in my revolution I wouldn't shoot Prince Charles, maybe I'd just suggest he stopped trying to appear like a straight businessman and grow his hair long, wear an Afghan and become the spaced out hippie that he so wants to be. Only then would I consider shooting him and probably miss.

Al moving back into Massie Road was undertaken in a similar spirit. To begin with, we just shared the house together. Given the size of the place and the relative space, that was easy. I stayed in the attic and she stayed in our old bedroom. We cooked separately too and, wherever possible, avoided being in at the same time. I think we both needed this gradualism in our lives.

Then little things started happening, she would be in the kitchen in the morning when I was and offer to make me tea. Then, the next day, I might be down before her and, as I was making toast anyway, offer her some toast and vegemite. Or I'd be going to Waitrose and ask her if she needed anything and she'd decide she would come with me. This sort of thing went on in the run-up to Christmas.

One day we were in the supermarket together.

"I'd really fancy a proper veggie roast on Sunday, wouldn't you?" Al said.

"God, yes! You mean with all the trappings?" I responded enthusiastically, "and with a good bottle of red wine."

Al smiled. Her hair had grown back a bit too, so she was becoming more like the old Al. She peered at me over the top of her glasses.

"So why don't we do it? We'll cook together, then maybe, if you're up for it, we could go to the cinema afterwards, yeah?"

So that's how we started cooking together again, because after we shared one meal we both realised, although we never said it out loud, that we liked eating with each other. Then we graduated to the odd meal out and gradually we were easing back into living with each other.

A fortnight before Christmas and we started to get innocently physical. Not big things, just little things. Hugs, kisses, nuzzles. It all felt good. The big leap, sex, was a fair way off, but the Sunday before Christmas weekend we did share a bed together. Again, no sex, just sleeping, touching, holding each other which was, in itself something I never thought would happen again. In the morning, I felt like I'd had the best night's sleep in months.

Then we were both into the never ending week of works' Christmas parties. Surprisingly, neither she or I returned home drunk, or so late for it to be an annoyance. And all through that week we shared a bed together. We moved closer, our touching and kissing became more intimate. Sometimes she touched my penis, and occasionally she let me kiss her nipples, but we stopped short of anything too sexual.

Christmas Day was on a Tuesday. We both stopped work on the Friday and spent the weekend doing separate things. But by the Sunday we had agreed to cook and basically lock ourselves away for the next few days. So a late lunch on a dark winter's afternoon led to us sitting in the lounge, already fairly tipsy, talking, sort of civilised, sort of together. We were playing old CDs, everything from Leonard Cohen through to jazz classics, whole albums, individual tracks, whatever took our fancy. To add to the atmosphere, we lit candles. So the lounge was lit by a gigantic Christmas tree and half a dozen floating candles. The dark of the mid-winter was gently broken by the flickering lights, the warmth of times gone – and times to come?

We were getting mellower and mellower, and then Al suggested that we should have a bath together, something I always liked. So she went upstairs, lit more candles and ran a bath filled with what I usually called 'smellies' but most other people would call sensual oils. Whilst she did so, I decided to open a bottle of champagne, filled an ice bucket and took two glasses and the bottle up to the bathroom.

In the darkness of a winter night, we sipped champagne in the warm water together. We touched, we kissed and eventually, without too much shock, we ended up making love together. Properly, passionately, continuously.

And later I lay there, with Al satisfied next to me, and for the first time ever I had a feeling with Al that I had never had before. It scared me, it chilled me. In a warm room, in a house lit by scented candles, in a bed with a beautiful woman, in a house where the chill of mid-winter was dispelled and melted – I felt empty.

8 weeks. I've spent the past 8 weeks like this and I am fed up. Yes of course I am gradually getting better, gradually getting my mobility back, but the worst thing is it's so boring!

There is a scar on my arm where the glass from the windscreen cut through it. Apparently if it wasn't for the skills of the surgeon I may have lost it, but the break and lacerations are healing well. The longer haul problem is my fractured hip. It will take another few months before I regain full mobility. In the meantime I have to walk with the aid of a pair of sticks. Even then I can't get far.

I've met the owner of the horses. A bespectacled, owl-like pharmacist. She was really quite angry, understood that there was nothing I could do but was grieving for the loss of her mare. Apparently I or it collided with the car, the impact forced me upwards and then I just spun over a wall and into a field. I still get nightmares about it but they're gradually decreasing in their frequency.

I'm living at Kalpna's. It made some sense, I couldn't look after myself in the first few weeks after I'd been in hospital and whilst the agency have insisted I keep the tenancy on I am not too bothered in the circumstances. Yet here I feel like a guest, almost like a prisoner. Unable to go anywhere, unable to do much.

I am sat in the lounge at Hampton View. I'm watching the sun set. In three weeks time it will be Christmas, then a few days later and I'll celebrate a year in Hope Cove. I am surrounded by 'Get Well' cards, which are now being supplemented by more seasonal stuff. I am prone to low moods at the moment. I keep thinking that I moved here for a quiet life, a non-demanding job and the chance to rediscover my enthusiasm for things. Somehow this plan has been less than a universal success, to the point that we could almost describe it as a total disaster.

And there have been phone calls. Calls from work colleagues, calls from relatives, people I haven't spoken to in years.

Then I had a call from Jim at the Ship.

"Well Mr Garvey," he said "I bet you never thought living in Devon would be this dangerous now, did you?"

"You can say that again Jim" I responded wearily.

"Well, the countryside Mark – full of mystery you know?" he chuckled to himself.

"Erm yes – thanks Jim." Jim was odd at the best of times but this conversation just proved that he was very,very odd.

'Well.' and he pauses for a long time, so long in fact that I think the line has gone dead.

"Hello?!'

"It's OK,' he interrupts, "I'm just wondering how to phrase the next bit.'

"Happy Christmas?!' I say, getting irritated.

"Fucking shut up you spastic, and listen!"

'Christ,' I think, 'this isn't the usual Jim!'

He carries on. "Do you know how much fucking trouble you have caused eh? You and your fucking poncy Italian mate?"

"Jim!"

"Fucking shut up I said! OK?"

Eventually we are quiet again. I can hear him breathing down the phone, panting almost. He starts again.

"You're going to come and meet me. Christmas Eve, at the harbour, after closing time. Tell one of the pakis to drop you, tell them I'll bring you back.'

'I beg your pardon? Pakis?!'

He mimics what I have said and then gets angry again. "Are you a fucking moron as well as deaf?! You're in no position to negotiate, Mr fucking County Hall Garvey! Just get yourself there when I say, if you don't want any more trouble."

He slams the phone down. The line is dead. Nothing.

I put the phone down and just sit and stare. I even wonder if I have dozed off and that the last conversation was a dream, the remnants from an afternoon snooze? After all I am on some powerful pain killers. Could I have imagined it?

The phone starts ringing again.

I pick it up. It's Jim.

'Sorry.' he says, but he sounds like he doesn't mean it. "I need to tell you not to be stupid, to make sure you're alone, OK – you got that?'

"How can I trust you?" I ask.

He laughs 'That's the wrong question – I think the question you meant to ask yourself is, 'can you afford not to trust me?,' isn't it?'

I weigh up what he has said. Instinctively I get the impression he is right.

"Jim – I'll be there.'

He hangs up.

* * *

What would it be like to be a ghost? I've often thought about this. I mean, I'm sure you could have lots of fun, moving things in the middle of the night, hiding people's car key's, fractionally moving the ball off penalty spots just before Rooney kicks it. I guess though you would have to know you were a ghost before you could actually get up to this devilment. Even then, would you be certain of your ghost – like status? I have a hunch it would take a fair bit of time for the reality to click in. Maybe the first time you walk through a wall or are in a crowded room and realise nobody can see you. Who knows?

In the new year I tried to rekindle the experiences I had, the feelings I had, with Al. She seemed as earthly and real as ever and just as passionate. In fact, she was more passionate than ever and at times threw caution to the winds. Some days she would want to make love before work and as soon as she came home, then she would also want to make love after dinner and before we went to sleep. The side effect of all this was that I was too exhausted to even consider looking at other women.

In truth, though, I was not enjoying what I should have been. It felt even more meaningless than sex with Patrice because at least that was risky and pushed at the boundaries of acceptability. This had none of that. This was just empty. Drifting through the motions, wandering the deserted corridors of empty emotion, trying to find a way to find the feelings again that I thought could've meant something.

Our lives lost any shape too. We went to cinema, theatres; ate meals in good quality restaurants; had romantic weekends in Bordeaux, Berlin and Barcelona. But none of it had any depth for me anymore. In fact, it started to have the strangest of effects, it started to make me not be passionate with Al, to physically lose interest in her, to even not to want to hold or touch her. From being a tactile, warm lover, I began to distance myself from her. She commented on this once or twice.

One evening she returned from work.

"Hey, don't I get a kiss anymore?" she asked.

So I crossed the room and kissed her on her cheek.

"No, a kiss, come on!"

And she kissed me passionately. I was stood there, wondering if she could tell that there was nothing on the other side of the kiss, no emotion, no passion just a man kissing a woman. Yet she just shrugged – started telling me about her day – and left it there.

I tortured myself over all of this. The trips away, the meals, the theatre, were all attempts by me to find the trigger that would make me realise that I still loved Al. And I began to grow dissatisfied with everything around me. The house wasn't big enough; Massie Road was too suburban – neither city or country; my seat at the Hawthorns wasn't quite right, maybe I should pay more next season; my hair was too short; my hair was too long; we were doing too much that was routine; we had no routine. I became impossible.

Strangely, my face did not take on a grey powdery look. I wasn't given a white sheet to adorn myself with in the hours between dusk and dawn. Yet an impartial observer would have easily recognised that this was not life, this was a man who was at the very least living the life of a ghost. Over time, it would also become clear that the ghost was also a fool.

* * *

"Do you want me to come with you?" Geo asked.

"It would be too dangerous."

Geo went quiet for a bit. He had come down for the day at my behest. And we were sat in the lounge at Hampton View. He, Janey and Matty were going off to Barbados for a few weeks, his celebration for having landed a series of commercials as an Italian chef – *The Pasta Master*. It had taken some persuasion for me to get him down here. Yet I needed, at the very least, to share the information with him.

"He could be dangerous, he could do you some damage."

He was right on this point. I can barely walk more than a few yards on my sticks, never mind run away.

'I'll be OK – I don't think he is that dangerous.'

Geo doubted this.

"Sounds pretty fucking dangerous to me. You don't know what he's got planned, do you?"

I reasoned in my own mind that Geo was right.

"I think he may be psychotic, but only borderline psychotic."

'Well that's OK then – I mean if he's only borderline, he'll probably just hack you up in big pieces rather than small pieces and leave your body half buried rather than never to be found again."

"Geo, come on,' I tried to reason. "He's made contact with me. He wants to tell me something important."

"Really?!" Geo asks. "What – like he is planning to introduce a new kind of cat food – Social Worker flavour? Come on, Mark – you're allowing your professional fantasy world to put yourself at risk."

He's right about this too.

"I'll be OK – I promise."

"Bollocks!" Geo responds. "Listen – this isn't about you anymore, this is about some bastard who may be posting pictures of my son, my fucking son, yeah, on the internet. Stop being so ego-fucking-centric. Get some help. Call DCI Mellon, call Al Qaeda for all I care but don't go and meet that psychopath alone! Look, just go to the police. They'll sort this out".

And I know he's right and I know they will sort this out. So what's stopping me?

I make an excuse.

"I want some security," I say but this fails to sway Geo.

"Isn't that kind of the police's job? You know, security?"

Then Geo takes control.

"Look mate – I can't let you do this, so I am going to give you a choice. I'll talk to Mellon, get his advice. What ever he says, we'll both go with it, OK?"

'No,' I say firmly.

Then he loses it. "Well he's right then! You're a fucking Moron!"

He picks up his jacket, doesn't even look back, slams the door and leaves. I hear his car start, the engine revs and he drives off, leaving me alone to face my tormentor.

* * *

We were in the Cotswolds, 12 weeks in to the new year, the Saturday before Easter. I had persuaded Al that it would be right if we moved out of Birmingham and to the countryside and I think that by this point Al was doing her best to keep me happy. If I'd have said we should move to the outer Hebridies and dress as Zulu warriors, I was under the impression that she would have gone along with this too.

We'd got details from various estate agents and ended up wanting to view a few places. That's the trouble with property details; they take on a life of their own once you take them out of the envelope. We were looking at spending silly amounts too; for the price we were paying you could buy a decent central defender for the Baggies. So instead of the two sides of A4 we got when we were looking at Massie Road, we were given brochures with glossy pictures, details of local schools, and all manner of information that was superfluous as far as we could see, but which you knew meant you were in serious territory and no longer seen as a step up from new-age travellers by estate agents.

So we found ourselves that Saturday viewing a property in Cleve Prior, a converted post office. Al loved it; it had rooms everywhere, three bedrooms upstairs and a gorgeous attic that ran the length of the house. It also needed a bit of work so we knew we could probably afford it.

In the car on the way back, Al talked excitedly about the prospects of the place and tried to work out what we could raise. She had some money her dad had left her, just £20,000, but she thought it would just about get the work done that needed to be done. So slowly a plan took shape that would involve selling Massie Road, moving to the countryside and basically changing our lifestyle. As Al got more excited by these prospects, I got more resistant to the idea as a whole. It took 35 minutes to get back home.

"It will take ages for me to get to the Hawthorns from there," I said with a sigh.

"Yeah," said Al, "but think of the improvement in our quality of life, you know, walking, we could even get a dog, don't you think a dog would be great?"

I really didn't want a dog. I mean I've always liked them, they're great fun, but a dog? For us? No, it made no sense. By the end of the weekend the dog had a name, Rex – which was meant to be a sort of ironic post-modernist statement – we'd discussed a walking rota, where Al would do more because she was nearby at Evesham, and I would compensate by walking Rex at the weekends. Al had decided that we could do all our shopping online, so this wouldn't be difficult and before I knew it the future was more or less sorted. I may have got this wrong but I think we even practiced opening cans of dog food and mixing it all together just to get us used to meeting Rex's needs. Bliss it was not.

Monday came, Al gave me the details and we agreed we'd put the offer in. If I talked to the estate agents about the old post office, she would sort out getting Massie Road marketed. It got to mid-morning and she called me excited and full of beans.

"Any news?" she asked excitedly.

"No, they said they would get back to us and put our offer to the owners." I lied. I hadn't even called.

"You know," I continued, "it's best to leave it for a bit, otherwise they'll think we're desperate and they'll reject the offer."

"Ah, but I'm so excited Mark! Make them accept our offer!"

I had the audacity to laugh at this.

"Come on," I said. "Calm down. I'm sure if it's meant to be it will be."

I put the phone down and wondered why I had lied. Why didn't I just say that I didn't want to move to living in the middle of the country, surrounded by outcasts from *The Archers*? Why didn't I come clean? Was I too afraid to tell her that the whole house hunt was just another example of a displacement exercise? Look for other things to do?

That evening, on the way home, I bought Al a huge bunch of flowers. I got home before her, put some wine in the fridge to chill and waited. I think she knew from the flowers that the news wasn't good. Lately I had stopped doing things like this.

"Hey, flowers," she said flatly, "does this mean what I think it does?"

I nodded. "'Fraid so," I confirmed, "the agents said that they have had a better offer with another agency. And the people have already got their property under offer."

She looked desolate.

"But I want a home for me, you and Rex," Al said. I could see she was near to tears, which didn't exactly make me feel like a good guy.

"I know," I said gently, and kissed her lightly on her forehead.

"Piss!" she shouted "Piss and fuck and all of that sort of thing!" I knew that she was accepting it. So a bunch of flowers seemed a cheap option compared to spending shedloads of cash on a property I didn't want.

I went to work the following day, convinced that I was such

a smooth operator, I was so clever. I'd managed to go through the motions and still comfort and show concern to Al. So generally I was feeling good. I must admit I was not feeling very noble, but bollocks to nobleness.

Late morning my phone rang.

"Me" said Al in a tone that was not friendly.

"Hi sweetheart," I said "How's your day."

"Shall I tell you? I mean do you really, really want to know?"

"Of course I do." I said sensing a blow was coming.

"Well I got a call at work about the old post office".

'Fuck,' I thought, 'I thought the agents were calling me!'

"Oh," I said.

"Er yeah, and like they said that they wanted to know what we thought of the place and if we would be making an offer."

This was not going to be good. But Al was determined to go through to the end of her speech.

"So I said that you had phoned them and been told that the place was sold, wasn't that the case Mark?"

I didn't answer.

"Look, I can't talk now, I've got a team meeting to go to".

One of my admin team looked across at me incredulous. She started shaking 'no' and must have thought, 'please not a team meeting, they're so tedious, I'm sure you've got it wrong!'

"You lied to me! You fucking lied to me and you even went through a charade of buying me flowers and every-fucking-thing else."

I shifted uncomfortably in my chair. This was worse than I thought it could be.

"So when you come out of your team meeting, work out where you're sleeping tonight, OK?"

She slammed the phone down.

I needed to move from my desk, so I went to the loo, yelled

at a few people ~~to make me feel a bit better~~ and eventually came back to get on with work.

I'd been sat there for a couple of moments and the phone rang again.

"Mark Garvey," I said.

"Aren't you meant to be in a team meeting" Al shouted down the phone. "Or was that just another lie?!"

Before I had time to respond she started again.

"One other thing I forgot to mention," she said, "I'm pregnant. Oh and this time I'm keeping it!"

The line went dead. I think I was at a total loss as to what to do next and for no reason other than it felt like the right thing to do I went and yelled at a few more people until I felt a bit better. Somehow or other, though, I knew that the yelling and bawling people out was no substitute for not dealing with the growing realisation that this ghost, whilst not causing fear, not making things go bump in the night and not causing penalty spot mischief, truly was a category A fool.

* * *

I'm am confused; tomorrow is Christmas Eve and I still haven't decided if I will meet Jim. I have been quiet, unnaturally quiet and withdrawn.

Alpha is around and has been helpful but she's noticed I'm a bit low.

"Come on," she said yesterday. "You're not always going to be like this. Chill out, yeah? I'll take you out."

I thought at the time, 'If only she knew,' but another part of me is pleased that she doesn't.

So Alpha loads me into her battered Ford Fiesta and before I know it she is driving me to The Ship.

Alpha

"Al No! Please this isn't a good idea."

But she just takes this as me being a grouchy old fart.

"Rubbish! You know you love The Ship!"

As I walk in, the look on Jim's face is not a happy one. However, he manages to hide this from Alpha – so disguising his mood. Jim pipes up:

"Hang on to your drinks – it's Dangerman!"

Luckily though there is nobody else in here, it's late afternoon and everybody else is too busy with Christmas shopping. Just me, Jim and Alpha.

"Quite the comedian, aren't we Jim?" Alpha responds.

She is icy, showing her best contempt for him.

"Now, now madam. I've a complimentary glass of mulled wine for you and a free pint for Hopalong here."

"Let me park the car," she says, "but no more jokes at Mark's expense."

He waits until she is outside again.

"What the fucking hell are you doing here now, you deaf twat!" he says.

"Tomorrow night after fucking closing time, deaf prick!" Each word is annunciated slowly, menacingly. He seems totally deranged.

"I may not come," I say defiantly.

"You'll come or Missy there will find that the brakes on her car will be mysteriously failing over the holiday period."

Alpha re-enters the pub.

"What were you saying about my car?" she asks.

"Just how amazed I am that it's still so roadworthy," says Jim, playing the innocent.

"And your point is?!" Alpha asks, just too aggressive for my liking.

"Come on, let's go," I say to Alpha. "I don't want a scene."

254

"You'll be alright on your own with me, Mark – If you want my opinion, madam here has got a chip on her shoulder."

"And you've got a chunk of your pint-sized intellect missing, you arsehole," Alpha snaps back.

"Oi!" Jim says in mock offence. "Not very ladylike." He turns to me. "Come back on your own tomorrow evening Mark – we'll have a quiet drink together late on."

But we are already leaving.

"Now don't forget Marky – Christmas Eve – just me and you."

I am hobbling out through the door by now. I glance back and he is looking threateningly at me – a look I have never seen on his face before. "Don't spoil my Christmas, Mark!"

I hobble across the car park as fast as I can.

"That man!" Alpha says once we are both inside.

"I'll sort him out tomorrow," I say, and she looks back at me, aghast.

"You mean you're going back in there?!" I can see that she thinks I am either mad or stupid. "What are you going to do, club him to death with your crutches?" She is laughing. "People might pay to see that," she says.

I try to join in with her laughter, but the falsity stings, the falsity betrays my fear and I am left wondering what on earth Christmas Eve will involve.

* * *

A suitcase, a rubber plant, two stuffed toys and a portable CD player, all in the hall. They gave the distinct and correct impression of arrivals rather than departures. They were stood in the hall like aliens, inspecting their new planet and waiting for their all powerful leader to arrive and command them. Even as

255

they waited, they were being reinforced by a box of books, a collection of CDs and a few framed pictures.

What did the alien forms make of their new environment? Planet Massie Road was a landscape polluted by war. The terrain was pitted with the debris from relations that had soured and now the arrival of the alien presences was about to make matters worse. I had retreated to the attic but could see from the dormer window that the small Renault Clio craft delivering the hordes into the hallway was piloted by my old inter-planetary adversary, Joy.

The decline in my relationship with Al was swift. One moment we were looking at planning brave new worlds with a dog called Rex and a house in the countryside, the next we were at each other's throats. One moment I had nothing to worry about, the next I was afraid that my home was being turned into a feminist commune. And of course, because Al and I were not married, I had no rights over the child she was carrying.

"You'll be able to see it from time to time," Al explained, "but as far as I'm concerned, you've got no role in bringing up the baby. OK?"

The 'OK' was stated not as a negotiating point but as closing statement. Al was not negotiating, she was laying down terms. Her approach was dogged and her view was that I should put up and shut up.

The arrival of Joy was announced in a similar way to my paternal rights.

"Er, look," she said late one night when I was sat at the kitchen table, picking through the remains of an Indian takeaway, "Joy is moving in at the weekend."

"I have no say over this?" I asked, knowing the answer.

"No, of course not." No smile, no warmth. Just negativity. Then to add to the humiliation, "and we'll be sharing my room."

'my room,' I thought. 'Wasn't that our room once?' How quickly the joint possessive is replaced by a singular possessive. Doubtless it would soon become 'our' room again but never 'my' room for me.

I was less than impressed.

"Well, I hope you'll both be very happy together."

"We will be," Al responded curtly.

For a while after Joy moved in, life continued as normal. We didn't argue – there were no battles over who used the bathroom, who had the lounge. Bliss was it to be alive at that brave new dawn. This lasted for all of two or 3 minutes and it seemed that we could all get along well. But the optimism of a brief ceasefire was not fulfilled by a negotiated peace settlement. Just more shelling.

Joy came into the kitchen carrying a bottle of Bollinger.

"Do you know where the ice bucket is?" Joy asked.

Al appeared behind her. "No point asking Mark, he's spent years trying to find my clitoris so don't expect him to know where something that he never really tries to find is."

"Under the sink," I said, ignoring Al's comment.

"No," Joy said, "no wonder she's never been satisfied if you think her clitoris is under the sink."

And so it continued. Whenever we were present together, there would be some barbed comment, some cheap snide remark at my expense. Or we would fight over who would have the lounge, when Al was throwing a dinner party or some other bollocks. Increasingly I retreated to the attic, worked late, went to Baggies away games at the weekend and stayed away – thus learning that Grimsby is not really the best place in the world to spend a weekend in April – or visited Jane and Geo.

It got to the summer and I had begun to realise that this was all pointless. I had no home, just mortgage payments and an attic room to show for the expense. I was having lunch with Kay when I think it happened and I just started crying. It was quite embarrassing really. There we were, having a nice pub lunch in Kidderminster, the next thing I knew, I was moving in. Kay knew things were bad but not quite as bad as I eventually explained.

"Get a solicitor involved, stupid." Which I'd resisted doing and knew there was little point. "Come and stay with us." Which meant contemplating moving out of Massie Road and I knew once I did that there would be no going back. Then I wondered what 'going back' actually meant because the reality was hitting me. There was no going back, there was just going.

* * *

There is a cold wind that bites at my face as I make my way to the quayside. Jim had been quite clear that he wanted to meet me on the Cob, at 11.45 – after closing time – on Christmas Eve. I wasn't to come into the pub. I was to come alone. 'Nothing stupid' he had advised. I wondered about this. I toyed with the idea of turning up in fancy dress, just to prove that I could still do stupid things. It was a passing thought though and I guess I could have told Jim it was 'nothing sensible' if I had've turned up as a pantomime dame.

I am surprised as to how cold it really is. Decembers never seem to be like this any more, but for once the blue planet feels blue. If Jim doesn't turn up soon I will be the same colour, a little frozen deaf guy stuck to the quayside like a limpet.

Just when I think he isn't going to show, I sense movement away to my left, near the steps at the quayside. Jim is in an enormous trench coat that flaps around against his legs. As far as I can tell he is alone.

"Mr Garvey – Happy Christmas!" he says, over jolly and unnecessarily festive.

"Is that what you brought me here for – a Christmas greeting?" I ask him, barely able to hide my irritation.

"Now, now Mark – don't be cheerless eh?" he says more flatly – with a greater sense of menace.

We stand for a few moments, looking at each other, silently. It is almost like a scene from a gay movie. Two men, stood eyeing each other up – ready to do what we can only imagine.

"So what do you want?" I eventually ask. Then his mood changes.

"Oi! Fuck off! OK? I'm in fucking charge here, not you." He moves towards me his index finger outstretched – he jabs it into my chest.

"'You've got to listen – do you fucking understand?"

I hold my hand up to calm his aggression.

"Jim," I say calmly, "just tell me what you have to tell me."

He paces up and down furiously for a few moments and I genuinely wonder about his sanity. I know he has had a head injury, I know that people with head injuries can be dangerous, unhinged, I am starting to taste fear in my mouth, that metallic taste I get when I wonder if violence is coming.

"Why did you have to come here?!" he yells.

I'm confused. "Because you invited me," I say.

Then he's mad again. He comes up really close to my face. "No you deaf fuckwit, not tonight, why did you fucking come to Hope Cove? Why did you have to come and stay at Drake? Fucking why?!"

He is shouting, which I realise is to my advantage because people can probably hear what he is saying.

He doesn't allow me to explain. He doesn't really want the history of my childhood holidays, the dreams of a new beginning, all that bollocks.

Then he shifts mood again.

259

"Do you like it here Mark? Causing your chaos, getting old ladies locked up? Does it make you feel good?" He doesn't wait for a response, he just continues. "I had a deal you see, a good deal – with Mapp."

I wonder what he means. Was he selling pictures online? Was he somehow or other in partnership with her?

"Two year ago," he is in his flow now so I just have to listen, "I noticed that couples were coming into the pub a bit upset like, a bit worried. Anyway I eventually get talking to them and they complain that their kids have been worried by a flashing in the bathroom. Never when their parents are with them, just when they're alone. I mean, this isn't happening frequently, just about once every 5 or 6 weeks."

He pauses – looks away into the distance for a few moments – then he goes back to his tale.

"So one evening I decide to confront Mapp about this and I tell her that unless she comes clean with me I am going straight to the old Bill. Well, I gave her a few days, not an ultimatum, and the chance to meet me again to talk through what she's been up to."

'Why didn't you go to the police?' I ask.

"Because they've got better things to do, haven't they?! And anyway, it's better to sort these things out than get the law involved. That's how we do stuff around here, but you, Mr fucking Social Worker, wouldn't fucking understand that, would you? You'd want a fucking case conference and reports straight off, even if some old boot had only farted."

'So,' I think, 'he's not a fan of the profession, now there's a shock!'

"But you and that fat Italian cunt had to fucking interfere, didn't you?"

He's full of flattery now.

260

"Anyway, after a few days Wilma appears in the bar at The Ship. She's had a think and she wants to talk. So we come to an arrangement. I tell her that she has to get help for her little fetish, medical help, and then she can stop doing what she's been doing and I won't go to the boys in blue."

"And did she?"' I ask.

"Course she fucking did – she's a sensible woman, Wilma." He smiles. "She went to the local quack who was helping her."

He looks across at me and it hasn't really registered.

"Who might that be?" he asks with a smile on his face.

"Dr Kapasi!"

He nods, grinning to himself.

"You see – you can't trust them Mark, you just can't trust them – bloody pakis."

I want to hit him. I want to fucking punch his lights out but I know that in my current state I am no match for him. Most of all though, I want an explanation.

* * *

I felt, at best, like a man who had been exiled or at worst a fugitive. Kay's house was welcoming and she made me feel wanted but it was not home. Her kids were great too, pleased to have me and happy to engage me in conversation, but again it somehow missed the point. Here I was, a man turned 50, living with his big sister. It was like the script had been mistyped but nobody had the energy to sit down and rewrite it.

I tried my best to be 'normal' in abnormal circumstances, but everything was empty. Even the Baggies promotion back to the Premiership only got me happy, not ecstatic. I was as horny as hell too. So I spent that summer having a bonkfest because bedding women, no matter who they were, somehow or other gave me a respite from having to think about how empty and pathetic my life was. Was I looking for love? Or was I just pretending that everything was OK and I always did know the difference between where we kept the ice bucket and where to find the clitoris?

Kay was worried that I was becoming a bad influence on her kids.

"They think you're great you know," she said to me, "they really like having you around and have started taking bets on whether or not you'll ever bring anyone back." She paused and gave me a very firm look. "And I told them that if Uncle Mark ever brings one of his floozies back to our house he will end up sleeping in the local park for the rest of his life." Not a veiled threat and one that I knew she would carry out. Yet conversations like this didn't stop me.

My tastes seemed all over the place. There were fat women, skinny women, older women, women my own age, women 20 years younger than me, blondes, brunettes, bisexual women, one Afro-Caribbean woman and quite a few others whose names I forgot within 48 hours of bedding them and whose calls I never once returned. None of it was ever serious, it was all just a joke – I was laughing at me for being the biggest fuckwit on the planet because as well as this human menagerie there was also a sense of desperation, nights when I would crawl into bed knowing that I really had become a total joke. Then the tears would flow until I could've sold my salted cheeks to my local chip shop. None of them were Al, none of them were the person who meant most to me, and none of me would recognise this fact.

How much did she know? I wondered if reports of the stray heart I had become ever reached her. Did she keep any tabs on me? Did she even care? There was no contact, or at the very least most only limited perfunctory contact. Emails about bills that needed paying, text messages asking what I wanted doing with the post but nothing that would indicate any warmth, any real interest in the life that had been ours.

Eventually, after much badgering from Kay, I saw a family lawyer, who more or less advised me that I had few rights other than to ask for the sale of the house and for the profits to be split proportionate to our respective earnings and any residual investment. I had no rights of access to the baby but Al could, if she so wished, ask for maintenance through the Child Support Agency. This seemed unfair but not unsurprising. My response was just to continue what I was doing – bedding more women, drinking a little too much and simply shutting out the reality that was the life that mine had become.

I felt like walking down to New Street station, assembling my own account of all that had happened and displaying a sign that said 'All my own work.' All that stopped me was the certain knowledge that the most benevolent gestures I would have received would have been to have been spat at by the less viscous observers, most would be far harsher on me.

* * *

He is being led away. He is ranting at the world but he is restrained by two police officers.

"You're a fucking cunt Garvey!" he yells.

I am too stunned to respond.

At the point of mentioning Kalpna's name, he had a look of triumph on his face. A look of total satisfaction, like when a visiting football manager goes 2-0 up in a relegation game. He thinks he's won.

Of course he has. He has done the one thing I never thought he could do – create even greater distrust between me and

Kalpna. That was a clever prize for him, a neat little trick that implicated her and might even implicate me. Time will tell.

'I think you're lying,' I told him. And he chuckled.

'Really?!' he asked. "Why would I lie, Mark?'

I wasn't sure about that one. I hadn't worked out his motive for lying, in fact search my brain as much as I could and I couldn't really find one.

"You see Mark, you're just making things inconvenient for us all. You're interfering in the way that social workers fucking do with your theories of broken homes, your pathetic attempts to defend the indefensible, you're just professional arseholes."

"Should I leave it to well intentioned amateurs like you then Jim?'

He got mad again then. He came marching towards me and pushed me backwards sending me tumbling. Luckily I landed on the opposite side to my broken hip but I still yelled out in pain as my other side jarred as I landed.

He stood over me, "Don't get fucking sarcastic you fucking ponce!"

The pain was intense and I could hardly speak. I decided just to be silent while my head almost bursts with the pain that is stabbing at my sides. This might set my recovery back months. Lying on the ground I became aware now that I was in in a dangerous situation. This had been a stupid mistake, I started to realise that I might get seriously harmed.

'Did you kill Peter?' I asked.

He laughed to himself. "No – you did! You bought the same fucking car as him, you made him a target. You fucking killed him."

'He wasn't meant to be killed, anyway, just warned off. My guy didn't know it wasn't you'.

I pulled a goal back. 2-1.

"So you were behind it then? I mean – did you have the right to take somebody's life – even if you didn't mean to?"

"Why should I go to prison?' he asked

"Because you arranged to have Peter killed," I say quietly.

"Not for that! For Mapp. Why should I go to prison for her?"

"Why would you?" I ask – genuinely confused.

"I knew, didn't I, I knew what she was doing and yet I came up with my own solution. It would have probably worked but for you. I mean, yeah, she was occasionally prone to going backwards – but she was getting treatment for it."

"So what do you want? What do you want from me tonight?'

"I want you to see these".

He dropped some photographs down on the ~~floor~~ ground next to me. I had to push myself upright ~~so that I~~ to can see them and as I did he stepped back a few paces. There are pictures of me. Tied up and gagged. Naked.

"What would your friend, Mr Peterson, make of these?' he asked.

Then he continued, "and what about the local press – do you think they show you as a person fit to work as Director of Social Services?"

3-1 down now! This is not good.

I sat in silence for a moment. This is hard. How has he got these pictures? Has he persuaded Kalpna? Has he bugged our place in the same way that Annot had bugged Drake? What's Kal's role in all of this?

Before I ~~could~~ can speak I am aware of footsteps – people running towards the quayside. Then I get dragged to one side. Not by Jim though, by somebody else. It was Mellon. As I was dragged sideways I catch a glance of three or four other uniformed officers grappling with Jim. And then running along a little way behind the officers I saw Anna.

Now that Jim is being led away, she is beside me, helping me upright.

'Mark – are you OK?!'

She is concerned and has that worried expression she carries in her back pocket just for occasions such as this.

"Are you OK?" Anna asks, repeating the question, insistent.

I look at Jim – being pushed into the back of a van – swearing and cursing me, Mellon – glancing across to see if I am safe, and at Anna's big blue eyes set deep in her oval face. I contemplate the mess that is about to unravel, the compromising pictures scattered on the quayside in front of me. An image flashes through my mind, when football teams know they're beaten, when they know that it's all over, despite their best efforts. This is worse than bad; this is a disaster.

"No," I say. "No."

* * *

It was a short email. After the first reading I read it again, just to make sure I understood what it meant.

'Dear Mark,

Joy and I have done a great deal of talking recently and we have decided that our future isn't together, but then again my future is no longer here. I know that England no longer holds the key to my happiness and need to make a start elsewhere. At the same time, since my dad died, I have had the urge to be nearer to Mum because she is lost without my dad and that her grandchild would, maybe, give her the new lease of life that she really needs.

I would like us to either sell Massie Road or for you to buy my share of the house off me. However I need the market rate. If you can't do this, I would like us to sell it ASAP on the open market. We can split the profits accordingly. Once the house is sold, I am going to go back to Perth. Hopefully this will be before baby arrives. However if not I will go home very soon after this.

If you still have any love for me, I hope you'll agree to what I'm asking for. It seems to me this is for the best – for both of us – please.

Al.'

I read the email two or three times. A bit of me is angry that she didn't even have the decency to call me. And there is another part of me that totally understands. A phone call would have meant discussion, maybe even a negotiation. In her email she could be clear and not have to listen to my own prejudices.

It strikes me that modern technology removes romance and reduces chance. After all, if we had've had it when Al and I first started out, maybe there would have been less pining and a Christmas trip to Australia could have been exposed as the whimsy it really was. Then again, maybe all of this was how it should have been. There is no point pondering the impossibilities of a changed world. We do what we do at the time, we do it for all the best reasons possible. We just can't control the consequences.

Eventually I wrote a response agreeing to what Al wanted.

It was some point on the same day that I was glancing through a week old copy of *The Guardian* when I came across the Director's post at Devon. Such a ridiculous proposition made sense. A new job, more status, a new beginning. And just one e-mail to the recruitment consultancy meant that all the inconvenience of phoning for an application pack was replaced by the instantaneous gratification of an electronic application pack returned in seconds, sat there in my inbox, offering the potential for everything to be different.

When the world was slower, I could ponder my responses. Now the speed of things just sucks us up in such a way that we never really think any decisions through. Then again, we fool ourselves that when the world was slower we made better quality decisions when all we did was take longer over making the same mistakes. Easy to blame computers, harder to account for what we do or did.

* * *

Mellon leans forward again, fiddling with the tape machine.

"We got most of what he was saying" he says "and enough to know he was attempting to bribe you."

I am nonplussed. It may be shock, it may be exhaustion, but none of this seems to matter anymore.

"We've also raided his place – not much there really – a few more pictures, mobile phones – but nothing much."

We're silent just for a moment or two. I can hear the ambient background noise of the police station; police officers' voices occasionally can be heard in the corridor outside.

"I think he was responsible for Peter's death," I say.

Mellon nods. "I'd tend to agree with you. Trouble is it's not down to me or you – it's down to those useless pen pushers at CPS. We can get him on collusion with Mapp but that's about it at this point. Means the maximum he'll get is maybe 7 or 8 years and entering on to the sex offenders' register."

"What about bribing me?" I ask.

He looks at me knowingly.

"I don't think you should pursue that one," says Mellon, "there's too much to risk if you do. You know, reputation, your job – messy really."

I nod. He's offering me a way out.

"Won't it come out in any court case though?" I ask.

"Jim's a clever guy. He knows that we can do a deal with him and CPS about what gets mentioned in court and what gets left out – he won't cause any trouble."

Mellon clears his throat for a moment, a habit I notice he has before he delivers some unpleasant news.

"The trouble is," he pauses.

"Yes?" I ask.

"Well, Dr Kapasi, there is no way we can keep her from having to discuss what she knew."

"What about the Hippocratic oath?" I ask.

"Yes," Mellon says sympathetically, "that will keep most of her reputation intact, but she is still an important witness."

We both ponder this. I need to talk to Kal.

"The position is made even more complicated by the fact that Dr Kapasi was at Drake House when the camera was discovered. It won't look good, sorry."

I nod agreement.

We're coming to the end of our discussion.

"OK – there's not much point in continuing anything now – it will all be sorted out in the new year."

He gathers up his papers into a neat pile and stretches his hand across to mine.

"Happy Christmas, Mr Garvey."

I shake his hand.

"And to you DCI Mellon – I think you may well have saved my life tonight."

"No – I didn't. Giovanni saved your life. If he hadn't have called me, I think you would be dead. As it is his wife will now probably kill you!"

A few moments later I am hobbling out into the reception. Geo is waiting for me.

"Jane says to tell you you are a mad fuckwit," he says – but it is said seriously.

"I'm so sorry – I'm so fucking sorry."

"I'll take you home."

We are silent in the car, just the rain beating against the windscreen and the sound of the wipers.

Eventually we are outside of Hampton View.

Geo makes a call on his mobile. A few moments later, Alpha appears.

She opens the passenger door, leans across me and give Geo a peck on the cheek.

"Aren't you meant to be in Barbados?" she asks.

"Let's not go there! Just get Mark in, will you?"

I am led down the path by Alpha, Geo doesn't even say goodnight. As soon as I am out of the car he has driven off.

"Mum's gone to bed," Alpha explains.

I am shocked by this but no longer have the energy to discuss the events of the evening. Presumably she is aware as to what has happened but even at 3am on Christmas Eve I imagined that at the very least she might be there for me.

A few moments later I am sat with a glass of brandy in the lounge looking out across the bay – looking out over Christmas morning. Alpha has gone back to bed and I am left in the silence. I think about all the effort that has been made by all the families who have wrapped presents, bought turkeys and tried their best to make Christmas as happy as possible. I think about the fantastic Christmas Day they are going to have and I know that mine will be spent here.

I feel sad, alone and abandoned at Christmas and wish that I was far away from here. I want to be as far away as possible. I want to be somewhere in another time and place when Christmas day morning was filled with hope, passion, and Alyson.

* * *

Sometimes we don't know that the final scene has been reached and we certainly don't know that the end has arrived. Normally final conversations are not flagged as final conversations, it is almost a rare luxury reserved for deathbeds and those who await corporal punishment. So most conversations always take place as if the script will continue, that we will maintain a dialogue regardless.

Al and I met to discuss the boring details of the sale of our house in the boring bit at the end of all relationships. I had, until then, never understood what some people meant when they said that pregnancy suited some people, but it certainly appeared to suit Al. She looked fantastic, her eyes were bright, her hair was lively and she really did seem to glow. She was wearing a dress, an event unusual enough to have merited a press conference in the past.

We were in a café at the Mailbox. We had got to the point where we had to sign the sale of Massie Road, and agree to what fixtures and fittings were being left. So over cappuccinos we went through what either of us wanted and what could be taken. Most things were staying but unlike the dishwashers, washing machines and light fittings, we were dumping each other. There were a couple of technical details to be sorted and neither of us knew when the central heating had last been serviced, which under the circumstances seemed a ridiculous question for us both to answer.

"So when do you think you'll go?" I asked her.

It was the first personal question I had raised.

She patted her tummy. "I have to check with a few airlines about their policy of carrying 'lumps', but if this all goes through quickly maybe in the next two or three weeks."

"Your mum excited?" I asked.

"Oh yeah," Al said, sighing, "yeah she really is excited. She's a bit freaked by how things have turned out but yeah, she's OK."

I nodded and we sat in silence for a moment.

"Do you want another coffee?" I asked in an attempt to make the peace between us last for a few moments.

Al glanced at her watch.

"I'd better not," she said. "I'll be weeing all night if I have another coffee, and Joy will be picking me up in 10 minutes."

We were sat at a window table. It must have been 3.30 in the afternoon and the light had faded quickly from the evening sky. I wondered what we must have looked like to everybody else, but guessed that all we looked like was a couple having a coffee together, sorting through life's endless red tape.

"You heard about the new job?" Al asked.

"Interviews are next week," I responded.

"It's a bit of a change, isn't it? I guess I never saw you as living in Devon."

I smiled. "That's what everybody at work has been saying, but you know – it would be a promotion and as I said to them, if life only happened in the way that we envisaged it the world might be perfect."

Al nodded. "Yeah, maybe."

Then there was another long silence interrupted by her mobile chirping on the table next to her.

"OK, yep, on my way," she said gently to the phone and I knew by the tenderness of the call that it was Joy and that time was up.

She started reaching into her handbag for money for the coffee.

"Let me," she said, but I interrupted her.

"Hey," I said, "don't worry I'll get these."

Then we both stood up. I pecked her on the cheek and she smiled. She went quiet for a moment. She started pulling on her coat, getting her things together and then.

"Are you sure this Devon stuff is right for you?"

I really didn't know the answer to that question, I just knew I needed a new start, a new beginning, somewhere to get over all the mess and start again.

"I'll be fine and anyway, I haven't been offered it yet."

She shrugged her shoulders. "Well, so long as you're happy."

Then the phone rang again, interrupting any further dialogue, and by the time she finished explaining to Joy she really was on her way, I had started sorting out the bill for our drinks chatting to the waitress who had served us.

She made her way to the door and turned back to look at me before stepping out into the street.

'Take care' she mouthed. I nodded.

Then she was gone.

* * *

We're lying in bed. I am on one side and Kal is as far away as she can be. Each time we talk we argue. We argue about why she couldn't even share some of the background with me, not the detail. We argue about why, even after Wilma was arrested, she couldn't have mentioned to me or Mellon that she had been treating her, that she had been counselling her. We argue that she has put my career at risk and that I have put her career at risk. We argue that each one of us has fucked up big time – albeit I think it is her and she thinks it is me. Now the silence is like the end of a First World War battle. The coldness of the sheets between her and I represents no-man's-land. We are dug in to

273

our positions. There isn't much chance of a ceasefire.

The dull light of Christmas Day morning is trying hard to penetrate through the curtains. The bedside clock shows 10.15 and I imagine that the wind and the rain of last night hasn't gone away.

Eventually I make my move. Swing my feet out of bed, pull on a dressing gown and hobble to the kitchen. I make coffee – very strong black coffee – and sit at the breakfast bar looking at nothing in particular in the garden, just leaves blowing in the wind.

I am just getting to the bottom of my cup of coffee when Kal enters into the kitchen and starts fidgeting with the kettle. She won't make eye contact with me.

"What are your plans for the day?" she asks icily.

"It's Christmas Day," I say – which I feel is enough to explain everything.

"You think we should spend it together?!" she asks, obviously dumbfounded by the idea.

"Well you clearly don't, do you?"

"Don't tell me what I think," she shouts and storms out of the kitchen, slamming the door behind her.

I am aware that there is now an argument going on upstairs – between Alpha and her mum. Then there is more door slamming, more yelling and moments later Alpha appears in the doorway of the kitchen. She is dressed in a big t-shirt that stretches down to her knees but she is looking distressed.

"Mark," she gasps for air – then she starts crying but the words come out as blubber.

"Mark, mymumhasasked, my mum has asked, god I can't do this. My mum has askedmetoaskyou to leave!"

"What?!" I ask – not because I don't understand what she has said, but because I do.

Alpha is exasperated – she starts again thinking there is a problem with my comprehension.

"My mum has-" I hold up my hand, stopping Alpha.

"No," I say, "I understand Alpha – I just don't know why your mum hasn't said this to me."

Alpha wails again. "Whas goingon Mark! Iwaslooking." Huge intake of breath – "I was looking forward to us spending Christmas today together." She crosses the kitchen and throws her arms around me a mass of snot, t-shirt and confused 20 year old.

I stand there holding her but recognise that this is another exit. Another one of those final scenes, played out to tears and mucus that seems to haunt me. 'Happy' and 'Christmas' seem like juxtapositions, not linked words. I feel like a puppy, close to a life of happiness and fulfilment, but thrown out in the cold on 25th December because the proposition of dealing with all the shit and mess outweighs the reality of sharing time together.

* * *

I was at Geoff's. It was a couple of days after my leaving do. Geoff and I had been out for a farewell meal and back to his place for a nightcap.

He was distressed that I was going: thought I was making a stupid mistake and argued that I was being stupid going down to 'yokel' country. The argument was good natured, but it was honest too.

He had left the room to get a final bottle of red wine for us to share. It was well past midnight. I was sat alone for a moment as my phone vibrated. A text message.

'Just thought I'd let you know – arrived safely in Perth. Hope all is good, good luck with the new job. A xxx.'

Geoff returns. 'Surely,' I think to myself, 'tonight draws a line under all that has passed, surely."

* * *

"Come on Kal it's fucking freezing out here!"

Still no response and I wonder what I have to do to convince her to open the door. I wouldn't mind but this is the second time I have been down since being thrown out. I just want to talk to her.

I know somebody is home because I have seen a shape moving behind the shutters, casting shadows on to the wall behind itself, I just can't tell if it's Kal or Alpha. I knock again harder still.

"Alpha, if you're in there please open up, come on," I'm not shouting now – talking a bit louder than usual. I kind of hope that my appeal to her daughter may spring the door open to Kal's heart and home.

Then there is movement in the hallway and for a moment I wonder if I have finally done it, finally persuaded one of them to talk to me.

The letterbox is prised open from the inside.

"She doesn't want to see you Mark, and she won't let me see you OK!?" It is Alpha's voice.

"Al, please, I'm sorry, that's all I can say."

"It's better if you go Mark, just get out of here, I mean you're not coming in. She said she never wants to see you again. Never."

"Come on!" I say, noticing that I am now pleading with a pair of lips talking at me through a letterbox, "this can all be worked through."

She interrupts me. "Mark, I've called the police, so like you have about three minutes to get out of here or face charges. On top of all this, I don't think County Hall are going to be too impressed if the police arrest you, do you?"

She is right. She is absolutely right.

276

I turn to go and then the letterbox responds.

"I'm really sorry Mark, I really liked you, still do."

"Alpha, have a word with her, please."

"There's no point," the letter box responds "she says everything is ruined, spoiled. She doesn't want to see you anymore. She says she can't trust you ever again and, you know, when you think about it life is all about trust isn't it?"

These words strike me as being too wise even for Alpha. I turn back. Geo is waiting in the car for me at the end of Hampton View. I hobble back along the path, catching Hope Cove beneath me in all it's simple complexity. I can see a ship passing out in the Channel, it's lights bobbing on the waves, its crew doubtless tucking in to a festive dinner.

I open the car door.

"No?" Geo asks.

"'Fraid not," I say, and let out a long sigh.

"What now then?" Geo asks.

"Just drop me at home – I need to think."

We are silent in the short drive back to my place. I'm amazed Geo is still around, given that I nearly fucked up his marriage and ruined the family Christmas he had planned. But the guy isn't programmed to resent me.

He pulls up at my gate.

"Are you sure you're OK?" he asks, looking worried and concerned.

"I feel such an arsehole."

Geo nods. I am not sure if the nod is an agreement, as in 'yes, you are an arsehole' or if it is just an emphatic nod to show that he has heard what I've said. Either way, I don't have the energy or the will to explore the nuances of a small nod in the chaos that is all this.

"Look, I have to go back up to Bristol tonight. Give me a call in a couple of days. We'll meet up again." Again the implication is clear. 'You can't come and stay, Jane is still too mad at you.' I realise that one of my great skills, a party piece even, is pissing off women without ever intending to do so.

"You've given me too much time already, under the circumstances." I say, remaining tight-lipped and hiding my hurt, not just at Geo but at the world in general.

"We're mates," Geo says, "don't mates support each other through thick and thin?"

I have to fight back the tears at this. I nod. I get to the end of the path at Stockwell Cottage. He watches me hobble into the house and then I push my way in through the front door. I wave to Geo, indicating that he should go. He nods, gives me a thumbs up sign together with a brave smile and then drives off.

I close the front door. After a short scuffle with my coat, I manage to remove it and leave it crumpled and defeated on the lounge floor. A small victory in a year of defeats.

* * *

It arrived one morning, just before I was due to leave for Devon, whilst I was at Kay's. The mass bonking had stopped, I was much calmer, and the new job at Devon, offering a new beginning and a new start, was just around the corner.

I knew from the postmark that it had been posted by Al's mum, it certainly wasn't Al's handwriting on the envelope.

Inside there was a small white card, embossed with gold edging. In the top right-hand corner was a digital image of a small baby, a small life. Then some simple text.

'Al is pleased to announce the arrival of baby Joshua Mark – to be known as Josh – born on 14th December. All presents gratefully received.'

So there he was – Josh. Part of me, part of my past but not part of my future. I studied the picture carefully, did he look like me? It was hard to tell because as far as I'm concerned all babies look the same – scary! This one though was a little less fierce, a little bit easier on the eye.

I showed it to Kay.

"Looks like you," she said.

"When? When do I look like this?"

"When West Brom get beat, when you're sad," she said gently.

"You mean I always look like this?" I asked – turning her gentle comment into a joke.

"Don't you want to go and see him?" she asked, "I mean don't you have any desire to see him?"

I was silent. If I wanted to see him, I would have to see Al and to see Al would be too painful.

"No," I lied, "best to let sleeping babies lie," I said.

I think Kay knew but she never really pressed me on it. She probably knew me to well to press me on the most serious things in life, because being who I am it would just be turned into a joke, a throwaway comment from a throwaway life.

* * *

3rd January. I was due to go to a meeting at County Hall today to discuss my return to work. It will still be a couple of months away. However, I woke at 7 and just knew that there was no way I could face Exeter.

It is mid morning. I have been busying myself with a computer game on my laptop. A part of me thinks I am far too old to play strategy games, but this is a shoot em-up thing. Killing green evil monsters fills in the time, it is like heroin, taking me to a place where I don't really have to think about anything much. I have just defeated an invading army of green things on the planet Zukon when the phone rings.

"Mark Garvey?" a voice enquires.

I recognise the voice. It is Peterson.

"Henry – hello, how are you?"

"I'm most well, thank you, but very concerned. You were expected here at County an hour ago."

"Well," I begin, "under the circumstances -"

He interrupts me. "Under the circumstances you should have been here! No two ways about it, is there!?"

I am struck by his tone. It is aggressive.

"You seem," he continues, "intent on dragging the good name of Devon Social Services Department into the gutter," he pauses "and not to attend today's meeting is totally unacceptable."

I realise he is now reading from a prepared script.

"I think that's unfair Henry, I'm under a -"

"Please, Mr Garvey do not interrupt me!"

He continues. "It is usual when a member of the senior management team in an organisation gets themselves into this position for them to resign. The fact that you have not chosen to discuss the latest developments with myself or the leader of the council is tantamount to gross misconduct. Accordingly, I am suspending you on full pay until we have had a chance to review the circumstances and decide what course of action is appropriate."

I sigh, loud enough for him to hear me.

"Do you have something to say Mark?"

I start to order my thoughts but I am defeated by it all.

"No, under the circumstances I have nothing to say."

"Very well," says Peterson in his clipped tones. "I shall be formerly writing to you by recorded delivery later today. You are forbidden to enter Devon County Council premises whilst this matter is under investigation or to use the resources of the county council".

I interrupt him "What you mean I can't use the roads, or return my library books?" I know I am being sarcastic, but this is ridiculous.

He is taken aback for a moment, then he corrects himself. "Of course, I mean any of the resources you used professionally during the course of your employment. However all this will be detailed in my letter to you which I will send this evening."

"Henry, is this really necessary?" I ask.

He doesn't respond. Instead he continues:

"Once you have received this letter I will expect you to sign a copy and return it to me. We have set no deadline for the end of this investigation and I will be in touch with you in due course."

He pauses again expecting a response

"Is all that clear Mark?"

"Henry," I want to tell him to stick his fucking poxy letter up his under-oiled arse. Instead I resort back to the language of the bollocks.

I start again "Henry – I shall pass your letter on to my legal advisers and proceed from therein."

A few more unpleasantries and the conversation ends.

I put the phone down and gaze out of the window. My computer beeps. The planet Zukon still requires defending.

* * *

It was simple. Nothing spectacular, it just showed a little tree in the darkness, surrounded by snow. The tree had Christmas lights on.

Inside there was no rhyme, no silly verse, it was blank. Just a handwritten block of text.

'To Mark, all our love, Alyson & Josh.'

It arrived at Kay's the morning I left for Devon. It left me sad, confused and aware that escaping the past would be so much harder than shaping the future.

* * *

It is a hire car – automatic so that I can drive it – and I pack the final bag into the boot.

I glance upwards as a gull shrieks above me and know that I will miss being near the coast, I will miss the sense of space living by the sea has given me. Then again, when I weigh it up, there is more to life than picture postcard views of country cliffs and pebble beaches.

There is no one to say goodbye to as such, but Flo and Anna have used flexi-time so that they can come and say farewell. It is a Monday evening. I am going back to Kidderminster to stay with Kay on a promise that the one-eyed monster will be kept safely behind bars for the foreseeable future.

"You will keep in touch won't you?" Anna asks, and I can see that she is distressed.

"I'll send you emails once I know what I am doing, and I'll come and see you when the case begins."

But no date has been set, and I really don't want to sit through a court case that risks placing me at the centre of a media scrum.

Flo chips in "Mark, I wouldn't say you have been the best boss I've had but it's been very exciting working for you. For all the wrong reasons, but exciting nonetheless."

We laugh together at this.

Then, after a few pecks on the cheek, tears from Anna and Hugs from Flo, I climb into the car.

As I pull away, I see them reflected in the rear view mirror, waving me off. The car climbs up out of the village, onto the Exeter road. I catch a final glance of the sea and then it is gone. Me and the familiar country lanes travelling to some point far away from all this.

I turn on the car radio, which is so complicated I am convinced that a degree in computing wouldn't even get you past the first page of the mammoth manual. Eventually I find what I am looking for – football commentary. It is Everton, a cup replay.. They're playing Tranmere Rovers. The rhythm of the commentary, the intimacy of everything that is described, relaxes me, seduces me and even makes the future seem a little bit brighter.

* * *

I pick my bags up off the carousel. I am tired, really, really tired from the long flight. I am sleepy and can sense the tiredness that makes walking, thinking and much else surreal. Eventually, pushing my way through the crowds I manage to get to the car rental desk.

The paperwork seems inordinately complicated but simple once the smiling, attractive Australian girl behind the counter guides me through the form. Then I am making my way out to the parking lot where my car waits for me. It is warm, an April morning and I can already tell that today is going to be a hot one, a really hot one.

I have been constantly running through why this is happening and why I am doing this. It makes perfect sense amongst all the nonsense. Each time I try to work out what I am doing I end up in an intellectual cul-de-sac that brings me back to the start of everything. In the end, this just seems like the right thing to do. Everything else seems to have been wasted or destroyed. A promising career, flushed down the toilet; a new love wasted; a chance of a new future wasted for no reason other than my inability to see the world as a secure place. It all seems ridiculous. So buying a ticket to Perth, catching a flight out of Heathrow on a foggy April morning, knowing I had no career and no home to go back to seems a reasonable choice, given all that has happened.

I have an overwhelming sense that I have been betrayed, by Mapp, by Kalpna, by Jim, by Peterson, but most of all by myself. I allowed so many things to seduce me that eventually I was bedded by my own delusions.

I'm getting nearer now. I can only have been driving for 20 minutes and I am already near the house that looks onto a beach where once I argued about whether or not we would have cats and dogs, be happy forever or fail forever.

Eventually I stop the car. I have to. I know in my mind that killing the engine is about killing the past.

I push the door open and the warm sea air, perfumed by a mixture of salt and eucalyptus, is refreshing compared to the pressurised airplane cabin and air conditioning of the car. The warmth of the day shocks me. It was freezing at Heathrow! How can our planet be hot and cold at the same time? This little blue place is like a baked alaska floating near the sun but creating perfect and imperfect moments.

Then I see them. There is Al and there is her mum. Alongside them, a dog runs and fetches sticks. I wonder what the dog is called, Rex maybe? Then I see Josh, who is sat on a little rug under a parasol. I look at this life and know that I came in hope. I came to see that the part of me that will continue after all of this and to hope. I hope Josh will understand. I hope he'll know that his dad once really loved his mother and was just a fool to make all the mistakes he ever did and ruin the lives that he's ruined. Most of all, I hope he'll learn from my errors and learn that when he finds real love he should cherish it, celebrate it and never let it go. I hope maybe he will support West Brom, even play for them one day. More than anything I hope his life is a happy one, a good life that builds on the errors of mine and has as little pain as possible and that he will, like me, always love his mum for being who she is and who she was.

I turn towards them and wave, but they haven't seen me. In my head there are remnants of a phone conversation I had with Al at Singapore Airport. I explained I was coming, I explained that I just wanted to see Josh. That was all I wanted – some positive encouragement. Al hadn't said 'no', just told me where they would be on the beach.

I walk towards the beach; I carefully negotiate the wooden steps down so that I am now on a level with the Indian Ocean. My pace quickens, I'm running now, I am running towards her, I am smiling. I can see Josh giggling at me, and the dog stops chasing its sticks. It runs in my direction and is eventually alongside me, barking excitedly. The waves keep kissing the shoreline and all I can do is hope that Alyson has been playing a game of 'odds or evens' and that maybe, just maybe, I have been lucky with the waves and that we can make the future work.

Then I am aware of a beeping, a background noise that becomes louder. Heat is replaced by cool, brightness by half light, a beach in Perth – a guest room in a house in Kidderminster. I am drenched in sweat.

I am awake again, teased by sleep, tortured by my longing for all this crap to be undone, tortured by the love that I wasted, tortured by my dreams of what could have been. Tortured, after Alyson.